Operation: Mistletoe
Roxanne Rustand

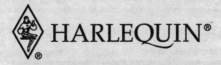

HARLEQUIN®

TORONTO • NEW YORK • LONDON
AMSTERDAM • PARIS • SYDNEY • HAMBURG
STOCKHOLM • ATHENS • TOKYO • MILAN • MADRID
PRAGUE • WARSAW • BUDAPEST • AUCKLAND

ISBN 0-373-71096-8

OPERATION: MISTLETOE

To those in law enforcement and the DEA, who dedicate their lives to making this world a better place to be.

And to dear friend Judy Roemerman, who first introduced me to romance fiction, gave me a computer and encouraged me to write. Without you, Judy, I wouldn't have pursued my dream!

ACKNOWLEDGMENTS:

Many thanks to the wonderful people who patiently answered endless questions. Any errors in detail are mine alone.

Harry Daugherty, Chief of Police, Marion, Iowa
Baxter, Minnesota, law enforcement officer LuAnn Becker
Minnesota attorney Mary E. Strand
Minnesota fisherman and outdoorsman Skip Schmitz
Weapons experts Nancy and Dave Nicholson

CHAPTER ONE

WHEN MRS. YVONNE WEATHERFIELD hesitated at the corner of Poplar and Main, spared one disdainful glance at her and kept on walking, Sara Hanrahan knew she was finally home.

She also wished she wasn't.

The trip from Dallas, more than eleven hundred miles in a rusted Bronco with a cantankerous transmission and a faulty heater, hadn't been bad. Her stay in Ryansville promised to be much less fun.

This time, she was back with a whole new attitude and a lot less tolerance. Straightening out a few people would do her heart good. But she needed to blend in, not set the townsfolk back on their heels. She knew her job too well to make that mistake.

"So what do you think, Harold? Just the place you'd like to be?"

He looked up at her, his eyes wise and patient, letting her know that any place on earth was fine as long as he was at her side.

Reaching down, she rubbed him under the collar, then grinned when the old dog leaned against her leg and wagged his tail. "At least *you've* got good taste."

She sensed, rather than heard, someone very large come up behind her. *Too close.* With the instinct born of three years with the DEA—Drug Enforcement Administration—and three years before that as a city cop, she spun on her heel and took a step back into a slight crouch. Swiftly assessed the man who'd approached.

Tall, dark and startled, wearing the navy-blue uniform of a county deputy, he was assessing *her* as if she just might be a criminal who'd come into his territory.

Her gaze riveted on his and she gave him an embarrassed, helpless smile. "Y-you surprised me, Officer. I, uh, had my purse stolen a few months ago, and I get nervous whenever someone comes up behind me."

"Sorry, ma'am." He didn't look particularly sorry, though he did appear a tad suspicious.

She glanced at the name badge on his uniform, then stared at him, taking in his raven-black hair, the squared chin, the high cheekbones. If Elvis had stepped out of the telephone booth at the end of the block, she wouldn't have felt greater disbelief.

The local resident deputy, a man named Roswell, had been mentioned during the DEA briefing, but she hadn't thought to associate him with the Roswells who'd dominated the local country-club-and-champagne set for generations. "Roswell? You're Nathan Roswell?"

A corner of his mouth lifted in wry acknowledgment, and suddenly she knew that his career choice hadn't gone over well with his wealthy family. His parents had probably been horrified at the thought of their precious son wearing a badge.

"You're…a Hanrahan, right?" He paused, considering. The corners of his mouth turned down. "Kyle's sister?"

An easy guess, given her family's propensity for freckles and strawberry-blond hair, but she had to give him points for remembering her surname and managing to maintain a neutral expression. As a teenager, Kyle had given the local law-enforcement officers a run for their money. And their father…he'd been entirely too memorable, as well. "I'm Sara."

"Just passing through?"

"I'm not sure."

"The job market around here is sorta tight."

Hearing a veiled warning beneath his words, she wondered what he'd do if she flipped out her ID. Instead, she gave a nonchalant lift of one shoulder. "That would affect my plans, I guess."

Standing there, tall and lean and resolute, with a gun strapped to his hip, he reminded her of a sheriff from the Old West. She half expected him to add a piece of friendly advice about not making any trouble in town.

Instead, he bent over and ruffled Harold's gray fur. "Nice German shepherd. Had him long?"

"Just a year."

He gave her an approving glance. "Pick him up at a shelter?"

Sara hesitated. The truth could spur questions heading down paths she couldn't walk. Not until she knew for sure that he didn't have connections to the suspected drug operation just outside of town.

Preliminary reports from the DEA indicated that

the deputy wasn't a shareholder in the company she'd come to investigate, but turning a blind eye had been a lucrative deal for the local cops in several cases she'd been on, so it didn't pay to take chances. "The dog's owner…passed away."

"I'm sorry."

So am I. Even now, more than three years later, the memories sometimes slipped into her thoughts at unexpected moments. Gunfire. Blood. *Oh, God. So much blood.* If only he'd waited a few minutes for her to get into position, Tony might have walked away from that warehouse. They might have married. And she'd probably still be a street cop in Dallas.

Nathan eyed her closely. "Are you okay?"

She shook off the memories and gave him the breeziest smile she could muster. "Just a little tired." She snapped her fingers at her side, calling Harold to attention. "We'd better get back home."

With a vague wave of farewell, she turned and continued down Main, past the restored 1880s' stone storefronts housing businesses that sure hadn't been here while she was growing up. Fiber artists. Potters. A glass studio. A custom jeweler. A charming coffee shop offering espresso and café latte, its prices and flavor variations offered on an antique chalkboard at the front window.

Progress, she thought dryly. All geared to the waves of weekend bumper-to-propeller traffic flooding through town toward the best of Minnesota's eleven thousand lakes. The summer migration must be a hundredfold greater these days if the new, upscale shops were any clue.

At the corner of Birch and Main she waited for the town's sole traffic light—another new development—to turn green, then started across the street. An uneasy sense of awareness crawled up her spine.

She turned slowly and looked over her shoulder, expecting to see the deputy observing her progress. Making sure, maybe, that she wasn't as light-fingered as her brother had been. The deputy was nowhere in sight. Surprised, she surveyed the sidewalks on both sides of the street.

Several women were window-shopping half a block down. A farmer in overalls studied a farm-auction flyer posted on a store window. Just a normal, quiet late-Saturday afternoon.

Except for a gaunt old man hesitating at the open door of a battered pickup truck at the other end of the block. Hunched over, as if bracing against a stiff wind, he wore ragged jeans faded to white at the knees and a grease-stained denim jacket. Though his face was shadowed by a wide-brimmed hat encrusted with an assortment of fishing lures, he seemed oddly familiar.

The moment their eyes met, he seemed to freeze.

Curious, she stared back at him. Her holiday trips home were usually too brief to spend time cruising around town, and it had been a good twelve years since she'd left for college. Enough time for a man to age, and some men weathered the years harder than others. Had she known him when she was a child?

She hadn't moved three steps before he abruptly turned to climb into the truck, then slammed the door. Gears grinding, black smoke spewing from its tailpipe, the truck lurched backward into the street. The pile of twisted metal and dented fifty-gallon drums in the back of the pickup swayed precariously as the vehicle swung around and crawled up the steep slope of Main. Stark's Salvage was hand-lettered across the tailgate.

She'd be in town for several months, and she'd definitely look up Mr. Stark. But that would have to wait. This afternoon she had to unpack and go through Special Agent Allen Larson's preliminary report one more time, then take a nice casual run past the Sanderson plant.

And then, when she could delay no longer, she'd need to face her family.

"YOU'VE BEEN IN TOWN how long?" Bernice Hanrahan lifted a vein-knotted hand to her gray hair and smoothed it back, then dropped a tea bag into the cup of hot water in front of her. Even at sixty-eight, she still had to wrestle her natural waves into the tight confinement of the bun she'd worn all her adult life. The reproach in her voice hadn't changed much over the years, either. "I would have made a nice supper if I'd known you were here already."

"I decided to drive all night, Mom. I didn't get in until midmorning. Since then I've taken Harold for a walk and unpacked," Sara added, knowing her mother would want a full accounting. "And I didn't want you going to any trouble. I thought maybe I could take you out for supper."

"No…I think I'd rather just stay in."

No surprise there. "Maybe I could bring something

in? I noticed a new Cantonese restaurant on the edge of town.''

''I don't think so.'' Pursing her lips, Bernice deftly changed topics. ''Are you certain you want to stay in that…that place above the Shuellers' garage? I could certainly make room for you here.''

Sara glanced around the spartan, almost sterile kitchen. Not one utensil lay on the counter, not a single cup or plate in the sink. The white Formica table held the same avocado plastic napkin holder and salt and pepper shakers that had rested on her mother's table even at the old green house they'd lived in when Sara was a child.

All the other furnishings were familiar, as well, remnants of a happier time.

The tiny, spotless duplex might be perfect for a single person, but not for two, plus a good-size dog. Even now, curled up at the back door of the kitchen, Harold seemed to overwhelm the small room. ''I appreciate your offer, but I figured the two of us would be a bit much.''

''You could tie that dog outside.''

''Night and day?''

Her mother sniffed. ''Wouldn't that be best?''

Bernice's tone implied that Sara had chosen the welfare of a dog over that of her own mother, but so be it. ''He had a long career as a drug dog, Mom. He deserves better than a chain and a doghouse.''

As if he knew what she'd said, Harold lifted his head and looked at her, thumping his tail several times against the floor in agreement. He'd never fully recovered from the last injury he'd received on duty.

Cold mornings and damp weather bothered him, even though he slept on soft blankets next to Sara's bed every night.

"How are you doing these days, Mom? Are you getting out a little more?"

The old, familiar distance settled between them. "I get out as much as I need to."

"What about church? Does Millie come to pick you up? I know she would."

Bernice silently fussed with her tea bag, catching it with her spoon and wrapping the string over the bag to drain the hot liquid back into her cup.

Sara tried another tack. "How's Kyle? I e-mail him now and then, but he never answers."

"Your brother isn't much of a letter writer."

"But he's okay?"

"Far as I know."

Sara gave a quiet sigh of relief. Both she and her boss back in Dallas, Zach Forrester, had siblings with drug problems. His sister's connections to that world had contributed to her death. Since then, Sara had prayed every day that her brother could stay clean. "I hope I'll get to see him while I'm back. Does he come home from college much?"

"Not often." Pain flickered across Bernice's face. "But Minneapolis is over four hours away."

Not that far—and not a reason to avoid ever coming home. She glanced at her watch. "How about it, Mom? Chinese takeout, or live a little and come with me to that little restaurant out on Lake Ryan? They serve great walleye at Josie's."

"N-no. My head is pounding." Bernice gave an

agitated sweep of her hand in the air. "I think I'd rather just lie down awhile, maybe have some soup later on. You go ahead."

"Please?" *It's been twenty-five years. Can't you let it rest?*

Bernice rose stiffly, took her teacup toward the sink. It fell from her hands and shattered on the vinyl floor.

Ignoring the shards at her feet, she braced her hands on the edge of the counter. "You've never understood." Her voice grew harsh. "I think you should leave. I…I just don't feel well."

Sara had come back to Ryansville on the pretext of visiting her family and starting a new life back in her hometown, but she'd known from the first that this would be the most unrealistic cover she'd ever had.

As much as she wished things were different, coming home was the hardest job the DEA had ever asked her to do.

NATHAN GRINNED across the chessboard at Clay Benson. "Gotcha."

With a deep sigh, Clay leaned back in his chair and laced his hands over his belly. His snowy brows beetled together as he studied the board. "Not yet, pardner. Day's not over till the mule's back in the barn."

Nathan laughed. The retired sheriff now seemed more like a congenial grandfather than his former boss, and had become a good friend over the past few years. "That's what I like, a man who can hope despite impossible odds. Shows real character."

"Nope. Sheer intelligence and skill." Clay glanced at the wall clock above Nathan's desk. "It's after one. I'd better skedaddle, or that barber is going to skin me bald for being late."

"Same time tomorrow?"

"You betcha." Clay shoved his bulk up out of the chair. "Noon sharp. Be prepared to lose your shirt."

Careful not to disturb the chess pieces, Nathan lifted the oak chessboard from his desk and settled it on the credenza against the wall behind him. "I've been meaning to ask you about something."

Clay stopped at the doorway, turned. "If you're going to harass me again about my cigarettes, don't. I plan to outlive every nonsmoker in town by at least five years."

That wasn't likely. Nathan had seen Clay when he'd claimed to have "just a twinge" of chest pain, and knew Clay's wife, Dora, and their family doctor had been after him for years to quit. The grim prospects for his future already filled Nathan with a sense of loss. "You remember the Hanrahans, don't you?"

"Hard to forget. Why? That boy Kyle back in town causing trouble?"

"No. One of them is back, though." Nathan sat on the edge of his desk. "I ran into Kyle's sister on Main last Saturday."

Clay rubbed his chin. "Never had any run-ins with her. Expecting trouble?"

"She doesn't seem like the type, but she was sure jumpy when I happened to come up behind her on Main."

"Run a background check on her?"

"I haven't had cause. Not yet, anyway."

Clay snorted. "I was county sheriff thirty-six years before moving back here to retire. Believe me, keep a close eye on that one. Apples don't fall far from the tree—especially a bad one like her father."

"I remember hearing something about the Daniel Hanrahan murder case. That was him?"

"Yeah. Frank Grover was a wonderful guy. He'd do anything for this town and the people in it, and he was a damned good friend. For him to die that way, out on some back road with a bullet in his gut..." Clay shook his head. "It still makes me sick thinking about it."

"Was there ever any question about the murderer?"

"Hell, no."

"The evidence?"

"Daniel Hanrahan was found at the scene. We got his fingerprints off the gun, and he had blood on his clothes."

"I'd long since been shipped off to boarding school, then. What was the local reaction?"

"I don't think anyone here ever forgave what the bastard did to Frank—or for the fact that he took his own life before going to trial. If his widow'd been smart, she would've moved someplace far, far away." Clay glanced at his watch. "See you tomorrow."

Nathan nodded to Clay as he left, then crossed his office to the bank of files along one wall. *Interesting.*

Ryansville had maintained its own local police chief and a deputy until four months ago. After the voters opted to contract law-enforcement services through the County Sheriff's Office, Nathan had been assigned back to his hometown.

Most everything was on the county's computer system now, but local cases going back twenty years or more were still filed away—handfuls of yellowed documents, tattered notes, old photographs crammed into folders.

He'd intended to work through all those files and review every case soon after arriving, but with a hundred square miles under his jurisdiction and just one relief deputy, he'd only made it through three years' worth. Now he thumbed through the files looking for the Hanrahan case.

Ollie Neilsen, his part-time secretary, rapped lightly on his office door, then stepped inside with a handful of mail and a package. He'd always thought she could play the perfect Mrs. Santa Claus, with her snow-white hair and grandmotherly face, but he knew better than to ever say so. Ollie still jogged a mile every day, wore spandex pants and silver shoes, and had recently earned her brown belt in tae kwon do.

"It's one o'clock." She held out a box of DARE—Drug Abuse Resistance Education—materials. "These new brochures just arrived, and you're due at the middle school in fifteen minutes."

"Thanks." He thumbed through a few more files from 1977, found the one he wanted and tossed it onto his desk. "I'll be back around two-thirty."

During his third year with the Minneapolis Police Department, he'd been specifically trained and then assigned to community education, but here in Ryansville he covered a variety of assignments during the week. This Wednesday-afternoon class was one of his favorites.

"You watch out for those young teachers, now, you hear?" Ollie winked at him. "Down at the beauty shop, I heard that a few of them have their eyes on you."

"Thanks," he said dryly. "But I doubt that'll be a problem during my class."

Or any other time. The sweet young things just out of college were just so…young. The others in town who'd flirted with him seemed to be either bitter over their latest divorce or a little too desperate, and as resident deputy, he could hardly go around having affairs without rumors flying.

Not that he took much notice of rumors, but the disrespect of the town's young people wasn't something he wanted to earn.

Handing him the box, Ollie bustled over to his desk and laid the stack of mail dead center. She drew in a sharp breath, then turned. "I…I'm sorry, Nathan. You know I don't like to pry."

"You're the soul of discretion." He couldn't help but grin. "I still say you should look into being a private investigator. You have a better eye for detail and more patience than any guy I know in the field. You could also probably beat up anyone who dared look at you cross-wise."

Usually she shot back a comment about how he'd never manage without her in the office, but this time she hesitated, her mouth working and eyes filled with pain, as if unsure of what she should say. "I couldn't help but notice the file you just pulled,'' she said finally.

''I've been going through old cases whenever I have a spare minute. You remember much about the Grover murder?''

''Franklin was my second cousin.'' She took a deep breath. ''The dearest man who ever lived, and he had so many plans to make this town a better place. There's not a person here who doesn't remember him.''

''Clay said the case was open-and-shut.''

''How much more proof could there have been? Daniel had the motive, opportunity and the murder weapon in his hands when he was caught.'' __

''Motive?''

''To steal Frank's wallet, I suppose. Or maybe things weren't going well with Daniel's new job at the factory. No one found any reprimands in his personal files, but Frank wasn't a confrontational sort of man. He would quietly take employees aside and give them a hundred chances before letting them go.''

''Opportunity?''

''Hanrahan got off at eleven. Franklin had been at a late meeting at the plant and was the last to leave, at about midnight. He left through the back entrance, but then his car broke down on Dry Creek Road. We figured he must have started walking back to town.'' Ollie's voice broke. ''For a billfold and thirty bucks, Daniel destroyed a brighter future for this town and devastated our family.''

Nathan reached over to rest a hand on her shoulder. ''I'm sorry.''

She looked up and gave him a watery smile. "Twenty-five years, and it's just like yesterday."

"Hanrahan's daughter turned up in town last weekend."

Ollie stiffened, stepped away. "Her brother was a real hellion. Theft, joyriding, booze and drugs. Teetered on the edge of being sent away for years. All we need is another Hanrahan around here to stir up trouble."

"It's hard to believe this gal came from a family history like that—she sure doesn't look like much of a hell-raiser to me."

Ollie's voice hardened. "If you're thinking the wrong man was blamed back in '77, think again. Opening old wounds will only bring back all the anger and won't change a thing. Leave it alone, Nathan. We'll all be better off."

CHAPTER TWO

"You sure walk your dog a lot. Can I help?"

Eight-year-old Josh Shueller, son of Sara's land-lord, stood at the door of her apartment and looked up at her with such hope that Sara grinned down at him. "I can't let you take him by yourself, but you could come along. If it's okay with your mom."

"Be right back!" He spun around and thundered down the outside flight of stairs from the one-bedroom apartment Sara had rented over the garage.

Maybe taking him along was a good thing, Sara decided as she sat at her kitchen table and tied her running shoes. The boy's presence might add a further air of innocence to her travels through town.

Not that what she'd done thus far was the least bit obvious. During the past week she'd gone for a daily run through town, ending at the southeast corner, where she ran around the perimeter of the Sanderson Company plant. If anyone asked, she could say she was getting into shape for long-distance competitions.

Now she knew the layout of the facility better and also had a fair idea of traffic flow. The original two-story brick building housed just the offices, but was connected by a new, fully enclosed walkway to the manufacturing area. Attached to that was an even newer warehouse.

According to the reports she'd seen, the warehouse had been added two years ago when the company began producing its Aunt Emma's Soaps and Scents—a venture that now eclipsed the line of home-cleaning chemicals it had produced for more than forty years.

Today she was going up into the hills above the plant to check out a small outcropping of rock overlooking the entrances and parking areas. It looked like a perfect place to start doing nightly surveillance. A person alone might look suspicious. A woman out to gaze at the stars with a friendly old dog would seem harmless.

She'd barely finished tying her second shoe when Josh rushed back up the stairs and knocked on her screen door. "Come in," she called.

He stepped inside, his freckled cheeks pink, his carrot-orange hair windblown. "Mom says yes but she wants to talk to you first," he blurted. "Then we can go. Where are we going? Can I hold the leash?"

"I think maybe I'd better hold on to Harold. At least for now." At the boy's crestfallen expression, she reached out and ruffled his hair. "Sometimes he gets a little excited."

"Next time?"

Sara laughed. "We'll see." She tapped her thigh with her hand. "C'mon, boy. Time to go."

Harold rose from his warm place at the base of the refrigerator and came to her side, where he obediently sat while she snapped a lead onto his collar.

"He is sooo cool," Josh marveled. "The neighbor's dog mostly goes the other way when you call him. Did you know that we can't have a dog on account of dad? He's allergic."

"He is?" Sara looked down at Josh in surprise. There hadn't been any hesitation in Bob's voice when he'd handed her the key. "And still he let me rent this apartment?"

Josh shrugged. "Mom said you needed a place. Said that you needed a break. 'Cause maybe no one would…" He stopped, his cheeks reddening.

Rent a place to the daughter of the town's most infamous criminal?

Sara remembered Josh's mother from childhood. Zoe, several years older, had been a quiet girl who'd endured a lot of teasing because of the dark port-wine stain on her face. Now Zoe had a left-side weakness—from a stroke at such a young age? Life had been unfair to her, but apparently she'd grown up to be a braver, more fair-minded adult than some of the others in town.

Sara smiled. "I suppose a lot of people wouldn't want tenants with a dog. They don't know, though, what a well-mannered old guy Harold is."

Josh looked uncomfortable. "Well—"

"Let's go, okay? I'd like to follow the trail in the woods east of town. Have you ever been up there?"

"With my dad once."

"Good, then. You can be my guide."

Down by the Shuellers' house, Zoe met them at the back door with a baby on one hip and a cell phone in her hand. "Sure you don't mind having Josh tag along?" she asked with a smile.

"Not at all. It's a perfect weekend to be outside, isn't it? Maybe you'd like to come with us. We aren't going to be moving very fast."

"Not a chance with this little guy." Zoe blew her bangs out of her eyes. "Timmy needs to go down for a nap, and he's too cranky to put up with a stroller. Otherwise, I might have come along." She gave a rueful glance at her baggy shirt and sweatpants. "Heaven knows I could use the exercise. Where are you two going?"

"Down Oak, then up the trails into the woods," Sara murmured. "We'll be back in an hour, if that's okay."

The baby, initially entranced at the sight of Harold's plume of a tail waving to and fro, threw back his head and howled.

"I know, Timmy. You're teething and you're tired. Guess we'd better get you into your crib." Zoe reached down and rested a hand on Josh's shoulder. "Be good. No wandering off—stay right with Sara. And try not to talk her ear off, promise?"

"Promise." Josh darted off, then paused at the corner of the house, dancing from foot to foot.

"It's nice of you to let him come along," Zoe said, her voice low enough that only Sara could hear. "He's been bursting with excitement over that dog ever since he learned you were moving in."

"No problem." Sara lifted a hand in farewell and headed after Josh.

They walked east on Third, then turned south on

Oak. In a few minutes, they'd left the residential area behind.

"I love Saturdays," Josh said. "Don't you? Sundays, too, but on Saturdays you have the whole day in front of you and it seems like it could go forever."

Before Sara could answer, Josh launched into a monologue about a school project he was planning on the life cycle of toads. He fell silent for maybe a minute as they left the road and started up a path leading up the hill above the Sanderson plant, then he abruptly stopped, turned toward her and flashed her a toothy smile. "Do you like Ryansville? Are you gonna get a job and stay here? Maybe you could hire me to walk Harold every day. That would be so cool!"

Sara studied him, taken aback. She hadn't been around many kids over the years, but this child seemed…unusual. Did eight-year-olds really talk *this* much? "Hmm…I'm not really sure how long I'll be here."

The wide path led them to a grassy, sunlit meadow, then past a heavy stand of pines before twisting up through a tumble of heavy boulders and rocky outcroppings. Harold trotted happily at Sara's side, his tail wagging and nose lifted to catch smells of things only he could detect.

The scent of dust and pine needles, kicked up from the trail by their feet, followed them as they climbed higher.

Half a mile up the slope, next to a fallen pine tree, an almost invisible path veered off to the right. "Let's check this out,'' Sara said to Josh. "Where do you think it goes?"

It led, as Sara had hoped, to the outcropping of rock she'd noticed from below.

Josh surveyed the small level area, then snorted impatiently. "This trail doesn't go anywhere. Let's go back to the other one. Maybe we can get to the top of the hill."

"Sure. Just a second, though." Sara paced off the area—maybe ten feet by five. Estimated the height of the drop-off. Then she counted the steps back to the main trail.

She'd be coming back as dusk faded into night, and one wrong move could mean a fast drop in altitude— a good hundred feet to a dry creek bed below. But this was a good place for observation. Probably no one else would be on the trail at night, and few would even notice the turnoff to this spot.

They hiked to the top of the hill, then traversed the long, level area at the top and stopped under an old, massive oak tree to share bottled water and a package of crackers. Josh's chatter about his parents, school, friends and Timmy continued, punctuated by questions about Harold and Sara, until they returned to the Shuellers' house.

At the front steps Josh pulled open the front door, shouted that he was back, then gave Sara a big grin. "Can I go next time, too?"

Her head spinning, Sara replied. "Um…we'll see, okay?"

At Zoe's throaty chuckle, Sara raised her eyes and found the boy's mom standing in the doorway.

Zoe unlatched the screen door and held it open. "Josh, Timmy is sleeping, so you need to be really quiet. Can you go into the family room and pick up your Scrabble game? It's still scattered all over."

Josh gave Harold a big hug, then trudged into the house and disappeared. The abrupt silence was nearly as distracting as all the chatter had been.

"He's a good kid," Sara ventured. "I can't remember ever hearing kids talk about their parents as much as he does. Especially in such a positive way."

Zoe's eyes filled with tears. "Really? He never complains, but I know my condition sets him up for a lot of teasing from the other kids."

"It isn't fair."

Slipping out onto the porch, Zoe closed the door behind her and leaned against the railing. "He's not very big for his age, and he has such a good heart. Too good," Zoe added, her voice laced with grief. "He wants to defend me against the world, and when the other kids taunt him about his 'monster mom,' he gets into fights he just can't win."

Sara's heart turned over. "I'm so sorry. I guess kids aren't any kinder now than they were when we were growing up."

"It seems worse, because it's my son and not me— and I can't always be there to defuse the situation." Zoe sighed.

Sara wanted to ask if she'd sought newer treatment options as an adult, but hesitated.

Zoe gave her a knowing look. "No, the newer laser methods weren't available up here when I was a kid, and my doc says I probably wouldn't get good results now. I learned to live with my appearance long ago, but didn't realize that birth-control pills can cause greater risks for women with port-wine stains."

"What happened?"

"Blot clots, and I ended up with a stroke." She smiled, but her smile was off-kilter. "Having a disfigured mom is a big burden for a young boy."

"Did you go through rehab?"

"Everything I could afford. The therapists worked miracles, really. I still have a noticeable limp, but I'm truly thankful that I don't need a cane any longer."

All the way home, Sara thought about the people who had everything and appreciated little, and about Zoe who'd endured more than her share of pain yet could find ways to be thankful. And wished there was something she could do to help.

Borne on a chill October wind, ragged clouds scudded past the sliver of moon, shifting the patterns of shadows on the scene below.

Sara settled next to Harold on the blanket she'd brought, put a navy ball cap on her head to cover her light hair, then set up a small telescope at her side. With luck, no one would see her. If someone did, she was ready.

Anyone thinking a woman alone might be easy prey would learn differently soon enough. Years of self-defense training and the Beretta semiautomatic in the holster at the small of her back were good insurance. The retired K-9 Patrol dog at her side was even better.

Besides drug detection, Harold had been trained for

building searches, tracking, apprehension and personal protection. He'd be a formidable ally in any confrontation.

Pulling out her night-vision binoculars, Sara scanned the parking lots to the south and east of the buildings. A handful of cars remained, nosed up to one of the side doors of the largest building like pups at a food dish. These didn't belong to overtime workers, whose cars would still be in orderly position within the painted lines of the lot.

Light shone from windows on the third floor of the building, but even with her powerful binoculars, she couldn't detect what was going on behind the closed vertical blinds.

A Lexus—black? dark blue or green?—and stopped at the well-lit west entrance. The driver punched something on the keypad at the gate, and the gate slid open. He drove without hesitation toward the group of cars. Scanning the empty parking lot as he stepped out of his car, he paused, then hurried to the door and disappeared inside.

Interesting. A meeting could run late, but one still drawing attendees at midnight hardly seemed likely. Reaching into her backpack, she withdrew a tiny voice-activated tape recorder and began describing what she was looking at. Then she pulled out her old Minolta, loaded with 1000 ASA film to make maximum use of the dim light, screwed on a 300-mm lens, and snapped a series of pictures.

The distance was probably too great to pick up anything significant on night photos of those license plates, even if the photos were enlarged, but this was still the best position for surveillance.

On the ground, she'd have to cross a wide stretch of barren field to get close to the well-lit perimeter fencing, and she'd still be too far away to pick up those numbers. Any security guy glancing out a window would easily see her.

So far, she'd logged arrivals and departures of delivery trucks during the day. Learned the hours of the formally attired office workers and of the more casually dressed employees in the manufacturing area or warehouse.

She'd need to start making frequent trips up here at night, to start logging any activities that occurred after the employees left. Were there many late-night deliveries? Shipments? And she needed to gain access to the buildings without raising suspicion.

Despite the deputy's warning about the local job market, it might not be too hard. Allen Larsen's report and her casual jaunts during the day had helped her identify some of the employees, and even though she'd been gone for more than twelve years, she'd recognized the names and faces of a few.

Small towns, she thought dryly as she stroked Harold's soft fur. For good or for bad, everybody knew everybody else, and everybody else's business, as well. Perhaps Sara could call in a favor that was long past due.

THE CARS DIDN'T START leaving until after two in the morning. Cold, stiff and tired, Sara removed the roll of film from her camera and tucked it into an inside pocket. She slid in a new roll and took a few pictures of the trees and rocks nearby.

She gathered her things and surveyed the small area. The rocky ground was ideal—there was no crushed grass to reveal her presence—but she took one last look to make sure she hadn't left any evidence behind.

Shouldering her backpack, she picked up Harold's leash and started down the trail back to town.

She'd gone maybe a dozen yards when branches rustled behind her. Her heart thumping heavily in her chest, she warned Harold to stay quiet. Then she reached for her weapon and spun around.

A split second later, two does and a massive ten- or twelve-point buck bounded across the trail. They froze at the other side, as if they sensed her presence. Then in a heartbeat they were gone.

Harold whined eagerly, his tail wagging, some remnant of primitive instinct drawing him to the hunt despite his life as a well-fed urban dog. "Sorry, buddy," she whispered. "Not a good idea."

The rest of the way down the hill, she moved with greater stealth, her senses trained on the dark undergrowth at either side of the trail. There were no wolves in this part of the country. Black bears prowled the deeper timber, but avoided humans and were rarely aggressive unless one inadvertently stepped between a mother and her cubs.

But there were other predators who were far less predictable—the two-legged variety. The deer had reminded her of her vulnerability.

An awareness brought into sharper focus, because

the farther she walked, the more she sensed that she wasn't alone.

Someone—or something—was out here with her.

She felt it in the uneasy prickle at her nape. Knew it for a fact when Harold began walking closer to her, bumping her right leg, the hair raised along his back. Now and then a low growl rumbled through him.

Ahead, the timber thinned into an expanse of underbrush, then opened into the broad meadow she'd crossed on the way up. The open area offered no cover for anyone stalking her—but afforded her no protection, either. She broke into a fast jog, Harold loping along beside her, then slowed as she entered the heavier darkness of the hardwoods and birch at the other side.

She looked back. There was no one on the trail behind her. For anyone to follow unseen, he or she would have had to skirt the perimeter of the meadow. Had it all been her imagination?

Her heart rate slowing, she followed the trail down to Dry Creek Road. Within a few hundred yards it intersected with Oak, the street running in front of the Sanderson plant, and soon the edge of Ryansville's residential area came into view. In ten minutes she and Harold would be back in her snug little apartment.

They were a block from there when she heard a car coming up the street behind her. Without headlights—not a good sign.

She scanned the area, judged the distance back to the Shuellers' place. In this part of town the homes were mostly old story-and-a-half clapboard structures, with clotheslines and large gardens in back. Few of the yards were fenced. She could cut through them, if need be.

Preparing to run, she glanced over her shoulder as the car eased up behind her. Her heart sank when she saw the light bar on the roof and the reflective graphics emblazoned on the side—Jefferson County Deputy.

If this was Nathan Roswell, he'd already seemed suspicious of her the first day she'd arrived. What would he think now at two-thirty in the morning? Worse—she was licensed to carry, but how would she explain the Beretta if he searched her?

The car rolled smoothly past, then stopped. The door swung open and, sure enough, Nathan stepped out. The frown on his face didn't bode well.

"Kinda late to be out walking, isn't it?" His gaze swept her from head to foot, then settled on her bulging backpack.

She smiled up at him and lifted one shoulder. "Insomnia, I guess. I worked night shifts while I was in college and never did get my sleep straightened out."

Accustomed to mentally recording minute details about her surroundings and the people she encountered, Sara remembered that his eyes had appeared green when she'd run into him downtown. Now, in the darkness, they appeared deep brown, with an almost eerie intensity that made her think he could see right through to her deepest thoughts.

She'd bet a nickel that most suspects probably folded and confessed on the spot when faced with an imposing guy like this one.

"Where did you work?" he asked casually, though she bet he'd be following up on the reference first thing in the morning.

She used the company that she and her colleagues often used when undercover. "Allied Computer Systems, Dallas."

"Even in a small town like Ryansville, it isn't always safe for a woman to be out alone this time of night."

"I suppose things have changed since I was a kid."

A corner of his mouth briefly tipped up. "A few people even lock their doors."

He'd been sent away to boarding school as a kid, she recalled. Before that she'd occasionally seen him in elementary school, though he was two years older than she was. Such an age difference when they were kids had been akin to living on different planets.

But even though she'd despised boys at that age, she remembered Nathan, with his dimples and his coal-dark wavy hair falling over one eye. He'd been quiet, and nicer than the little toads who made spitballs and told crude jokes at recess.

The fates that had given him those cherubic dimples as a child had definitely smiled on him as an adult. In the light of a street lamp overhead, his sharply sculpted cheekbones shadowed a lean hard face. Where once there'd been cute little dimples, slashes deepened in his cheeks when he grinned.

Not that he'd smiled at her much. Right now, his dark brows were lowered and he seemed particularly interested in her backpack.

"I noticed you coming up Oak. Have you been walking long?"

He wanted more than a simple answer—he wanted to know exactly where she'd been. "We covered a lot of backstreets," she said, with a vague wave of her hand. "We've been out a couple of hours, maybe."

"Happen to wander through the trailer court south of here?"

"Nope."

"Not even close?"

"Nope—we didn't go that far. Why, was there some trouble?"

"See anyone cruising around?"

"Not for the last hour or so."

He waited quietly, an age-old tactic designed to spur people into nervous chatter just to fill that awkward silence. When she didn't, he sighed. "Do you always carry a heavy backpack when you walk in town?"

"I take night photographs sometimes. When the light is just right."

His brow lifted.

"Of *nature,* not someone's open window. I'll give you the roll of film in my camera if you want proof. I also do some stargazing when I get away from the streetlights in town. I'm carrying a small telescope and a blanket, as well as a camera."

"Into the constellations, are you?"

"The worst amateur, but I try." Harold bumped his nose on her thigh. "Well...if there's nothing else..."

Nathan tipped his head in acknowledgment and turned back toward his car. At the door he paused. ''Be careful. There were a couple of burglaries in the trailer court tonight, and you never know who you might run into. Help isn't always close by.''

Breathing a sigh of relief, she watched as his cruiser pulled away and headed up the hill.

The last thing she could afford to do was attract the attention of the law...or anyone else.

CHAPTER THREE

ON MONDAY EVENING Nathan climbed down the ladder, relieved when his feet hit ground, and lifted a hand to shade his eyes against the evening sun. "What do you think?"

His godfather, Ian Flynn, studied the two-story Victorian and nodded in approval. Trim, impeccably dressed in a charcoal wool suit and his trademark Italian loafers, he'd carefully stayed on the paved walkway leading to the double front doors. "You're getting a lot done. You've had it what—six months, now?"

"Seven. I thought I'd be further along by now."

Ian pursed his lips, studying the ornate scrollwork at the gables, the lacy fretwork above the balcony. "You aren't trying to do all of this yourself, I hope."

"I had someone else replace the roof and the highest trim." Nathan unbuckled his toolbelt and draped it over a nearby sawhorse.

"So at this rate you'll be done b—"

"2010."

Ian clapped him on the back. "Believe me, these projects are never done. I like the color, by the way." The house was now as it had been before, pale buttercup accented with crisp white gingerbread trim and touches of deep yellow and delft blue.

Nathan had drawn the line at painting the front door its original bright red, though, a touch of whimsy typical of his eccentric great-aunt who'd toured Europe at ninety-three and had had her ears double-pierced in celebration of her hundredth birthday.

"It's a shame it passed out of the family's hands." Ian glanced around the yard. "Have your parents been over?"

"I've invited them, but they haven't stopped by."

"Your mother was always one stubborn woman. But Patrick?"

"We're all pleasantly polite. I make my appearances at holidays and birthdays." Nathan tipped his head toward the patrol car parked in the drive. "They still take my career choice as a personal affront. Especially now that I'm back in the area."

Ian snorted. "Salt on the wound?"

"They think I should be an executive, not a cop, but that isn't going to happen." Nathan shrugged. "My sister Meredith is much better suited to take over the Roswell-family companies than I ever was, anyway."

He'd certainly never met anyone with more competitive drive, which was one reason they'd never been particularly close. As a child she'd been given to long sulks over something as simple as losing at Monopoly.

"Your parents will give up one of these days." Ian glanced at his watch. "Guess I'd better run. I've got a board meeting tonight."

Nathan grinned. "I thought you'd retired. As the company owner you should be basking in the sun in Cancun."

"I can't let go." Ian smiled ruefully. "Mostly I just check in."

"Everything going well?"

"Robert can be a pompous son of a gun, but Sanderson hasn't had to lay off anyone this year. That's more than a lot of companies can say these days. Sales of our Aunt Emma's product line are looking strong." Ian jingled the change in the pocket of his slacks. "I'll do whatever it takes to keep my company and this town going. Good to see you again, Nathan. Maybe we can have dinner sometime."

"I'd like that." Nathan waved as Ian stepped into his car, then turned back to the front of his house and studied his handiwork.

At least here he could accomplish something and see immediate results.

He hadn't found evidence linking anyone to the break-ins at the trailer court over the weekend. The Hanrahan woman had been nearby, but there'd been nothing edgy or evasive in her manner when he'd questioned her on the street. Either she was innocent, or she was the most accomplished liar he'd come across in a long while.

Some aspects of his job were frustrating, blocked by dead ends, alibis and legal red tape that could set a guilty man free. But this house—this entire place— filled him with a sense of peace and satisfaction he hadn't felt in years.

Two hours of work, and he could have a section

of fence fixed. Another three or four hours and he could reclaim an overgrown flower garden or give another part of the exterior a fresh coat of paint.

Ian had spoken of the potential here, and he'd been right. Nathan felt it every time he drove down the curved lane and parked in front. He was building a home, a good life for himself, and pursuing a career he loved.

But now he found himself wondering about a certain red-haired woman. A pretty, self-possessed woman with an air of mystery that had intrigued him from the first moment he'd seen her on the streets of Ryansville last Saturday.

What sort of woman went jogging in the middle of the night or had the courage to return to a town where people associated her name with the worst local crime in the past fifty years?

THE NEXT MORNING, Sara was up by seven, dressed in a simple black skirt, peach-colored blouse and low heels. She took Harold for a brief walk around the block. He wagged his tail forlornly as she grabbed her car keys and headed for the door. "Not this time, buddy. But I'll be back soon." She rubbed his ears. "Wish me luck."

Given the droop of his head, he'd be sitting patiently at the door until she returned.

Minutes later she parked her car in Sanderson's visitors' lot and surveyed the building at close range.

She vaguely remembered the old section of the facility from her childhood. The security lighting and high perimeter fencing were new, but the old brick facade and cracked cement sidewalk leading to the front door were the same.

Her dad had worked here before his death. She remembered sitting with Mom and Kyle under the big old maple near the side entrance, with Dad's forgotten lunch box in her hands. When the noon whistle blew, he'd stride out to greet them with a twinkle in his eye and big smile on his face. "How's my best girl?" he'd tease before lifting her high.

He forgot his lunch often, and looking back from an adult perspective, she realized he'd wanted the company of his family during his lunch break as much as he'd wanted those bologna-and-cheese sandwiches and homemade chocolate-chip cookies.

Where had everything gone wrong? True, she'd been just a child that summer, but she couldn't remember anything out of the ordinary. Yet just a few months later—right before Christmas—Daniel Hanrahan had been found standing over the body of Frank Grover with a gun in his hand.

She'd been only seven years old the day her dad killed a man, then hung himself in the tiny Ryansville jail.

Shaking off the memories, Sara stepped into the cool, dark entrance to Sanderson's front-office building and paused to let her eyes adjust to the dim lighting.

The central hallway was flanked by oak doors, each with opaque, pebbled glass windows bearing old-fashioned gilt letters. Main Office. Accounting. Manager. Mail Room. She walked down the hallway until she found Human Resources.

A heavyset brunette in her midthirties—Mrs. Webster, according to the name plate on her desk—looked up from some documents in her hand and gave Sara an apologetic smile. "I'm sorry, but we're not hiring right n—" Her eyes widened. "Sara? Sara Hanrahan?"

Sara saw now that the woman did look vaguely familiar. Take off fifty pounds, change the hairstyle…

"It's me, Jane Kinney…Webster, now." She set the papers aside and gave a self-deprecating wave of one hand. "A lot older, a little heavier, but hopefully a little wiser. I was two years ahead of you in school, remember? When you worked at the Dairy Queen, I was next door working at Whidbey Dry Cleaners. I left town for quite a few years, but now I'm back for good."

Allen's preliminary report hadn't mentioned Jane, but she might be an even better lead than the ones he'd listed. "So now you've got a job here," Sara said. "Good going, Jane. You've obviously done well."

"Maybe…but not with everything." Her broad smile faded to rueful acceptance as she held up her left hand and wiggled her bare ring finger. "Divorced."

"I'm sorry. Kids?"

"Someday, I hope. What about you?"

"Single. Came close a couple times, but things didn't work out."

"Well, good luck finding someone in Ryansville." Jane rolled her eyes. "Unless you like spending weekends in a bass boat, a duck blind or an ice-fishing shack in the middle of a frozen lake. Me? I prefer movies and dinner to mosquitoes and frostbite.''

Since Sara planned to stay in town for just a few months, any romantic entanglements were unlikely and would probably be more trouble than they'd be worth. Suddenly an image of Nathan flashed through her thoughts. Not that possibilities existed there now or at any other point in this lifetime.

Whatever he did for a living, he was still one of the Roswells. He'd hardly bring home the daughter of a seamstress and the factory worker who'd murdered his boss. And while even a single afternoon with his wealthy, snobbish family was unimaginable to her, she knew they'd enjoy the situation even less.

''I'm not looking for a guy,'' Sara said with a smile. ''I just need a job. Any openings in accounting?''

Jane's face fell. ''I'm so sorry. We haven't hired anyone in months.''

''Even for something like a bookkeeper? Secretary? I'm not choosy, really.''

Jane shook her head, then shot a glance at the door and lowered her voice. ''We've been lucky not to have layoffs. We lost a few accounts this past year, and business has been slow.''

''Sounds like bad news for the town.''

''Oh, not yet,'' Jane quickly assured her, her hands fluttering like frightened birds. She clasped them together and dropped them to the blotter on her desk. ''Like I said, no jobs have been lost or anything. I shouldn't have said that. A friend over in the business office told me that we'll even be getting our Christmas bonuses again this year.''

"I won't repeat what you said, honest. Could I fill out an application, anyway? Or could you put my name on a waiting list?''

"Of course.'' Jane stood and walked to an open doorway in the corner that led into a small storeroom, then returned with an application form, clipboard and pen. "You can just sit right where you are to fill it out, and I'll sure let you know if anything opens up.''

Five minutes later Sara had completed the form, using prearranged references that would be forwarded anonymously to DEA staff. She handed it back. "Any chance I could have a tour just to see what the place is like?''

"No, we don't do that. The owner says it's disruptive and unsanitary, having people walking through. And Robert Kelstrom—he's the manager who really runs the place—says it could be a risk for company secrets.''

"Secrets? About hand lotions and cleaning solutions?''

"There's a lot of competition out there, you know,'' Jane said defensively. "It could happen.''

"Of course. I wasn't thinking.'' Jane's caution and loyalty might be a problem, but she'd be a good initial contact. Sara rose to leave. "Thanks for letting me fill out the application.''

At the door she stopped and turned back. "It's been a long time since I've lived here. Maybe we could meet for lunch sometime? I could pick you up.''

Jane brightened. She was probably a very lonely woman, Sara realized.

"I'd love it!" Jane pulled a business card from her top desk drawer, wrote something on the back and held it out. "This has my direct line at work and the company's hours, plus I've added my home address and number. Call me anytime!"

As she walked out to her car, Sara felt a twinge of guilt about using Jane for information. But with luck, the entire investigation would turn up nothing at all, and Jane would never be the wiser.

That is, unless she proved to be far less innocent than she appeared.

"YOU DON'T HAVE a microfiche?" Hoping she'd heard wrong, Sara stared at the elderly librarian. "You know, a way to store old documents and newspapers?"

"I know what it is," Miss Perkins sniffed. "We just don't have one." She lifted one gaunt arm and pointed toward a massive wooden door at the far end of the corridor. "The newspapers are through there, up one flight. First door on your left. Put everything back as you found it. Don't forget to turn off the lights."

"You're open for another two hours, right?"

"Tuesdays until nine for the past seventy-five years."

And she'd probably been at her desk for every one of them. Sara remembered visiting the library as a child and seeing Miss Perkins in her position of power at the main desk, guarding the library with an eagle eye. She hadn't mellowed much with age.

"Thanks, Miss Perkins."

"No gum in the library, Miss Hanrahan. And no more overdues on those Black Stallion books, you hear?"

Sara looked over her shoulder and caught a hint of a twinkle in the old woman's eye. "You remember?"

"I don't forget the children who show promise, Miss Hanrahan," she said crisply.

Before Sara could reply, the librarian turned her back and began sorting through the stack of mail on her desk.

Smiling, Sara headed down the hall and up the narrow stairs. Who would have guessed that the woman known as the "Witch of the Ryansville Library"—at least by the kids in Sara's high-school class—actually had a sense of humor?

A musty smell assailed Sara as she opened the door to the room containing the newspaper stacks, flipped on the switch and stepped inside.

The single light fixture, a two-bulb affair suspended from the ceiling, illuminated an oak desk in the center of the room. The stacks themselves loomed deep in the shadows.

Sara worked her way down the aisles, squinting at the spidery writing on the small cards tacked to the end of each aisle: 1895–1905, 1906–1915. 1916–1935…

As the years passed, the *Ryansville Gazette* had evolved from something akin to a newsletter to a standard newspaper format with a substantial number of pages.

She'd come to research articles over the past five years regarding the Sanderson Company, but when she reached the 1976–1985 issues, she took a sharp breath. Everything would be here—the details of her father's arrest, the reports of Franklin's death. She'd been so young back then and had understood little of what was going on.

Moving down the narrow aisle, she found 1977, then the issues for June…July…August. Her heart skipped a beat. September…October.

Here was the event that had altered her life forever. That had changed Bernice from a busy mother of two who'd attended church and the PTA to a silent, embittered woman who survived as a seamstress and rarely left her home.

With trembling hands Sara lifted the September and October issues and took them to the table. She stood there for a moment, afraid of what she'd find and unable to make the first move.

From the corner of her eye she glimpsed someone large step into the room. Startled, she moved away from the table, turned and found herself looking up at Nathan Roswell—who apparently hadn't expected to see anyone else up here, either.

She gave an embarrassed laugh. "I'm sorry—you surprised me!"

"Same here." An easy grin deepened the dimples in his cheeks. When he wasn't frowning at her, the man had a nice smile. "I wasn't sure anyone ever came upstairs."

"It's...uh...my first time up here." She shot a quick glance at her collection of papers on the table, then leaned over to scoop them up. He leaned over at the same time and their fingers collided.

He must have felt the same sensation, the same flicker of surprise she did, because he stilled, lifted his gaze to meet hers.

"I'll...just put these back and get out of your way," she managed after an awkward silence.

He looked down at the stack of papers on the desk and apparently recognized the significance of 1977, because his brows lowered. So he knew about her father, then. Was that why he'd looked at her with such suspicion both times they'd met? Did he figure she was just as capable of criminal acts?

"That was a tough year, wasn't it? I'm sorry about your dad," he said quietly.

"Thanks." She shelved the newspapers and turned to leave, not wanting to face questions she couldn't answer.

"I wasn't living here when it happened," he continued, "but I remembered hearing rumors. Clay Benson gave me the details. I can imagine how hard it was for you and your family."

No, you can't, she thought. A young boy of wealth and privilege wouldn't have had a clue back then, and the man he'd become wouldn't be able to do much better. What would be a tragedy in his life—a day when the Rolls didn't start? A downturn on Wall Street?

She gave him a grim smile. "We're all doing fine now. See you around."

The casual words of farewell were exactly right, leaving no room for further discussion and no hint of encouragement. Any interest in this man would only spell trouble on a personal and professional level.

But something in his eyes kept her from slipping out the door. Something dark and compelling and masculine, calling to a part of her that had been dormant for a very long time. For just a heartbeat, she imagined things that could never be.

And then she turned and walked away.

CHAPTER FOUR

NATHAN DROVE SLOWLY up Poplar, past the noisy crowd forming in front of Walker Elementary School, and pulled to a stop in front of the deputy's office in the next block. He climbed out of his patrol car and stared back down the street.

Christmas. Bah, humbug, he thought grimly.

Here it was, the second Saturday in October, and peak fall color had hit with the enthusiasm of a child with a new box of paints. On his drive into town, the riot of crimsons, brilliant oranges and fluorescent yellows set against the deep emeralds of the pines rimming Lake Ryan had been breathtaking, the air crisp and cool with the sweet scents of evergreens and burning leaves.

And instead of enjoying this perfect fall day, half the population of Ryansville was standing in the schoolyard, arguing over just how commercial they could make Christmas this year.

Slamming his car door, he pivoted toward his office and nearly fell over the Shueller boy, who was a riot of color himself, from his bright carrot hair and freckles to the tips of his paint-spattered sneakers.

"Hi! Are you coming to the Christmas meeting?"

The eager light in Josh's eyes couldn't be mistaken, even through the kid's thick glasses.

"I don't think so." At Josh's crestfallen expression, he added, "I think they've got more than enough help over there, don't you?"

"Yeah, I guess." The boy's expression brightened. "But this is gonna be the best ever. There's gonna be a parade and a Christmas show and a contest for the most Christmas lights on a house. And they want real animals and people to be in the na…na…"

"Nativity scene?"

Josh's broad grin displayed a number of missing teeth. "Yeah. Doesn't it sound cool?"

Maybe to an eight-year-old. But the less Nathan had to do with it, the better. Yvonne Weatherfield had already pressured him to head up a planning committee, but he'd managed to decline. If he could withstand the coy demands of Ryansville's most prominent socialite, he could manage to sidestep one small boy. "Good luck, Josh. I hope you get a starring role."

"Well…guess I gotta get over there."

Nathan watched the boy trudge across the street. At the other side, however, the Christmas spirit apparently took hold of him once again, because he took off at a run to join the others.

Each year a new chairperson promised bigger-better-brighter than ever, and each year, the local businesspeople and women's groups rallied with ever-greater fervor, all in the name of attracting heavier shopping traffic during the prime weeks of December.

Where was the true meaning of Christmas? Not in fancy decorations and busy cash registers.

Childhood memories assaulted him. His mother had always made the family home a dazzling wonderland for as long as he could remember. As a kid, he'd been warned countless times never to touch anything, and he'd sometime wondered if the candlelit splendor she re-created was meant only to impress those who attended her Women's Auxiliary Christmas tea.

Once inside the small brick building, he rolled the tension out of his shoulders, picked up the scattering of mail beneath the slot next to the door and strode to his office in the back.

The place was blessedly quiet—Ollie worked only on Mondays, Wednesdays and Friday mornings—though the answering machine light blinked steadily and a stack of new faxes waited in the tray of the machine.

Nothing urgent in either case, he knew. All 911 calls in Jefferson County were routed through the sheriff's office in Hawthorne, and both his two-way radio and the pager on his belt had been relatively quiet all morning.

Lifting the faxes, he thumbed through them for new Crime Alert Network notices. A couple of liquor stores had been hit in the next county, a runaway, a stolen Ford pickup down in Fergus Falls, some lakeshore cabins had been burglarized over in Detroit Lakes…

Still studying the notices, he settled into his chair and hit the answering-machine button.

Yvonne's voice cut through the silence. "Just wanted you to know that we're still hoping you'll chair the—"

He hit the erase button.

"Hi, dear, this is your mother. We're leaving for

Florida tomorrow and hoped we might see you tonight at supper. Six o'clock.''

Hitting the erase button again, he sighed. She'd already asked him, and he'd already agreed to be there, barring any emergency calls, but why she still invited him so often wasn't entirely clear. Neither she nor his father seemed particularly pleased when he showed up.

These dinners were inevitably chilly affairs, his father shifting uncomfortably in his chair, his mother making awkward attempts at conversation.

Neither Patrick nor Elena Roswell had forgiven their son for turning down a position in one of the family companies, and neither one had given up hope that he would come to his senses and return.

And when his sister Meredith was there, it was painfully clear that she feared he might succumb to their wishes someday and thus undermine her own position of power.

Which would happen when cows flew.

Only Ruth, the housekeeper, seemed genuinely glad to see him, and for her wonderful cooking and heartfelt hugs he would have driven to the other side of the Dakotas.

He listened to the rest of the messages, jotting notes in his planner, returned several calls, then started on his IRC's—initial complaint reports—that still had to be written for each of his call-outs on the previous day.

At the sound of the front door opening, he glanced up to find Yvonne Weatherfield approaching with a sultry sway of her hips and an assessing gleam in her eye. Her soft ivory sweater clung tightly to her curves; the matching skirt ended at midthigh. In all of Ryansville there didn't exist a more determined woman.

"I'm so glad I caught you, Nathan," she murmured, her full lips curving into a pout. "We so wanted you at our meeting to help us decide just what to do."

"I'm working today, Yvonne. Sorry."

She smiled brightly. "It's not too late, really. I have to head up the entertainment committee. Would you be willing to help me, just a little?"

The walls of the office seemed to close in on him as he imagined the meetings, the endless phone calls. The very thought made him shudder. "I'm sorry. Another time maybe, but not this year." He stood up and grabbed his keys from the desk. "I'm afraid I have to leave. Good luck pulling a team together. I know you'll do a great job as always."

He ushered her to the door, then closed it behind him and locked it.

"But, Nathan—"

"I really have to go, Yvonne." He strode to his cruiser, unlocked the door and settled behind the wheel.

Across the street, Sara Hanrahan jogged up the steep incline with her dog at her side. In black leggings and an old Dallas Cowboys sweatshirt, her hair hidden by a ball cap, she couldn't have looked more different from Yvonne, yet there was something about her that made him stare. Her easy grace, maybe, or her obvious disregard for what anyone thought.

Damn shame about her dad. He'd read through those newspapers out of curiosity, and the case seemed as clear as Clay had said. Murder, followed by a jail-cell suicide.

She spared his car a brief look, glanced at Yvonne, and kept going without a break in stride, but he could have sworn that her mouth curved into a faint smile.

JOSH DRAGGED HIS FEET up the steep slope on Poplar, his gaze fastened on the cracked cement sidewalk and his heart heavy as lead. The voices of Thad and Ricky Weatherfield still rang in his ears. *Yeah, right, Shueller, like anyone would choose you. For a* Planet of the Apes, *maybe. Or* Return of the Dead.

A lot of the older girls had giggled, and though some of the adults had turned around and frowned, the Weatherfield brothers had just snickered. Usually they were careful not to let anyone else hear their taunts, but they hurt all the same.

It was as if they'd made Josh their prime target—waiting, planning for the chance to be mean. At least they hadn't said anything about his mom this time. If they had, he would have barreled into them again and tried to do something about it. Of course, that would probably have gotten him a detention, and he'd have no chance of being Joseph in the play.

Because no matter what, the Weatherfield boys always stuck up for each other.

"Hey, Josh. What's happening?"

He looked up, surprised to hear Sara Hanrahan's voice and see her standing just a few feet away with her head tipped and a curious look on her face. Harold sat at her side with his tongue lolling out one side of his mouth.

"You look like you just lost your best friend."

He pulled to a stop and scuffed a toe against a broken slab of cement. "Nah."

"Feel okay?"

"Yeah." He watched as her mouth curved into a smile and a nice twinkle gleamed in her eyes, and suddenly he felt a little better. "How's Harold?"

She dropped a hand to the top of the dog's head. "Doing good. Want to walk with us? I was headed out to the Dairy Queen at the edge of town. My treat, if you want to come along."

"Sure!"

With her other hand she reached for her back pocket and handed him her cell phone. "Call your mom and make sure it's okay."

"I'm in fifth grade," he protested, feeling his cheeks warm. The boys had just taunted him about being a mama's boy, and their words were still ricocheting around in his brain. "I don't have to ask her everything."

"No treats if you don't call," Sara said with a wink. "I don't want her mad at me. She might raise my rent."

Josh glanced around, then took the phone and dialed his home number. His mom answered on the second ring.

"Hi, honey. How'd it go? Did you get the part?"

His heart fell at her enthusiasm. Mom was so sure he was bright and talented and popular, but what did she know? Nothing. Nothing about how things were really like, anyway. "The committee's gonna decide in a couple weeks."

"They couldn't pick anyone better than you, Joshie."

He winced at his childhood name, glad that no one nearby could hear it, then rapidly told her about the Dairy Queen, disconnected and handed the phone back. "It's okay."

They fell into step and were halfway to their destination before Sara grinned and bumped into his shoulder. "You still look down in the dumps. What's this about a committee? Are you running for mayor?"

"Joseph."

"Who?"

"You know, for the nativity program downtown." He allowed himself to imagine it for just a moment—the pride on his mom's face, the feeling of being a star, even if it was for just a few hours. The vision faded almost as soon as he conjured it up. "I think there'll be live animals in the display for a few days before Christmas, but on Christmas Eve actors will be there, and they'll get to say their parts."

"I see. So what are the chances of your being Joseph?"

"Probably zero."

"Why? I think you'd be a great Joseph. How is this decided? By a vote?"

"Nah. The committee. But Mrs. Weatherfield—" the name tasted sour on his tongue "—is head of it, and she'll make sure they pick one of her boys."

Sara raised a brow. "That hardly seems fair."

He started to say that it never was, but just shrugged and bit back the words. Whining was a big waste of time, and nothing would ever change. What the Weatherfields wanted, they got.

At the Dairy Queen Sara bought a small cone for Harold and hot fudge malts for Josh and herself, and then they shuffled through fallen leaves at the small park across the street to sit at a picnic table.

"So you're already thinking ahead to Christmas, are you?" Sara asked after a few minutes. "Does your family do special things?"

Josh licked his spoon. "You bet."

"Put up the lights and decorations?"

"Not just that. We have a tree and stuff, but my mom bakes for weeks, and we decorate cookies on Sundays after church. We take 'em to the old people who live alone, and to the nursing home."

"Sounds like fun."

"Then we make a lot of our presents for each other, and we make our cards and—" He stopped, suddenly embarrassed.

"Please, go on."

"My mom sings a lot. She's got a really cool voice, and she sings all the Christmas songs. The funny ones, too. My dad and I sing along, but we sound awful." Warmth spread through his chest at the memories. "Then we have lotsa Swedish food on Christmas Eve, cause my dad's Swedish, and always go to the candlelight service at church before we open presents. I guess everyone does all that stuff, though."

Sara gave him a small smile. "Not everyone."

"So what do you do?"

She stood and tossed her paper napkin into a trash barrel a few feet away. "Not nearly as much."

"You have a Christmas tree, right?"

"Um…sometimes."

"And mistletoe?"

"Nope."

"Do you come back here, then?"

"Not always. Sometimes I'm too busy working."

Her Christmases sounded awful. "I can give you some special mistletoe, if you want it. We get lots, and it's the best kind of all. My uncle Pete hunts it with a shotgun."

She laughed aloud at that. "A what?"

"A shotgun," he repeated patiently. "Mistletoe grows way up in the treetops where he lives in West Virginia. It's too high to climb after, and it's real bad for the trees. So he blams it with his 20-gauge."

"Really."

"Then it falls to the ground." She gave him a look that said she didn't believe him, but that was okay. Tonight he'd e-mail Uncle Pete and ask him to send extra. If anyone needed Pete's magic mistletoe, it was someone who spent Christmases alone and didn't even put up a tree. "It's cool that you get to be up here for Christmas this year, right? You can be with your mom!"

She didn't answer for a long time. "Count your blessings," she said finally, reaching out to tousle his hair. "You're a very lucky kid."

Every year since he could remember, Josh had looked forward to Christmas with feelings that seemed to bubble up out of nowhere until he could barely stand to count off the days. Not because he knew there'd be huge presents under the tree—he'd learned long ago that they didn't have that kind of money.

But it was something else much better. The beautiful lights on the tree at midnight, when all the other lights were off and just the embers in the fireplace remained. The smell of baking and the beautiful music and the feeling that everyone else in the world was happy at this very moment.

Yet Sara and Deputy Roswell didn't seem to share that feeling a bit. How could such cool grown-ups be so messed up?

He studied her when she wasn't watching and wished he could do something to help.

MONDAY MORNING, Sara knocked on her mother's door and waited patiently. Then tried again. "It's just me, Mom. Are you in there?"

After a moment she heard the sound of slow footsteps, a hesitation that told her Bernice was peering through the curtain, then two dead bolts slid back and a safety chain jingled loosely against the door frame.

The door swung open and her mother stood before her in shades of gray, from the gray hair scraped into a bun to her house dress and sturdy lace-up shoes. On a foggy day, she would have disappeared in the mist. "I see you didn't bring that big dog of yours," she said disdainfully.

"His name is Harold, Mom, and he's a very well-trained dog."

"You're dressed up."

"Yes, well..." Sara glanced down at her navy silk blouse and beige slacks. "I thought I'd go down to the plant and ask again about job openings in the main office."

Something flashed in Bernice's eyes—could it be delight?—but disappeared quickly. "Humpf. Not that it will do much good. I don't think they've hired anyone new in a coon's age."

They stood looking at each other until Sara gently

asked, "How about some tea, Mom? We could visit awhile before I go."

"Oh. Well, sure." Her mother gave a flustered flap of her hand and stepped back to let Sara come inside, then she methodically fastened each lock and bolt.

Sara moved into the kitchen and started a kettle of water on the stove, then leaned a hip against the sink. She'd been in town more than two weeks already and had stopped in several times, but Bernice had yet to agree to having lunch somewhere or even to taking a drive out to see the fall leaves. Maybe it was time to face the past.

"I went to the library last week," Sara murmured, watching her mother's nervous movements as she collected tea bags, cups and spoons. "I'd never been up to the newspaper room before, have you?"

"No." Bernice arranged the cups on the kitchen table, with the handles turned precisely at the right angle.

"I couldn't believe that Mrs. Perkins remembered me after all these years." Sara chuckled. "She's still in complete control of the place, too."

"Always was methodical, even as a girl." Bernice paced to the window, then back to the table, smoothing her apron as she walked.

"Older than you by quite a bit, though."

"Well, yes. But the town was smaller then. We all knew each other very well."

And there were many in town who would still be friendly toward Bernice if she'd give them a chance. But since her husband had died, she'd walled herself away from everyone—her neighbors, her siblings, her children. Especially her children.

The kettle whistled. Sara carried it to the table and poured two cups, then set the kettle on a back burner. "Come sit here with me, Momma."

Bernice finally sat down and began her careful ritual with her tea bag, giving it her undivided attention. Dipping, inspecting. Dipping, inspecting.

Unable to wait any longer, Sara gripped the handle of her cup and took a deep breath. "I went to the newspaper archives to look up something. When I walked past the aisles of newspapers I came across the stacks from 1977."

Bernice stilled.

"Mom, I found the December issues."

Her mother's face blanched, her gaze riveted to the teacup in her hands.

"I was just a kid in second grade," Sara said gently. "I heard people talk, but I never really heard it from your angle. It's a hard thing for us to keep inside for so long. Don't you think so?"

Bernice's spoon slipped from her grasp and hit the table with a clatter. *"No."*

"I didn't read those articles. Someone came up there, so I left." An image of Nathan's arrival flashed through her mind, but she immediately suppressed it. She'd fled the room like a scalded cat. "But I need to talk about this, Mom. When Dad died it changed everything—you, me, Kyle—and nothing was ever the same again. Look at you now. Do you ever go out? Ever try to have some fun?"

The older woman's lips formed a hard, pinched line. "You know the facts."

"But I don't know *why,* Mom, and for twenty-five years this subject has been completely off-limits. Why would a loving father go out and kill one of the nicest old guys in town and then kill himself hours later?''

"What does it matter?" Her voice shaking with anger, Bernice fumbled with her cup as she rose, then crossed the kitchen. Her cup clattered into the sink. "He had a nice home. Children to support. He betrayed us all—and for what?" She gestured sharply around the room. "He left us with nothing."

Bernice disappeared into her bedroom and shut the door behind her. And that, as Sara well knew, meant that she wouldn't be back out for hours.

Years had passed, but her mother's bitterness was as fresh as the day Daniel Hanrahan died.

However, Sara would be home for a good three months this time, and she was going to delve into the past to find out what had happened to her gentle father on that cold December day.

Because even after all this time, none of it made sense.

CHAPTER FIVE

ON THE WAY DOWN to the Sanderson plant, Sara pulled to a stop in front of the post office. Though her daily communications with Special Agent Allen Larson at the regional DEA office in Minneapolis were exchanged by FAX and e-mail, she still checked her post-office box daily.

She'd forwarded some magazine subscriptions, and then there were always the credit-card bills that never seemed to end. Especially not when one owned an aging Ford Bronco that made mechanics smile with glee. When this case was over, she'd go back to Dallas and do some serious vehicle shopping.

Lost in thought, she crossed the sidewalk and opened the door of the post office only to find herself staring at a broad chest clad in a dark-blue deputy's shirt. Damn.

She lifted her gaze to meet the amused expression on Nathan's face.

"Preoccupied?"

"Um...no. Actually, yes." She jerked her chin toward the Bronco. "Just thinking about when my old pal and I can part ways."

"Usually I see you out walking." He glanced at

her silky blouse and linen slacks, and a corner of his mouth lifted. "You must have big plans."

A young mother with two boys came up behind Sara, so she stepped farther inside the building to let them pass. "Not really. Excuse me—"

She started past him toward the mailboxes along the back wall, but he followed her and leaned a shoulder against the wall as she retrieved her mail. Two Visa bills, a utility bill for her apartment in Dallas. One from Amoco with her expenses for her trip north. Fortunately the DEA was picking up the tab.

"Had any luck finding a job around here?"

"None yet. See you around." She started past him.

"Whoa! What's the rush?"

She lowered her voice. "It's nice seeing you again, and all that, but I really have to go. I—"

"Coffee? Bill's Coffee Shop is right next door."

Several other customers glanced over at their conversation, and one of them gave her a wink.

Great. Just what she needed—people talking about Nathan getting cozy with the new woman in town. What were the chances, if she ever did get a job at Sanderson, that she'd be privy to any illegal activities if people linked her with the deputy sheriff?

"Please?"

The genuine concern in his eyes stopped her short. The simple courtesy of that word made it nearly impossible to say no.

"I'd like to," she hedged. "But I need to get down to Sanderson again."

"You got an interview?"

"No, but—"

He shook his head. "Do they have your name and number?"

"Yes, but it still won't hurt—"

"Believe me, they haven't hired for a long time. I would have heard." He gave her a lopsided grin. "There's nothing you can't find out at Bill's, and hiring down at the plant would be headline news."

And walking into Bill's on Nathan's arm would likely add her to the daily news, too. The possibility gave her the willpower to decline an invitation she wished she could accept.

"I'm sorry," she said firmly. "But maybe you'll give me a rain check."

She spun on her heel and strode out of the post office to the Bronco, unlocked the door and climbed in without looking back. She could feel Nathan's curious gaze, though, even after she'd started down Main.

Not that she imagined he cared about her particularly. She'd simply been convenient, someone from outside this small town who might be interesting to talk to for a while.

Maybe the shock of being refused would do him good.

After stopping by her apartment to give Harold a quick walk, she drove down to Sanderson. Good timing, probably. The noon whistle would blow in just fifteen minutes, and with luck, Jane Webster would be happy to have some company.

The secretary had already opened her bag of lunch at her desk when Sara walked in. "Hey, Jane—guess you aren't in the mood to go out for lunch?"

Startled, Jane looked up from unwrapping a sandwich. A broad smile lit her face. "Sara! Good to see you again." Her smile dimmed. "I'm real sorry I haven't been able to call you about any jobs, but nothing has come up, honest."

"That's not your fault. I just came by to see you, though. Can you leave?"

"Jeez, I wish I could." She tipped her head toward the phone. "I have to stick around to answer the phone, because Mr. Flynn's secretary has gone. Otherwise I could."

"There's no one else? Maybe in accounting?"

"Nope. This week it's supposed to be either Marcy or me." She held up a good-size lunch sack and gave Sara a guilty smile. "I overdid my lunch today, though. Want to join me here?"

Even better. "Sounds great." Sara pulled a chair up to the front of the desk and accepted a sandwich and a bag of chips. "Sure you have enough?"

Jane rose and patted her ample hips. "You're doing me a favor. Coffee?"

A quick glance around the room didn't reveal a coffeepot. "I'd love it, if you don't mind."

When Jane left the office, Sara listened to her footsteps heading down the hall and then eased out of her chair and surveyed the room. A bank of file drawers filled one wall. An older-model tape-backup unit sat next to the computer monitor on Jane's desk, and a handful of disks were scattered on the credenza behind her chair.

She leaned forward. Reached toward the tape backup machine, which would likely contain more information than she could have ever hoped to gather in one fell swoop.

"Can I help you?"

The cold male voice cut through the silence like a scalpel and nearly stopped her heart.

She grabbed an apple from the open lunch sack on the desk and turned around slowly, holding it out for the man to see. "I'm an old friend of Jane's. We're eating lunch together and catching up on old times. And you are...?"

He was slender with short silver-gray hair, an expensively cut suit and an air of command. Behind the designer wire-rims, his eyes were hard and suspicious. "Where's Jane?"

Jane's footsteps came down the hall, and she appeared in the doorway a moment later, a look of confusion and worry on her plump face. "Oh, dear. I hope you don't mind, Mr. Flynn. My friend just stopped by, and I thought we could have lunch together. I'm still watching the phones. I...I haven't done this before."

"You and I will talk later, Ms. Webster."

Jane paled. "I didn't realize. I'm so sorry, I can ask her to leave if it isn't okay."

He gave a sharp wave of his hand. "Finish your lunch, Ms. Webster, but I do want to talk to you after Marcy returns."

He gave Sara a long, searching look, as if cataloging her every feature for future reference, then disappeared down the hallway as quietly as he'd come.

When Jane handed Sara the coffee, her hands were trembling. "I'm sorry—I hope he wasn't too upset when he found you here. I really didn't think it would be a problem.''

"I think he was more startled than anything," Sara said easily. "Finding a stranger alone in the office would look suspicious to any manager. I don't blame him a bit." She waved a hand toward the computer and the banks of file cabinets. "You probably have tons of sensitive business data in here, right? The scoop on everything that goes on?"

Jane sank into the chair behind her desk and gave a gusty sigh. "Just human-resources information. Records of staff problems and dismissals. Everything else is down in accounting. I honestly can't imagine anyone being interested—it's hard enough for me to deal with this every day."

"I suppose. So was that the big boss?"

"You bet. Ian Flynn is the owner. When he retired, he promoted Robert Kelstrom to take over, but Ian still comes in almost every day."

"Is Kelstrom good to work for?"

Jane tried to smother a laugh. "Let's just say that he knows every aspect of this business and runs a tight ship. Without him, who knows? Some people figure the company wouldn't be in business if it weren't for Robert."

"Nice guy to work with?"

"Very efficient. Particular." She grinned. "I think he's sort of cute, too. He's even available."

Interesting. "I wish you luck, then."

They finished the sandwiches, then munched on the chips and fruit, catching up on old news around town. At twelve-thirty, Jane gave a sigh of contentment.

"This has been fun," she said wistfully. "Maybe we can get together sometime for supper, or lunch on my day off? I haven't had much time for fun since I moved back here."

"I'd love it." Sara eased her conscience by telling herself that she might have befriended this lonely woman, anyway.

Once outside, she sauntered out to the Bronco as if she hadn't a care in the world. But the hairs at the back of her neck prickled, and she knew someone was watching. Jane, maybe? As she opened the door, she glanced casually over her shoulder, prepared to wave to her old friend.

There was someone standing in the shadows at an upstairs window, all right. But it wasn't a woman.

FOR THE REST of the week, Sara continued her surveillance of Sanderson by night and her observation of the town by day.

She received faxes directly from the state Crime Alert Network just as Nathan probably did at his office. If a steady stream of drugs were being routed through this sleepy little town, it wasn't obvious.

New information in Allen's daily messages had tapered off, though he'd recently relayed rumors about a large shipment planned in several weeks.

Long-term surveillance or undercover work could be boring, frustrating and go on for months on end without any real excitement, but this case—set in the town of her childhood—carried with it a sense of the surreal.

Maybe if things had been different, she would have

felt at home and enjoyed the time away from Dallas, but she had few connections here. The tragedy of her father's death, her mother's reaction and the public outcry against her family's name had changed everything.

Friday night she glanced out the window of the apartment, then whistled Harold to her side. Darkness had fallen, and it was time to leave.

Up on the hill overlooking the plant, she settled into her usual spot with Harold curled at her feet, withdrew her binoculars, notebook and penlight, and waited.

The nights were cooler now—mid-October had brought a hard frost last night. Sara remembered that winter snows sometimes started as early as Halloween. With luck this would be a milder winter than most.

Over the past three weeks she'd continued her surveillance, documented activity at the plant, faxed daily reports. Repetitive details, but if the tip about major drug shipments coming through this town was true, destroying this pipeline would mean one more battle in the war on drugs had been won.

For that, she'd stay here as long as it took.

At midnight Harold stirred. A low growl rumbled through his body and vibrated against her calf.

She stilled. Listened.

The skeleton crew of night employees had been outside smoking around eleven, but all of them were back inside now.

A flash of light caught her gaze, and she leaned

forward with the binoculars to check the back gate—one rarely used, except by the lawn crew.

A dark truck eased toward the back of the plant, its headlights off. When it pulled to a stop, three figures darted to the back of the vehicle and swiftly unloaded several dozen packing cartons.

Harold's growl rumbled louder. He rose into a sit, his ears pricked and his hackles raised.

Sara lifted her camera and snapped off several dozen photographs.

The vehicle left with the same stealth as it had arrived.

Bingo.

At 4:00 a.m., still on an adrenaline high, Sara packed up her things and started down the trail, with Harold at her side.

Bad timing to be heading home. She could hardly claim to have been stargazing or to be up for an early run at this hour. But the good deputy of Ryansville was undoubtedly snuggled in bed, and nothing ever stirred around this town before five in the morning.

Which was why the sound of soft footsteps sent a chill straight to her heart. She stopped abruptly. Slipped off the trail to the left and crouched, placing a warning hand on Harold's neck, her senses on high alert.

The faint sounds drew closer.

This was no deer or bumbling raccoon. These were human footfalls, carefully placed to avoid detection.

"No," she whispered to the dog, resting a hand over his muzzle.

Harold remembered his training, but his entire body shook with anticipation.

A man came into view, his features indistinguishable in the dark. Ten feet away he stopped. Stood in complete silence for an eternity. Then slowly moved on, as if he, too, were wary of others in the dark.

Had he heard her? Possibly seen her in the distance—though he surely couldn't have identified her.

She waited another half hour before finally resuming her cautious trip home, and even then she halted at every sound.

CHAPTER SIX

IT HAD BEEN a successful week. Nathan had made it through dinner with his parents last weekend, and now they'd left for Sanibel Island off the coast of Florida, for three weeks of sun and margaritas on the beach. For which he was thankful. They could enjoy the sun, and he could enjoy the peace.

His mother had given him her usual talk about family responsibility and the fact that his law-enforcement career was both far too dangerous and far too beneath his potential. Nothing new there.

This morning, Ollie had given him her weekly lecture about finding a suitable wife, so at least that was out of the way, as well.

On the law-and-order front, there'd been no domestic disturbances, no major accidents out on the highway. A recent string of lakeshore-cabin burglaries had been solved when one of the owners arrived in midweek, found his cabin door ajar and turned his rottweiler loose for an investigation of its own.

The two cowering teenagers, who'd driven all the way from Newbrook, had been more than happy to surrender when faced with the dog's teeth. They'd confessed to the trailer-court break-ins, as well.

So why did Nathan feel a nagging sense of frustration?

The answer came to him as he watched Clay move a knight and neatly eliminate his bishop.

"Your move." Clay lounged back in his chair with a triumphant gleam of satisfaction in his eyes. "If you can."

Nathan studied the board, considering and discarding half a dozen options. "I can always move—it's just a matter of whether or not I want to speed up the end of the game."

Clay gave a bark of laughter. "That's what I like. A man who knows when he's whipped and doesn't prolong the agony."

"I didn't say I was defeated. In fact—" Nathan moved his remaining bishop and retired Clay's queen "—I think you got a little rusty while you were off gallivanting in Chicago with your wife these past two weeks."

"Anything interesting happen while we were gone?"

"No headline news. I did a little research on the Grover murder, by the way."

"That's old, old news."

"While you were gone, I went through the case files, then stopped at the library to look at the newspapers from back then. When I walked in, Hanrahan's daughter was just about to do the same thing."

"Probably curious. She was a little mite back then, too young to know what was going on." Clay gave a noncommittal shrug, but a muscle ticking along his jaw betrayed his sudden tension. "You won't find anything now that we didn't find back then."

"Maybe not. But why would a quiet family man with no record, no history of conflict with his boss, suddenly turn on the man and kill him?"

Clay studied the chessboard for a long moment, then lifted his gaze to Nathan's. "There's logic to this game, but with some crimes, there isn't any. You'll never know why a guy was fine one day, then snapped the next." His gaze chilled. "Grover and Hanrahan are dead and buried. Second-guessing a good investigation is a waste of time."

"I'm not implying there were mistakes."

"You won't find any. Looks to me," Clay added with a grim smile, "like life up here is a lot less exciting than down in Minneapolis, if you're dredging up old cases for something to do."

Maybe the old guy's defensiveness came from pride, Nathan thought. Maybe it came from insecurity now that his career was over.

Or maybe he was right.

"The report says the Mitchell boys heard something out there and called for help."

Clay shifted impatiently in his chair. "They'd been out at the sledding hill back of the plant with their friends and a case of beer. If the case had come to trial, the fact that they were drunk as skunks wouldn't have helped their testimony much."

"They didn't see anything, though, right?"

"You read the case files. They heard loud voices, then two gunshots. Scared the hell out of them—they lit out in the opposite direction, skirted the eastern edge of the plant and ran for home. Never did have another problem with them and their beer parties in those woods.''

"So there were no witnesses."

"Nope."

"And when you arrived?"

"I was working late, so I got to the scene five minutes after the call. Hanrahan was still there, kneeling by the body."

"He couldn't have just come running to the scene and tried to help?"

"The man *confessed,* dammit."

"Right on the spot?"

"No—at the jail." Clay's lower jaw worked. "What is this—a test? It's been twenty-five years, dammit. Go back and read my report."

An image of Sara and her little brother as children flashed through Nathan's mind. During the week before Christmas they would have been excited about Santa Claus and shaking presents under their tree. Then the day before Christmas Eve, their world fell apart. Their father had been accused of murder and had committed suicide. What had that done to them during all the Christmases that followed?

And why had Daniel done it? Had Frank Grover quietly told him he'd be fired if he didn't straighten up? Had Daniel been that desperate for money?

But Clay clearly wasn't interested in rehashing the past. Nathan gave him an easy smile. "Sorry. I guess seeing that pretty Hanrahan gal in town got me thinking about her background, that's all." He tipped his head toward the board. "Your turn?"

Clay studied the chess pieces in silence for several minutes, then heaved a big sigh and shoved back his chair. "I'd better go pick up the missus. She goes to Mae's every Saturday morning and it's always the same—those hairdressers get someone in their chair, then gossip for hours. When I go down there and sit a spell, things speed up a little."

"Want to go another round over lunch on Monday?"

"You betcha." He gave Nathan a wink as he shrugged into the jacket he'd draped over the back of his chair. "That'll give you more time to stew over the outcome of this here game."

He was at the door of the office when he stopped and turned back. "Just a piece of friendly advice. I've seen that Hanrahan girl around, too, and don't deny that she's damned pretty. There's something… different about her, though. That edgy look, like she's no stranger to trouble."

"She's living alone. She's bound to be a little wary."

"It's more than that. Don't get mixed up with her, Nathan. Nice packaging doesn't justify the risk."

Nathan heard Clay banter with Ollie out at the front desk for a few minutes, then the front door opened and he was gone.

Long afterward, Nathan sat in his chair, leaning back with his hands laced behind his head, and stared out the window.

It wasn't the packaging. Not at all. It was the rest of Sara Hanrahan that intrigued him—her rare level of confidence and that no-nonsense attitude, as if she owned the world and no one was going to stand in her way. That, and the fact that she not only ignored him, she seemed to go out of her way to *avoid* him.

Since coming back to Ryansville, he'd been pursued by a lot of women who probably gave more thought to his family tree and monied background than they ever gave to him. In the city he'd been anonymous, but here he seemed to be a like a trophy walleye that a lot of single women—and a few married ones—hoped to land.

Sara Hanrahan clearly didn't, which made her all the more intriguing. When he'd inadvertently surprised her in the library, he felt an unexpected, soul-deep spark of interest that he'd have sworn she'd felt, too. So why did she barely give him the time of day?

Maybe next time he'd make it harder for her to ignore him and see what happened.

SARA SAUNTERED up Main with Harold at her side, nodding at people as she passed, moving over when someone came up behind her at a faster pace.

Lots of people were out on this beautiful autumn afternoon, jogging, walking their dogs or pushing strollers under the canopy of gold and ruby leaves.

This could well be the last weekend of the year for such heavy tourist traffic. Soon cabin owners would be busy locking up their cabins and hauling their boats out of the water, and some of the smaller lakeside resorts would be closing for the year after next weekend. Already, the nights called for two blankets and a hot cup of cocoa before bedtime.

Window-shopping for her mother's birthday gift

was proving to be an interesting challenge. There were dozens of shops in town now, ranging from quaint to wildly modernistic, and the store windows were filled with merchandise that was both beautiful and unique. None of it, however, would appeal to her mother.

When she and Harold moved to one side to let yet another guy pass, he slowed and fell into step with her.

"Hi."

Startled, she glanced over and found Nathan Roswell walking next to her as if he had all the time in the world.

In faded jeans and a beige cotton sweater, he looked lean and tall and way too handsome for his own good. She'd always had a weakness for men with thick dark hair and chiseled features, and for a split second she imagined what it might be like to actually date him.

But anyone as blueblooded as this guy was definitely not in her league. And given his profession, he was the last one she ought to hang around with. "What—no uniform?" she asked mildly, stopping at the front window of the Clay Pigeon to check out a display of pottery. "I didn't think you wore anything but dark blue and shiny badges."

"I'm taking the rest of the day off."

When she didn't answer, he didn't take the hint and keep moving. Instead, he stopped next to her and studied the pottery, too. In his reflection on the glass, she saw his brow furrow.

"I think I'd go with the basset hound," he mused.

"Or maybe the sheep. Graceful lines, don't you think?"

She'd intended to ignore him, but when her gaze landed on those two pieces, she could barely choke back her laughter. "The sheep?"

The basset hound was adorable—sway-backed, its chest touching the shelf, long, floppy ears trailing along behind it. The sheep was a round ball of clay atop four splayed feet, only the tip of its nose protruding beyond its heavy wool.

Nathan rubbed his chin thoughtfully. "I'm sure I've seen work by that artist at the Minneapolis Museum of Art."

"If that's true, then I know a few thousand kindergartners in line to make a fortune with clay." She glanced up at Nathan and found his eyes brimming with amusement. Who would have thought he had a sense of humor? She remembered him as a quiet kid, one who'd seemed aloof and unapproachable. Now she wondered if he might have just been shy. "Don't let me hold you up if you want to rush in and buy it before someone else does. I should be on my way, anyhow."

He flashed her a smile. "I'll take my chances and wait. I'd rather walk with you."

After watching Yvonne Weatherfield bat her baby blues at him last weekend, that was a little hard to believe. Maybe he'd grown curious about why Sara was really here. Maybe he'd already figured out a little too much.

She lifted a shoulder. "Whatever."

When they started walking again, he sauntered

along as if he didn't have a care in the world. Almost everyone they passed greeted him, and then looked at her with open interest. *Great. Really great.*

"It's been fun," Sara muttered after they'd gone three blocks and run into half the population of Ryansville. "But I think I'd better head home. See you around."

The man was either obtuse or he had an agenda, because when she turned down Birch, so did he. "Don't you have something to do?" she snapped when she stopped in front of the Shuellers' house.

He feigned surprise, but she could detect a twinkle lurking in the depths of his gaze. "I just did it. My mom always said I should take a lady to her door."

"That," Sara said coldly, "is if the lady is a *date.*"

"Which brings up an interesting point. What are you doing tonight?"

"Laundry."

"Tomorrow night?"

"Busy."

"Okay, then—" he thought for a moment "—I have meetings on Monday and Tuesday evenings. Wednesday?"

"Can't."

At the lift of his brow, she found herself adding, "It's my mother's birthday." *And if I have to drag her out of that apartment, she's going out for a nice meal.*

"Is your brother coming home for it?"

Outright flirtation she could have breezily dismissed. At any hint of disapproval or condescension she would have automatically shot back some dis-

dainful remark and left. But the unexpected sympathy
in his voice weakened her defenses. "I...don't know.
Why do you ask?"

"It's a small town," he said quietly. He reached
out as if planning to brush his fingers along her jaw,
but then dropped his arm. "People talk."

All around them, maple and oak leaves drifted
down on a soft breeze like giant snowflakes of rust
and amber. The distant, sweet scent of burning leaves
reminded her of a time long ago, when her father had
come home with his lunch pail and a smile. When
everything seemed stable and secure.

"Being back in Ryansville always brings back
good memories and bad, but nothing can ever change
what happened."

"No," he conceded gently. "Though only your father was responsible for what he did. Maybe the rest
of you need to put it in the past."

"In the past?" Her mother turned into a bitter recluse. Her brother had gone through one of the most
notable teenage rebellions in recent history. And even
though Sara would never believe that her father had
killed Frank Grover, she'd buried herself in a demanding, often dangerous career more than a thousand miles away. *Oh yes, we've all dealt with the past
very well indeed.*

"There are some people who haven't...forgotten,
even after twenty-five years." He rested a gentle hand
on her shoulder. "Call me if you have any trouble.
Promise?"

She already knew about the lack of acceptance a
Hanrahan faced in this town. At the age of seven,

she'd learned that a tough skin and casual indifference were her best defense. But was he hinting at something more—something like police protection?

Either way, she could handle herself just fine. She'd had years of experience in dealing with criminals that the people of Ryansville couldn't even imagine. And her Beretta was more than enough to deal with any physical challenges she might face.

What could prove more challenging was the fact that just the weight of his hand on her shoulder sent a sensation of warmth straight through her, calling to a part of her that she'd closed off ever since Tony had died.

Because even after this investigation was over, there could never be anything between her and a man like Nathan Roswell.

EVER SINCE SHE'D RUN into him on Saturday, Nathan seemed to show up everywhere she went—except at her late-night sessions in the hills overlooking Sanderson. Now she left later and checked carefully before stepping outside. If he happened to be patrolling in the area, he would undoubtedly have stopped and insisted on walking with her to keep her safe.

She chuckled softly as she cleaned her Beretta at her tiny kitchen table on Tuesday morning, wondering what he'd think if he found out she wasn't quite so defenseless, after all.

Twenty minutes later she and Harold walked down Oak, past the front gates and parking lot of Sanderson, and turned east at Dry Creek Road on the pretext of taking a pleasant little jaunt on a crisp fall morning.

Nathan wasn't the only one she'd been running into around town. Three times now, she'd spotted old Earl Stark watching her from a distance.

Yesterday evening, when she'd stopped, pivoted and started back up Poplar toward her apartment, he'd been sitting in his old truck just half a block away. Watching her again.

The startled look on his face told her all she needed to know. He *was* following her.

A mile down Dry Creek Road, the road curved around a small pond, where morning mist rose like wisps of smoke from the still, dark surface of the water. Only an occasional car and the eerie cry of a loon broke the silence.

Another quarter mile down the road, Stark's Salvage came into view. Sara stopped in the shade of a gnarled oak by the mailbox and looked past the locked, dented aluminum gate to the cluttered property beyond.

Two corrugated steel buildings and several Quonset huts rose from a graveyard of antiquated farm machinery and the rusted skeletons of old cars and trucks. In the middle of it all sat Stark's ramshackle house.

A typical setting for a town's most prolific pack rat, except for the strains of ''Für Elise'' rising to a crescendo from a piano in that little house, each note delivered with timing that made Sara hold her breath with anticipation. It seemed impossible—how could someone living in that house be capable of playing so well?

The tattered curtains at one of the windows fluttered, and Sara caught a brief glimpse of Earl's face peering out. A few seconds later the music abruptly stopped.

The screen door of the house squealed open and then slammed shut as a huge, stooped figure in overalls, arms hanging limply at his sides, shambled out onto the porch.

A dim memory surfaced of Earl at the gas station in town, filling his old truck. She'd been about six or seven, with two precious quarters in one hand and Kyle's chubby wrist in the other, on their usual Saturday-morning quest for strawberry cream soda from the station's pop machine.

When a pale, round expressionless face appeared at the window of Earl's truck, she'd stared back in wonderment, and when that vacant gaze lowered to her bottle of bright-red pop, she'd edged closer and held it out. Though the boy must have been in his twenties, he'd appeared as childlike as little Kyle.

But then Earl had rounded the truck and seen them, swore, and told her to "git." Faced with his unshaven, frightening face and bellowing voice, she and Kyle had run most of the way home and collapsed in an exhausted heap beneath the lilac bushes in their backyard.

Rumors had surfaced now and then about Earl's strange child roaming the woods, or about social workers who'd gone to the Stark's place and returned without seeing any sign of the boy. A recluse, Earl wanted no interference in his life.

Could the giant on the porch be that boy from long ago?

"Hello!" she called out, lifting a hand in greeting.

The man lifted his head to look at her, and even from this distance, she was sure.

"Is Earl home? I'm...I'm looking to buy an old desk."

He stared silently back at her. Then with slow, hydraulic movements he lumbered down the steps and crossed the cluttered yard toward her, his gaze never wavering.

Despite the gate between them and a dog at her side who would attack on command, a chill slid down Sara's spine as he drew closer.

He'd appeared huge on the porch, but the perspective hadn't done him justice. A good six foot six, he had to weigh at least 250 pounds—and that mass was in his upper body, not his belly.

When Harold whined, she reached down to calm him, then did a double take.

The dog wasn't whining with anxiety. His tail was sweeping slow arcs in the dust, as if he was welcoming the man who now towered over them both from the other side of the gate.

"Are you Earl's son?" She gave him her friendliest smile. When he didn't answer, she added, "I'd like to talk to him, if that's okay?"

He extended a meaty fist over the gate, turned it palm up, and opened his fingers to reveal a crumpled note. Apparently aware that she might hesitate to take it from his hand, he laid it on the flat surface of the fence post at the gate, then turned back to the house.

She waited until he was inside before she reached for the note.

It was hastily scrawled. Nearly illegible.

I got something you need. Midnight in the park by the trailer court. Don't bring nobody else, and don't come out here no more.

E.S.

She'd been on a lot of stakeouts. Though she was capable of firing her gun in the line of duty, the thought of going out alone in the dark, where Earl and his son might be waiting, was enough to give her pause.

Why did Earl want to meet her—and what could he have that she needed?

CHAPTER SEVEN

SARA COULD WILLINGLY have wrung her brother's stubborn neck. How could Kyle have blown off his own mother's birthday without a word?

She'd been calling his number in Minneapolis for the past several days and leaving voice messages. In the last one, she'd given him the time and name of the restaurant, had asked him to call her if he planned to come. There'd been no response.

Now she stood alone in her mother's living room with gaily wrapped packages in her arms. "I couldn't get a hold of Kyle, Mom," she said. "But this is your birthday, so you and I are going out."

Her firm tone had cowed a lot of tough suspects through the years, but Bernice Hanrahan was made of sterner stuff.

"No."

"Yes, Mom. I made reservations at Josie's out on Lake Ryan. It's small and quiet—hardly anyone will be there at six on a Wednesday night. We'll get a nice table overlooking the water."

Bernice gave a vague wave toward her stove. "I've got a little casserole baking."

"Is it done?"

"Well, yes."

"Good. Then you can toss it in the fridge and reheat it for tomorrow night." Sara set the gifts on the little bench by the door, then sidestepped her mother and reached into the front closet. "Tell me," she called out over her shoulder, "how many times I've made it back to Minnesota on your birthday over the past fourteen years."

Bernice folded her arms across her chest.

"You never know, Mom. It could be another fourteen before it happens again." Sara slipped her mother's long wool coat off a hanger. "It's a little chilly tonight."

They stared each other down for several long moments before Bernice's mouth worked and her gaze slid away. "I don't go out much anymore."

Which was the understatement of the year. "It's time, Mom," Sara said gently as she held out the coat. "Put this on and come along. It means a lot to me."

Bernice frowned and pursed her lips. "Where's that dog of yours?"

"He's at my apartment, and he'll be fine until I get back."

After a final moment of hesitation, Bernice went into the kitchen and took the casserole from the oven, then allowed Sara to help her with her coat. "We won't be late?"

"I would love to take you shopping after dinner, but we can come right back if that's what you want."

"What I want is to stay right here, not chase all over creation," Bernice grumbled as they walked out to the Bronco. "At my age, arthritis and cold weather are a bad mix."

She maintained a stubborn silence all the way to the lake, but as they stepped into Josie's Steak House Sara heard her draw a shaky breath. "It's okay, Mom. You'll be fine."

The evening crowd hadn't arrived yet, but there were a few couples in the main dining area. Several people looked up and nodded in greeting, then turned back to their menus.

"Isn't this pretty?" Sara continued. "I love the rustic decor. Look—that little alcove over there has a great view of the lake."

Sara had checked out the place earlier and reserved that table knowing it might be a more comfortable setting for her mother. And sure enough, Bernice nodded in agreement.

Over their salads, her mother sat stiffly in her chair, her face pale. But by the time their dinners arrived, the tense set of her shoulders had relaxed a few degrees.

Sara closed her eyes to savor another bite of fresh walleye. "I'd forgotten how wonderful this is."

"More than I could possibly eat, though," Bernice responded. "And more than I could ever afford. Not you, either."

"But this is your birthday, Mom. While I'm here, I'd like for us to go out more often and have a good time."

"How can you pay for this?" Bernice frowned at her twice-baked potato. "Did you find a job?"

Sara couldn't reveal, not even to her own mother, that she was on a DEA assignment. Over the years, she'd allowed Bernice to believe that she had a government office job in Dallas. "I've been careful, honest."

"Humpf," her mother snorted. "And what happens next week or next month? What will you do then?"

"I'll be fine. Really." Soft strains of Rachmaninoff filled the air, reminding Sara of the music she'd unexpectedly heard the day before. "Mom, do you remember Earl Stark?"

Bernice stilled, a forkful of asparagus in midair. "The junkman? Of course."

"He had a son, didn't he? I don't remember ever seeing him in school."

"He must have been a good ten, fifteen years older than you. I don't think he went to school very long."

Sara laid her utensils at the side of her plate. "But surely—"

"One of the kindergarten teachers was a customer of mine. Leon was big for his age, and he viciously swung at her in class one time. Tore the sleeve of a lovely wool dress I'd just made for her and gave her an awful bruise."

"A *kindergartner?* But why?"

"I think she was trying to get him to hang up his coat. He'd gotten out of control a few times before, but not as bad. After that incident, she said Stark never sent him to school again."

Sara thought about the huge, silent man who'd shuffled across the yard to hand her that note. If angered, he'd be nearly unstoppable, yet there'd been no sign of hostility in those pale, blank eyes. "But the law—"

"The county sent out some social workers and even the sheriff, but Stark insisted the boy had gone to live with relatives and no one saw him around town for a long time." Bernice shrugged. "I don't think the county was very good at following up back then, though. After a while everyone just forgot about it."

"I think I saw Leon yesterday out at the salvage yard."

Bernice frowned. "Why in the world were you down there?"

"Harold and I were out walking again. When we went past the Stark place I heard the most beautiful music. I could tell it was coming from an old piano, though, and not a CD."

"Well, it must have been your imagination. Earl never got past fourth grade, and from the strange way he behaves in town, he's probably slipping into dementia—no surprise, given his heavy drinking. Folks say Leon is retarded."

"Maybe they had company?"

"No one with any sense would stay more than five minutes in that house. Some members of the town council wanted to condemn it years ago, but old Earl fought 'em."

They ate in silence for several minutes, watching the sun slip beneath the ragged, pine-studded horizon.

"Ready for dessert?" Sara asked, waving at their waitress. "I hear they have something interesting."

"No. I couldn't." The restaurant had been filling up while they ate, and now Bernice cast a nervous glance at the crowded dining room behind her. "I think I'd rather go home."

The waitress bore down on their table with a bright smile and a small birthday cake ablaze with lit candles. Behind her, a ripple of applause and cheers rose from the other patrons.

Bernice's cheeks reddened. "It's time to go, Sara. I want to go home."

The little waitress grinned. "Don't worry, ma'am. They always clap when they see a birthday cake go by. Should we all sing happy birthday?"

Bernice's eyes filled with horror. "Please, no!"

Sara reached across the table for her mother's hand. "It's okay, Mom. It's just a little cake. No big deal."

"No? You don't think so? What do you think people say behind my back when I go downtown? What happens when we stand up to leave and they see who I am?"

"They see a woman who has lived here all her life, who went to school with their parents and raised her family the best she could," Sara said quietly. "They see a woman who handled tragedy with a lot of dignity. You don't need to hide yourself away, Mom. Not anymore."

Her eyes filled with unshed tears, Bernice whispered harshly. "You have never understood, Sara. All these years you've tried to make it all sound so simple, but you were just a child back then and you haven't lived here for a long time."

"But, Mom—"

"No. The man I loved betrayed us all, then took the coward's way out and left us destitute." Anger glittered in her eyes. "Do you have any idea how hard that was? What I went through? This town turned against us then, and I have no use for any of them now. *Take me home!*''

AFTER AN HOUR at her mother's house, the atmosphere was still cool. Sara gave Bernice the gifts and served the cake she'd brought from the restaurant, then wished her mother good-night and left. *So much for renewed bonds. At this rate I'll be lucky if she's speaking to me when it's time to head for Dallas.*

At least Harold was happy to see her when she got home. He'd become accustomed to their late-night outings, and by ten o'clock he started whining at the apartment door.

Sara paced the kitchen, waiting for the phone to ring. She'd checked in earlier with Allen Larsen, but he hadn't left any messages. Where was her DEA contact? Why didn't he call?

She couldn't ask for local backup—not yet. Not until she knew without a doubt that Nathan had no connections to anyone involved in the suspected drug shipments.

But meeting Earl at midnight without backup would be a very stupid thing to do. She probably could handle Earl, but Leon was another story. If he caught her by surprise, she wouldn't have a chance— especially in the secluded place Earl had chosen.

The park was a block-square patch of scrub grass down by the trailer court. A few trees, a single scarred picnic table and a set of swings hardly made the area a nice place for kids to play, and the overgrown lilacs rimming the south and east sides effectively isolated the area from any watchful eyes.

"Ring, dang it," she muttered, eyeing the phone as she paced the small room.

Maybe Earl did plan to meet her alone. Maybe he had an old grudge against the owner of Sanderson and held important information. In the note he'd warned her not to come back to his place again—did he fear being discovered? And why was he so sure Sara would be interested in whatever information he had?

Could he be working for the other side? Maybe he'd seen her spying and been told to dispose of her.

At eleven-thirty Harold whined again at the door, and thumped his tail on the carpet.

"Okay, okay. You can do your business here one more time where it's safe, and then we're taking a little drive."

After a few minutes in the yard, Sara whistled Harold into the Bronco, where he took his favorite spot on the front seat beside her. She cruised slowly down Birch, past four blocks of neatly kept houses and several open lots at the bottom of the hill.

To the left, lit by a solitary street lamp, lay the small park. The weak illumination went no farther than the old picnic table at base of the light, and the splinter of moon overhead left the rest of the area in darkness.

She pulled to the curb, made sure her doors were locked and doused her headlights, but left the engine running. "What do you think, buddy?" she asked, reaching over to scratch Harold's ears.

The old dog whined and turned awkwardly around on the seat next to her, then stared out into the darkness.

"We aren't going out there," she murmured. "Let's just see what happens, okay?"

Earl hadn't indicated any particular area of the small park, but he would surely hear the Bronco and approach it. With backup she might have been more aggressive about searching him out, but a special agent didn't reach retirement age by being stupid. If the man wanted to talk to her, she was here.

Five minutes ticked past. Ten. At twenty minutes after midnight she considered shifting into drive and heading home.

Headlights appeared over the hill behind her. A vehicle slowly approached and pulled up a car's length away from her rear bumper. She stilled, her heart kicking into overdrive, as she quickly reviewed the situation.

This could be her lucky—

When orange grill lights started flashing on the car behind, she swore softly under her breath. If Earl had been anywhere nearby, he'd take off now for sure, and as the seconds ticked by she knew the deputy must be running her license plates on his MDC— mobile data computer.

Not that he'd find anything that might jeopardize her operation here in Ryansville. The Bronco was registered in her name and her driving record was clear. There weren't any outstanding warrants on her, nor would he find any reference to her job.

Harold whined and scrambled around on the seat, clearly excited by the flashing lights.

"Does this bring back old memories, buddy?" she murmured. She reached over and caught his collar to quiet him. "This won't take long, and then we'll be on our way."

Previously Nathan had taken her "insomnia" at face value, but sooner or later he might start getting suspicious. From the look in his eye when he finally got out of his car and approached the driver's side door of hers, that time had come.

He braced one arm on the roof of the Bronco and waited for her to roll down her window. "A little late, isn't it?"

"Sure is," she retorted. "I took my mom out to dinner, but when I got home Harold still really wanted his evening walk. It was so late that I felt better about just letting him run a few minutes in the park."

Nathan raised a dark eyebrow. "Down here?"

"Things do look spookier in the dark," she admitted. "I've only been down here during the day."

He peered into her car. Harold, now sitting at full attention on the front seat, was still panting with excitement. "Would your dog defend you?"

If Nathan only knew. "I...think he would. Shepherds can be pretty protective."

"Just don't rely on it. This isn't Mayberry, and one resident deputy can't keep constant watch twenty-four hours a day."

A feeling of warmth slid through her at the concern in his tone. He was just doing his job, but how often was someone worried about *her* safety? Usually, it was the other way around. "I suppose I'd better head home."

"I'll follow you."

"It's just a few blocks," she protested. "I'm in a

locked vehicle, so I'll be fine." But he was already striding back to his cruiser, and she knew he would escort her home no matter what she said. Damn.

For sure, if Earl had seen the deputy pull up, talk to her and then follow her home, he'd hesitate to come forward again.

His note said not to come back to his place, but tomorrow she'd try cruising past to see if he might be outside, because she'd already checked the phone book and found no listing for Stark's Salvage. What sort of business operated these days without a phone?

If he had documents of some kind for her, maybe he could just hand them over. If he needed to talk, they could arrange another meeting.

Back at her apartment, she pulled into her parking space in back. Nathan was at her car door before she had it open all the way.

"You're staying home now, right?" he asked. A corner of his mouth tilted up into a half smile. "No more late-night walks?"

"Absolutely not." Harold jumped out of the vehicle and came to stand at her side as she glanced at her watch. "Heavens—it's twelve-thirty."

Her sweater snagged on a rough edge of her door when she climbed out of the Bronco, and Nathan reached out to cup her elbow as she freed the loop of yarn. Just a casual contact, nothing more...but instantly she felt her pulse kick into high gear.

"I'll wait here to make sure you get inside." He glanced around. "With all these pine trees, your apartment entrance is completely hidden from view—

even from the Shuellers' house. You need to be careful.''

He stood close enough for her to catch the compelling scent of his woodsy aftershave, and his low, smoky voice sent a shiver rippling across her skin.

A sense of disorientation slid through her as she found herself focusing on his beautifully sculpted mouth and then looked up to find heat sparking in hazel eyes that had darkened with sensual awareness.

The powerful, unspoken masculine promise in his gaze made her heart skip a beat.

So he felt the same, unsettling attraction she did.

With a sharp, dismissive shake of his head, he stepped back. ''Keep safe,'' he growled. He waited until she was inside, then turned back to his patrol car.

From her kitchen window, she watched as he drove off. Clearly she hadn't been getting enough sleep—or maybe she just needed a good, long vacation after this was all over.

She'd just imagined something that he would never offer and she could never accept. If the secrets she held close weren't enough, she had only to look at her own dark past.

Though perhaps it wouldn't hurt to dream.

CHAPTER EIGHT

AFTER EARL FAILED to show up at the park Wednesday night, Sara had driven past his place a number of times. From the cover of the underbrush and trees along his fence, she'd spent hours watching for any activity.

The gate across the rutted lane leading into Stark's Salvage had remained locked, and she'd seen no sign of Earl or Leon.

If Allen had called back in time with an offer of backup assistance, she might have been able to make contact with Earl in the park. But Allen and the other agents had been involved in a major raid north of St. Paul, and his answer had come too late.

Had Earl been spooked by seeing Nathan drive up behind her SUV?

If so, finding him was all the more worthwhile. An inner voice told her something was wrong—terribly wrong—or she would have seen some sign of him in the past two days.

"Back to square one," she muttered as she approached the side door of Sanderson at five-thirty on Friday.

She'd parked a block away, watching as the office personnel drove out of the main gate at five o'clock.

Now, only Jane's red Subaru remained in the front lot, while the second-shift factory crew's vehicles were parked behind the building.

Sara waited another ten minutes, then drove in and parked her Bronco between a couple of dusty pickups.

The windows of the office building were dark and the front doors would be locked, of course, but from her position up on the hill she'd often seen a cleaning crew use a side door. She walked casually up to the door, tried the handle and felt it turn easily in her hand. Gratefully, she slipped inside.

To the right, a double set of steel doors flanked by glass display cases led into the plant. To the left, gleaming terrazzo flooring stretched down the main hallway of the office area.

After waiting in silence for several minutes, listening for footsteps, Sara turned right and tried the door handles. *Locked.*

She started down the hallway, quietly testing doorknobs and cataloguing the layout and distances.

The bathrooms—unlocked.

The employee lounge—unlocked.

Individual offices—locked.

She peered through the pebbled-glass door to the accounting department. This would definitely be a place to visit, she thought dryly, making out the blurry forms of numerous desks and computer monitors. To one side of the room, the frame of another door was visible—perhaps the office of Robert Kelstrom.

Since she'd started her surveillance, there'd been some surreptitious-looking late-night activity around the place, enough to convince her that the tip on drug shipments coming through hadn't been far wrong.

Finding out just what the operation was and who was involved would prove interesting. Perhaps there was a ring of cohorts out in the plant, but logic dictated that in a small company like this one, at least some of the top brass would have to know what was going on.

Ahead, a dim wash of light spilled into the hallway outside the human resources office. Sara moved to the door and surveyed the room through a window. Bathed in the glow of her computer monitor, Jane sat behind her desk, her head cradled in one hand and a sheaf of papers scattered in front of her.

Sara rapped lightly on the glass pane. "Jane? Are you in there?"

Jane sat up with a start. *"Sara?"*

"I thought I'd stop by and see if you wanted to meet for supper," Sara said, still speaking through the door.

A broad grin on her face, Jane glanced up at a wall clock as she rose from her desk, then crossed the room to unlock her door. "I didn't realize how late it was. This is such a neat surprise—but how did you get in?"

"I meant to get here sooner, but I saw your car was still in the lot. The side door was open." Sara gave the desk a look of amazement. "Sheesh. Your work must never end!"

Jane gave a little shrug. "I'm just thankful for the job, believe me." Her smile dimmed. "I'm really sorry I haven't been able to call you about any openings. Ian and Robert have been pretty upbeat lately, though. Maybe soon.''

''Don't worry about it. How much do you have left to do here?''

Retracing her steps, Jane stood by her chair and closed the program on her computer, then shut the system down and grabbed a ring of keys from the top drawer of the desk. ''I just need to slip some reports into Mr. Flynn's mailbox in the business office, and then I can leave.''

Sara closed her eyes and breathed in deeply. ''This place always smells so good—what is it?''

''A whole lot different than when we were growing up, isn't it? Back then the place just made cleaning compounds and there was a perpetual stench of ammonia. Now it depends on what product they're working on.'' Jane headed out the door toward the business office, and Sara followed. ''There's always the light scent of beeswax, but the herbs and florals vary. My favorite is when they're working on Emma's Original Hand Lotion. Lily of the valley, a touch of lilac—it's heavenly!''

Sara watched as Jane sorted through the keys. ''I guess all the products sell like wildfire.''

''Yeah, they do pretty well. Business is picking up because Robert recently went to some distributors' shows throughout the Midwest and signed up several new accounts.'' Jane unlocked the door and flipped on the lights, then slid several documents into one of the slots of the mailboxes mounted on the far wall. She waved toward a display of various salves, hand creams and specialty furniture waxes with the familiar green-and-white gingham labels of Aunt Emma's Natural Skin Care products on a shelf above a secretary's desk. "Changing the packaging sure wasn't a good move, though."

"Aren't those the same as always?"

"Oh, we're back to the originals now." Jane rolled her eyes. "Ian wanted to try something more upscale, and sales fell by fifty percent during the next quarter. I wasn't here at the time, but I heard that even our oldest customers failed to recognize the products. The company almost went under before everything got straightened out."

Which could explain the kind of desperation that could drive the owners into seeking alternative forms of income.

Back out in the hallway, Sara looked toward the manufacturing end of the building. "Can you imagine spending your day surrounded by all those beautiful scents? It must be wonderful," she said wistfully.

Jane chuckled. "I don't think you'd hear many of the guys agreeing with that. Robert says he can't even smell it anymore."

A pretty pink blush brightened Jane's full cheeks whenever she spoke the manager's name. *Interesting.* "Most everyone is gone… Do you think you could just give me a quick tour?"

"Well…"

Sara gave her a Girl Scout's salute, then crossed her heart. "I swear I'm not after any trade secrets. Honest."

"I don't know—Ian and Robert are pretty adamant about strangers coming through." Jane frowned.

"Maybe the shift manager wouldn't mind if I asked first—Phil's a pretty laid-back guy."

"I don't want you to get into any trouble, Jane."

The woman thought for a moment, her brow furrowed, then she strode into her office. "Good grief—what harm could it do?" She thumbed through a stack of papers on her desk. "I have a vacation-request form to give back to him, anyway. He'll be happy to see the boss approved it. Follow me."

Yes!

Jane led the way to the steel doors leading into the plant. Once inside, Sara carefully scanned the cavernous area, memorizing each detail.

The doors effectively muffled a considerable amount of noise, she realized with surprise.

This area, perhaps one hundred by two hundred feet with a twenty-foot ceiling, was almost chilly despite the steaming vats running through the center of the room and the steady drone of massive packaging equipment in full operation. At the far end, a man drove a forklift in quick, decisive swoops as he moved forward to snag filled pallets, then spun around to add them to the tall stacks along the back wall.

Conveyers moved bottles of amber liquid through a capper, then on through a curtained section, after which they reappeared with bright new labels—Aunt Emma's Original Beeswax Furniture Polish. There were maybe fifteen or twenty workers in sight, all moving with precision, all dressed in white coveralls and caps.

"I think Phil will be in his office," Jane shouted

close to Sara's ear. "I'll give this to him and then I'll
show you around."

Nodding, Sara watched her friend head to the small
office along the wall. Behind its glass walls she saw
Jane talking to a lean, gray-haired guy who looked
up abruptly to give Sara a piercing look, then shook
his head.

Time here might be short. Sara casually glanced
around, then edged toward the center of the floor.
She'd seen late-night shipments come in—over there,
on the south side. One of the workers nodded to her
as he walked past with what looked like a pH test kit
and a clipboard, and disappeared around the other
side of the vats.

There were four doors along that south wall. One
was marked *EXIT*, but the others were of heavy steel
with padlocks. Storerooms for chemical supplies—or
something more?

Jane appeared at her elbow. "I'm sorry—I can't
take you through. Phil says it's because of liability,
with all the equipment. From right here you can probably see most of what goes on, anyway. Let's go,
okay?"

Sara dutifully followed her back to the entrance,
aware that Phil was watching her with narrowed eyes
from behind the plate-glass walls of his office.

There would be keys in that office. Keys to those
storerooms—and perhaps evidence of exactly what
went on here during the wee hours of the morning.

But this wasn't the time to raid the place. Not yet.
Finding out who was involved was more important.
Already, Allen and some of the other agents were

following up on the license plates she'd seen arriving at odd hours.

"You can see how clean it is in there," Jane explained once they were outside the production area. "Besides concern over a visitor being hurt, they don't want to risk contamination."

There was concern about risk, all right, but Sara doubted it was just over a few stray germs.

JOSH GRINNED at Harold and gave the leash an extra wrap around his wrist. He'd gone on lots of walks with Sara and her dog, and she'd even let Josh hold the leash.

Early this morning she'd come to the back door and asked Mom if he could come over after school and take Harold outside. Just in the fenced backyard, Sara had said. Only for a few minutes.

But the day was so nice, and Harold had wagged his tail and looked so excited about going out, that Josh didn't take him into the yard, after all. What would it hurt to go around the block? Or maybe two blocks?

There sure weren't any dogs like this one around town. Harold was sort of old, but he'd been a police dog long ago. How cool was that? No one would dare give Josh any grief today.

Harold jogged beside him as Josh ran up Birch. When they reached Main, Josh hesitated. He started to turn back toward home…

And came face-to-face with the Weatherfields.

"Hey, scumbag," sneered Ricky. "Where'd you get the mutt? At the landfill?"

"Yeah—he's exactly the color of a big rat," said Thad. "I'll bet that's where he came from."

Harold growled, and the hair stood up along his back. "Easy, boy," Josh whispered. "It's okay."

"It's okay?" Ricky hooted. "There must be a law about bringing a big rat downtown."

Josh tensed his hold on the leash. A deeper growl rumbled through the dog's body and vibrated against Josh's leg. "Just leave me alone, okay? This dog doesn't like you much."

"Like we should care?" Thad scoffed. "Both you and that dog are probably gonna catch that disease your mom has. I can see it now, a kid and a big rat with matching purple spots."

Josh's fists tensed, and forgetting about Harold, passersby and everything else, he shot forward.

The dog was faster. Lunging to the end of his leash, he erupted into a gray blur of furious barking and snapping jaws.

The Weatherfield brothers screamed and took off at a dead run down Main and disappeared around the next corner. Harold strained at the leash and dragged Josh behind him in pursuit.

Around them, shoppers scattered. A woman shrieked. Everyone within two blocks stopped to stare in horror.

"No! No, Harold!" Josh cried. "Easy, boy. It's okay. Sit! Sit!"

The dog slowed, then quieted and dropped obediently to the cement. His eyes were still fastened on the point where the Weatherfields had disappeared.

"Holy cow," Josh breathed. He scrambled to his

feet and looked down at the torn knee of his jeans. Dust covered the front of his denim jacket. The scrapes on both palms stung, and one was even bleeding a little.

"That dog doesn't belong in town," shouted a woman still cowering in the entryway of Mitchell's Hardware. "Someone's going to get killed!"

Mr. Mitchell himself came out of the store. "I'm going to report this to the deputy, son. That dog is a menace. Are you okay, Mrs. Lund?" He shepherded her inside, then gave Josh a stern look. "You get that animal home and keep him there, do you hear?"

Nodding, a sick feeling welling up in his stomach, Josh said, "Heel!" and turned back toward home feeling the eyes of everyone in town staring at him.

What if Sara found out? If someone called the deputy, would he take Harold away and shoot him? Tears burned behind Josh's eyelids and he furiously blinked them away. A lump the size of a softball filled his throat.

Even Harold seemed to feel bad. His tail and head hung low, he looked just about as forlorn as any dog could get.

When they neared home Josh stared glumly at his front yard. By now, the phone had rung off the wall. At least five people would have told Mom about the killer dog and about how Josh had screwed up big time by bringing the animal near Main Street.

Mrs. Weatherfield had probably called, too, threatening some big lawsuit.

Josh sighed and kept walking. Maybe…if he waited long enough, Mom might even be worried about him and not be quite so mad when he did show up safe and sound.

At the bottom of the hill, he debated about where to go. The woods behind the Sanderson plant or the park by the trailer court?

At his side, Harold sat with his nose lifted to the soft fall breeze. He whined softly and looked up at Josh, then looked toward the far end of the park and whined even louder.

Uh-oh. After what happened in town, Josh already knew there'd be no holding the dog back if he started after a rabbit or something. "Easy, boy—let's go home, okay?"

He tugged on the leash, but Harold ignored him.

"Please! Come on, we need to—"

Harold jumped to his feet and bolted. The leather burned the fresh abrasions on Josh's hands, and he automatically let go.

In the blink of an eye, Harold disappeared into the trees at the other end of the park. Soon all Josh could hear was the barking fading into the distance.

Fear twisted Josh's stomach into a giant knot. What if there were kids playing back there? What if Harold attacked them? Or what if he ran away for good?

Josh took off after the dog.

At the edge of the wood he hesitated. Everyone at school knew about the stuff that went on back there— beer parties and drug deals and teenagers fooling around—but the sound of Harold's barking drove him on. "Harold! Here, boy!"

Spruce needles scratched at his face. Spiderwebs

stuck to his skin. Clinging wild-raspberry vines grabbed at his jeans.

When he finally broke free of the underbrush, he ran until his ragged breathing tore at his lungs and he had to stop.

Something thrashed through the bushes up ahead. Josh froze with fear. There were black bears out in the more isolated areas, but now and then there were sightings close to town—

Harold burst into sight, his tongue lolling out one side of his mouth as if he, too, was tired after such a long run.

"Good boy! Come here, boy—that's a good dog!"

But his tail wagging furiously, the dog bounded away again, and the sound of him crashing through the brittle weeds and branches made Josh's heart sink as he started after him again. *Stupid dog! Stupid, stupid dog!*

Suddenly all sounds stopped except for Harold's soft whines.

His heart in his throat, Josh slowed and tried to move quietly forward. What if there were really bad people back here—hiding stolen stuff or something? He parted some low maple branches…

…and found Harold sitting next to a fallen tree. Someone was there with him.

Josh stared, his stomach quivering and his knees turning to jelly. "H-here, boy," he whispered. "Please."

The dog didn't move so much as a hair.

Watching the ground for twigs that might snap and leaves that might rustle, Josh took a small step closer, then another, his heart battering against his ribs and his mouth dry as dust.

"C-come on, H-Harold!"

It took another few seconds for his eyes to adjust to the deep shadows. When he got a better look at the guy's floppy fishing hat loaded with lures, relief flooded through him.

He'd seen that hat in town. Maybe the owner was a little weird, but the guy had always been nice to him.

Grinning now, Josh moved forward and skirted the end of the log. "Hey, there! Sorry about the dog, mister. I hope he didn't scare you or anything."

He rounded a tangle of raspberry vines and reached for Harold's collar. "I'm sorry if Harold bothered y—"

Horror flooded through him as he looked at the guy to apologize.

And then all he could do was scream.

CHAPTER NINE

AFTER HAVING SUPPER with Jane at the little Chinese restaurant in town, Sara drove back to her apartment. She'd barely stepped out of the Bronco when she heard the back door of the Shuellers' house slam.

"Sara!" Zoe came running through the trees in the backyard with Timmy in her arms. "Josh is missing!"

"What?" Sara spun around, dread knotting in her stomach as a hundred grim scenarios flashed through her mind. "When? For how long?"

Zoe's face was pale, her eyes reddened. "H-he took Harold for a walk. Apparently the dog got really mean downtown, went after a couple boys who were teasing Josh and scared everyone to pieces. People said Josh started for home, but no one has seen him since." She took a quavering breath. "What if Harold attacked him? He could be bleeding to death somewhere. Bob has been driving all over town looking for him, and so have Josh's uncles. He's been gone almost two hours!"

"Did you call 911?"

"Half an hour ago." Zoe reached into her back pocket for tissue, then blew her nose. "The d-deputy said I should stay here in case Josh shows up, but waiting here is driving me crazy. I'm so scared!''

Sara reached out and took Zoe's hand. ''Believe me, Zoe. Harold would never hurt Josh. If he became defensive, it was *only* because he was protecting your son.''

''Then why isn't Josh home? It's nearly dark!''

''I don't know. I do know that Harold would guard Josh with his life, and if Harold is with him, he's okay.'' Sara thought for a moment. ''Does Josh have any special places he goes if he's upset?''

Zoe's lower lip trembled. ''H-home.''

''I told him not to leave the yard,'' Sara said gently. ''Maybe he figured he was going to be in trouble.''

''Bob already went to the school, and we've called everyone we know.'' Timmy whimpered as Zoe wiped away her tears. ''Where can he be?''

''I'm going out to look for him, too. Where have the others looked?''

''D-downtown. The schoolyard…the playground behind our church.'' She tipped her head and rested it against Timmy's, her shoulders bowed in defeat. ''They've been up the trail behind the Sanderson plant…all through the residential areas. Nathan called a bit ago to tell me that almost two dozen people are out looking.''

Sara lifted her key ring and tried to hide her own fears. ''Harold always responds to this whistle. We'll find your son.''

Taking the whistle off the key ring, Sara climbed back in the Bronco and began cruising the streets of

Ryansville, starting at the center of town and working in ever-expanding circles.

At each street corner, she stopped and blew the high-pitched whistle, then waited for an answering bark or the sight of Harold's powerful gray form approaching with Josh in tow. Nothing—except the occasional barks and howls of other dogs in town.

After thirty minutes, she ended up on the south side of town, where she'd parked the night she'd hoped to meet Earl. After this, she would check the trails above the Sanderson facility. But would Josh have headed to this dark and isolated area? It didn't seem likely.

She blew the whistle. Waited. Then tried again, louder.

From somewhere down in the trailer court, a beagle bayed and some sort of terrier barked shrilly. Amid the cacophony was another, more distant sound— Harold?

She tried again and this time heard him more clearly. Yes! But why on earth was he so far back in the woods? Reaching for her cell phone, she dialed Zoe's number and told her to call the deputy's office. Then she grabbed the flashlight in the glove box, checked the concealed holster at the small of her back and stepped out into the darkness.

"Josh! Are you out there?"

He was probably too far away to hear her, but even when she'd lived here as a kid, everyone knew that these woods weren't a safe place to be. *Please God, let him be okay.*

The prayer played like a litany in her mind as she crossed the dimly lit park and started into the woods.

Every few minutes she used the whistle and called out Josh's name, then adjusted her direction and continued on, fending off sharp pine branches with one upraised arm and holding the flashlight with the other.

She tripped over downed branches and rocks hidden by the grass and weeds. Barb-covered vines and stinging nettles grabbed at the tender flesh of her calves and ankles.

The terrain fell away into a strip of marsh. She cautiously made her way across, her running shoes squelching in the cold, reeking muck. Near the other side she stepped into a deeper spot and fell forward, both hands buried in mud and rotting vegetation. She lost hold of the flashlight, which sank into a brackish pool of water.

Darkness descended with grim finality.

Something gray and wolflike suddenly loomed huge on the bank above her, its eyes glowing, and in that brief moment of disorientation she nearly screamed.

The wolf-creature whined and scrambled down the bank, but danced back and forth at the edge of the bog.

"Oh, Harold!" Relief flooded through her as she made her way to solid ground and sank to her knees next to him. "Why on earth are you way back here?"

He bounded back up to the top of the bank and looked down at her, whining with impatience.

Cupping her hands at her mouth, she took a deep breath, then yelled as loud as she could. "Josh! Can you hear me?"

This time, she heard him.

She crawled up the steep bank, grabbing at exposed tree roots for balance, and finally found Josh at the edge of a small clearing.

"Hey, kiddo, how are you?" she asked softly. "Are you hurt?"

Weak moonlight filtered through the lacy branches overhead, revealing his dirty, tear-streaked face. "I-I'm sorry about taking Harold for a walk. I know you're mad."

She hunkered down next to him and ran a hand over his cheek. "Honey, I appreciate your help with my dog, and I know you did your best. Right now, the only thing that matters is that you're all right. What happened?"

"Harold got away from me and ran way back here. When I saw the dead guy, I got real scared and starting running for home." He moved his right leg and winced. "I hurt my ankle."

"Dead guy? Where?" She ran a hand over Josh's leg and gently examined his ankle. It felt warm and swollen.

"B-back over there." Josh shuddered as he jerked his chin toward the other side of the clearing. "He's sitting by that big log."

"Are you sure he's dead? Maybe he's just sleeping."

Josh shook his head violently at the memory. "His eyes are open, and he smells sorta funny. He didn't move at all."

"I need to go check. Maybe he's really sick. Harold will stay right here with you. Okay?"

The boy's eyes widened with fear.

She withdrew her cell phone from her jacket pocket and called Zoe. "I found him. He's okay—don't worry. Just a little scared."

"Thank God. Where…how? Can I come get him?" Her sobs and joyous laughter burst through the receiver. "Thank you so much. Oh, Sara, thank you!"

After Zoe calmed down, Sara gave her directions and asked her to notify the deputy to say Josh had been found, then handed the phone over to the boy. "Here, your mom is going to call back as soon as she reaches the deputy. You can talk to her while I go check out the guy you saw."

Josh paled. "Don't leave me, please!"

"I promise, Josh, I'll be right back." Sara ordered Harold to stay, then started across the clearing.

Once beyond Josh's line of vision she drew her semiautomatic. There were other possibilities besides a coma, illness or death. If the guy was strung out on something, he could be dangerous. If he had friends with him, that could be even worse—but Sara couldn't take the chance that she might be leaving someone to die.

Ahead she could see the form of a log. She scanned the area for any sign of movement. Nothing.

Moving slowly forward, senses on high alert, she studied every shadow. Every tree. Leaves rustled off to the right and she froze—until she made out the bulk of a raccoon waddling into the night.

She eased around the log, keeping a distance of five yards between it and herself, her gun raised and held in both hands. A man was propped against the log, just as Josh had said, but his features were hidden in the darkness. "Sir. Can you hear me, sir?"

He didn't move.

She scanned the entire clearing once again, then edged several feet closer. "Sir?" But even as she spoke, a familiar odor wafted toward her, and she saw the wind-tossed leaves that had blanketed his legs and caught at the collar of his jacket.

The clouds overhead slid past the moon, and a silvery beam of light filtered through the branches above to cast an eerie glow on his staring eyes and open mouth.

Earl Stark had the ultimate excuse for not meeting her two nights before.

NATHAN WATCHED as the county coroner's panel van pulled away, then turned to Sara, still amazed that she would venture so far back into the dark woods alone—even to rescue someone.

That she'd remained so calm after finding the body surprised him even more.

The Shuellers had long since picked up Josh and taken him to the local clinic to have his ankle checked, and now the Jefferson County crime-scene investigation team was searching for evidence.

"So what did the coroner say?" Sara asked, hugging herself against the cold. "Does he know how long Earl was out here?"

"We've had temperatures in the thirties and forties for the past several days, which slows decomposition, but the coroner thinks Earl died approximately forty-eight hours ago."

Sara shuddered. "Does he think it was murder?"

"So far, he hasn't found evidence of trauma, and based on the lividity and blanching patterns on the body, he says it doesn't appear that it was moved after death. He thinks this was probably a natural death."

"They'll do an autopsy to be sure, won't they?"

"Maybe. State law only requires an autopsy if he died under violent or unusual circumstances."

"Being found dead like this isn't *unusual?*"

Nathan reached out and rested a comforting hand on her upper arm, ignoring the spark that shot through him at the point of contact. "I know finding the body was frightening, but the coroner called the local medical clinic on his way over here. Earl was chronically ill. He had a long history of heart disease, alcoholism and emphysema. He probably died of a heart attack."

"You think that's what happened?" Her voice was tinged with disbelief.

"If the coroner has any questions, or if our crime-scene unit finds anything suspicious, there'll be an autopsy. In that case, I'd call in the BCA—the Bureau of Criminal Apprehension—to help us process evidence at the scene."

A flash of indecision crossed her face. "I...I was supposed to meet him two nights ago. He was healthy enough then."

"That was the night I found you down here and escorted you home?"

"Uh...yeah." Her gaze shifted away from his.

Why hadn't she told him the truth in the first place? "You said you were just letting your dog run in the park."

She hitched a shoulder impatiently. "I was. But I'd also received a message that he wanted to talk to me."

"You don't think it's risky to meet strange men in dark, isolated places?" He tried to keep his tone level, but she lifted her chin another notch.

"Of course, I do. I'm not completely stupid. I never got out of my car and the doors were locked."

"You couldn't have arranged something during the day in public?"

She raised her palms in frustration. "There was no phone listing for the salvage yard. I received his note the day before, and he made it very clear that he didn't want me coming anywhere near his place. I don't know why…I figured he was afraid of something."

"Of what?"

"I don't know!" she cried. "But I worried he might change his mind if I didn't do what he said. I…" She fell silent. When she spoke again it was a whisper. "I hoped he knew something about my dad."

Now it all began to make a little more sense. "Why would you think that?"

"What else would he want to talk to me about? I never had any business with him before. I figured maybe he knew something about what happened the night of Grover's murder and my dad's suicide."

"Why would he wait all these years? I've been through the old records, Sara," he said gently. "There's little doubt about what happened. Clay Benson and my secretary say they remember the case like it was yesterday.''

''But there could have been mistakes.''

''Earl was an alcoholic and might not have been the best historian. Every now and then he spent time at a mental-health facility down in Minneapolis.''

''That doesn't mean he couldn't remember something important,'' she insisted, tears glittering in her eyes.

''Even if he had told you about your dad, you couldn't be sure it was true—it might have been something he'd hallucinated.''

She bowed her head. ''Then all my hopes were for nothing.'' A solitary tear slid down her face as she turned away. ''If you don't need me anymore, I think I'll go home.''

''Wait.'' He gently caught her wrist. Through the denim fabric her bones felt fragile, and he felt an overpowering urge to protect her. ''I'm sorry. I just didn't want you thinking you'd missed your one chance to find out the truth.''

''I'm still not convinced.'' She pulled away from him and strode to her Bronco, where Harold watched her from the front seat. ''And I'm not going to stop looking for answers, either.''

Nathan followed. He caught the edge of her door as she opened it and slid behind the wheel. ''Will you be okay?''

She nodded. ''What about Leon? What will happen to him?''

''I'll go out to talk to him, make sure he understands about his father.''

"But will he be okay on his own?"

"I'll also alert the county so Social Services can send someone out to assess him. Given his mental status, he'd be considered a vulnerable adult."

"That poor man. Losing his father and then his home."

"Maybe. He might be able to manage there with some assistance and a conservator for business matters. If not, there are group homes in the county."

"He seems so shy. I doubt he'd like them."

"It could be a tough adjustment," Nathan agreed. "But who knows? Maybe he'd really enjoy interacting with peers in a home. I know the local social workers, and they're both top-notch. They'll do what's best for him."

"Will you let me know?"

"Sure." Nathan stepped back and shut the door for her, then waited as she rolled down the window. "About your dog... I didn't want to discuss this while Josh was here, but I understand there was some trouble in town."

Sara turned the key in the ignition and the engine roared to life. "Some boys taunted Josh. Harold was only being protective."

"I had several calls saying that the dog was vicious and completely out of control."

Sara turned to face him, her mouth set in a grim line. "Harold was *guarding* Josh."

"Maybe. But if there's any more trouble, Animal Control may need to pick him up."

She reached over to lay a protective hand on the German shepherd's shoulder. "There won't be, because I'll make sure Josh doesn't walk him again.'' She hesitated, then gave a resigned sigh. "Harold had a long career with a police department, and he's had training that would put any other dog in town to shame. Don't be thinking that he's dangerous and needs to be disposed of, because it isn't going to happen. Are we done yet?''

"I guess we are.''

"Good.'' She bent to release the parking brake.

"Just one question—how did you get him?''

"These dogs usually retire to live with their handler, as you well know. Harold was retired for several years before his owner was killed in the line of duty. The man was a...very good friend, and Harold already knew me well. So the department let me keep him.''

Nathan watched her turn the SUV around in a parking area at the other end of the park, then drive past and head up the street toward her apartment.

She'd handled his questions calmly, considering that she'd just been through the emotional trauma of finding a body in the woods. Everything she'd said seemed logical and believable.

So why did Nathan still get the feeling that there was a whole lot about Sara Hanrahan that he didn't know?

CHAPTER TEN

"WHAT DO YOU MEAN, he's been cremated?"

"Just what I said, lady." The voice on the other end of the line sounded bored. "We've got the documents right here—prepaid services signed by the deceased back in 1974 and notarized. I sold him the plan myself."

"But the man was just found yesterday," Sara said, trying to curb her frustration. "He died under suspicious circumstances. There should have been an autopsy."

"The body was brought in and nobody said nothing. He was ID'd as Earl Samuel Stark, and I did what we were paid by the deceased to do. End of story."

"But isn't there a law—"

"Look, everyone knew the old guy had a heart condition and was a heavy drinker. If you found him in the woods, I'm sure that upset you a lot, but all that means is that his ticker finally gave out. He signed a document saying he didn't want a funeral or any kind of services, he just wanted to be cremated."

"What about the coroner's report?"

"Lady, I don't know who the hell you are, but—" The pencil in Sara's hand snapped. "I'd like to talk to the owner of the funeral home, please."

"You just have." *Click.*

Sara held the receiver away from her ear and glared at it, then slammed it down on the cradle. Expectations of natural death in the elderly probably hid more wrongful deaths than were ever discovered, but until now she hadn't dealt with the situation firsthand.

Perhaps Earl *had* died of a heart attack. However, the timing, coupled with his fear of being seen with her, seemed damned suspicious.

She'd told Nathan about her failed meeting with Earl and claimed she was after information about her late father. Maybe it hadn't been such a bad move. If Nathan grew curious about her actions in town, he'd figure she was still looking.

But now she'd never know what Earl had wanted to tell her. Not unless his son had some answers—and that wasn't likely. Still, after she visited the retired sheriff, she would pay Leon a call.

She thumbed through the local telephone directory, found Clay Benson's address, then loaded Harold into the SUV and headed across town on the chance that he might be home.

Sure enough, he was raking leaves in his front yard when she pulled to a stop at the curb.

"Hi, Sheriff Benson," she called out as she sauntered up his sidewalk. "Beautiful fall day, isn't it?"

His breathing labored and his face ruddy with exertion, he leaned on his rake and watched her approach. "Guess it is."

She offered her hand. "I'm Sara Hanrahan. You probably don't recognize me from years ago, but I grew up here."

"I know who you are."

"Can I ask you a few questions?"

"I'm retired."

"I understand that, sir. But I'd like to ask you about the past." She nodded toward the wicker furniture on his porch. "Would you take a break for a few minutes?"

"You can ask me right here." His expression softened. "My wife, Dora, will give me hell if I don't have these leaves done by the time she gets home."

"You were the sheriff back in 1977."

"That's right."

"My dad…died back then."

Clay gave her a long, assessing look. "And you want to know what happened, and if there could have been some mistake. You don't believe he could have murdered Frank or committed suicide, because your daddy wouldn't have done something like that."

"Yes…something like that."

"Honey, I'd like to tell you that every bit of evidence was wrong. I'd like to tell you that I missed things in that investigation, that I didn't find your dad with the body and with Frank's blood on his hands." Clay's voice took on a harder edge. "But that would be a lie."

"I'm not questioning your conclusions, sir. It's just that I know so little about what happened. My mother would never say a word, and the newspapers…well—" she gave a little shrug "—sometimes reporters don't get the details quite right."

"Your dad didn't argue when I cuffed him and took him to town. He rambled on about Frank and his job at the factory and said something about getting even. Of course, a man who's liquored up will say things he don't mean. When we got back to my office, he blurted out a confession. I locked him up and left on a domestic call. When I got back, Daniel had hung himself with his own belt.''

A sick feeling roiled through Sara's midsection. ''Th-there wasn't evidence of anyone else at the murder scene?''

Clay's ruddy face took on a darker hue. ''I did a thorough investigation.'' He looked up at the sound of an approaching car. ''Dora will be home any minute, and I need to get back to work here. If you have more questions, ask the deputy to look up the old reports. It's been too long for me to remember all the details.''

''I understand.'' Sara started for the curb, then turned back. ''By the way, did you hear that Earl Stark died?''

Clay's gaze didn't flicker. ''He was an old man.''

''I guess so. He died out in the woods the other night. Sad, isn't it?''

''It happens.'' Clay turned away and started raking again, clearly dismissing her.

''I saw him around town just a few days ago, though. He looked healthy as a horse.''

''Old boozers like him don't live long,'' Clay retorted without turning around.

''Did you know him well?''

Clay gave an exasperated snort. ''*No* one knew him well. The man was a recluse.''

"Would you say he could be a reliable source of information?"

The old sheriff did turn around then, and his eyes were filled with contempt. "I don't know what you're getting at, but the man was a drunk. You could believe him just about as far as you could throw him—but given the fact he'd rarely took a bath, you sure as hell wouldn't want to try. I had to haul him off to a mental hospital twice, and my cruiser reeked for days."

"Well, thanks for your time, Sheriff."

He grunted an unintelligible response as he turned back to his raking, but now there was a stiffness to his back that hadn't been there before.

One of the things Clay had said kept playing through her mind, clashing with every memory she had of her father. *Of course, a man who's liquored up will say things he doesn't mean.*

She'd been just a second-grader when her father died, but she clearly remembered his comment after seeing Earl stumble out a tavern. "Only a fool drinks like that," he'd said. "Alcohol is a terrible thing."

Could her teetotaler father truly have been drunk the night of the murder? It just didn't seem possible.

SARA STOPPED by her apartment to pick up the cell phone she'd forgotten on her kitchen table. When she stepped outside again, she wished she hadn't.

Nathan had pulled in behind her Bronco and was leaning against the front fender of his cruiser with his arms folded and one boot cocked over the other ankle, as if he had all the time in the world.

Damn.

"I hear you've been busy today," he called out as she approached. "Now I've got one riled undertaker and a grumpy retired sheriff on my hands. They're asking if I've hired an assistant investigator."

She stopped at her car door and opened it. "Maybe you need to."

His grin widened. "Are you applying?"

"Me? What would I know about law enforcement?"

"You seem to have a knack for asking questions— and that's a good first step."

Slamming the car door shut again, she strode over to him and looked up at the twinkle in his eyes. "You think it's funny."

"No. I think it's interesting. They must do a lot of assertiveness training down in— Where are you from?"

"Dallas. Did you know that poor Earl has been cremated already?"

The twinkle in Nathan's eyes faded. "I just heard."

"Since finding him, I've thought about little else. When I called the mortuary, the guy said there hadn't been an autopsy."

"The coroner ruled it a natural death, given Earl's health history. The mortuary just went ahead."

"How could they do that?"

"Autopsies are pretty rare around here if someone dies in a nursing home or is elderly and has serious health problems."

"But Earl was well enough to live independently

and still run his own business. That doesn't sound like someone who was at death's door."

Nathan sighed heavily. "The crime-scene unit found nothing unusual. The coroner checked with the cardiologist who'd attended him in the hospital ER when he had a mild attack last year. Earl was told that he wasn't likely to survive if he didn't agree to surgery, and he basically walked out of the hospital against medical advice."

"So then it's all over. No one cares, and no one will look any further."

He looked down at her, his eyes filled with concern. "Look, I know this has been stressful for you. What would you say to just getting away for an hour or so?"

She'd been so focused on Earl that she hadn't been fully aware of just how close she stood to Nathan, or how keenly he was studying her. As if she actually mattered to him. "Getting away?" she repeated.

"Come with me," he said, catching her hand in his. "There's a restaurant on Hidden Lake, just past Newbrook, that has the best orange roughy you'll ever taste."

Maybe he was just being friendly, offering comfort. But her body read that contact in an entirely different way. "The best ever?"

"Absolutely."

Maybe it wouldn't hurt to spend a little time with him away from the watchful eyes of the townsfolk of Ryansville. "Just casual friends having lunch?"

He held up his hand. "Scout's honor. Nothing more."

She glanced around, but didn't see anyone else in a backyard. Then she climbed into his cruiser.

"I feel like I'm being arrested," she murmured.

He grinned at her. "I'd have you handcuffed and in the back seat if you were."

She glanced at the molded plastic bench seat in the back. "I think I like it up here better. What, the county can't afford upholstery for the back seat?"

He slid a wry glance at her as he checked the rearview mirror and backed into the alley. "Not for the drunks who leave all sorts of reminders of their trips."

"That's disgusting!"

"Believe me, you have no idea." He called dispatch and announced his lunch break, then headed out toward the edge of town.

As they traveled up the highway toward Newbrook, Sara continued to mask her familiarity with the equipment inside the cruiser. "Fancy laptop," she murmured, eyeing the mobile data computer mounted in front of the dashboard. "What does it do?"

"It accesses the state computers, so I can run warrant checks, vehicle registrations and driver's licenses, check for stolen vehicles, you name it." He touched the screen, and a county map appeared. "It has a global positioning system, too."

"Not your average little laptop, then."

He laughed. "Not exactly. One of these runs around ten grand. Few small towns have them, but our County Sheriff's Office has done well at getting special grants this past year. Since I'm covering a large area on my own, fairly distant from the central office, I got lucky.''

Sara settled back in her seat and studied him as he drove. Away from Ryansville and her responsibilities there, it felt good just to relax. Seeing Nathan's genuine pleasure over his career made her view him in a whole new light. The rich kid was now a fellow officer—one whose dedication and professional pride made him more appealing.

He shot a quick glance at her, then turned his attention back to the winding road leading from New-brook to Hidden Lake. ''What are your plans if Sanderson doesn't start hiring?''

''I expect I'll go back to Dallas in a few months. I'd hoped to stay here, but there's bound to be better accounting opportunities in a big city.''

''But you don't have relatives there, right?''

''Nope.''

''Close friends?''

''Sure, some.''

''Anyone special?''

''Not for a while.'' An image of Tony's laughing face drifted through her thoughts, but it wasn't as painful to think about him as it had been before.

Nathan gave her a knowing glance. ''Was that guy the one who owned Harold?''

''Yeah…it's been a few years now, though. I guess if he'd died of some disease, I might have had time to prepare. But when he was shot, I was completely devastated. You keep thinking just a few seconds difference either way, and maybe he would be alive. The unfairness of it hurts all the more.''

"I know. When my partner in Minneapolis was killed, I ended up taking almost a month off. I just couldn't concentrate."

Nathan flipped on the turn signal and took a left onto a narrow gravel road, then drove in silence until the road opened into a parking area adjacent to a low log building hugging the lake.

Though it was only eleven-thirty, there were at least a dozen cars already parked close to the door.

"Popular place," Sara said when a waitress seated them by a large picture window overlooking the lake.

"They don't take reservations, so by noon, there'll be a line of people out the door." After the waitress took their orders, he leaned back and smiled at Sara. "Was it the orange roughy or was it me?"

"That lured me here? Definitely the fish. No offense."

"So tell me, Ms. Hanrahan, what might entice you besides something with fins? Would it be good music? Dancing? Sunny faraway beaches?"

"It would depend on who was doing the enticing." *If it's you, almost anything,* she realized with a start.

Sunshine sparkled on the lake outside, and inside, the atmosphere was warm and intimate, the ambiance enhanced by soft flickering candlelight and the deep gold of rough-cut pine walls.

The subdued lighting shadowed the lean, strong planes of his face and darkened his eyes, and she found herself wanting to touch him just to be sure he was real.

"You're looking at me," he said with a low laugh, "as if I might be your main course."

"Must be the lighting in here," she shot back to hide her sudden embarrassment. The last person she ought to be ogling was the one man in town she had to avoid.

Grasping at the first change of topic that came to mind, she folded her hands on the tablecloth, leaned forward and said, "The former sheriff didn't seem very happy to see me."

Nathan canted his head slightly in acknowledgment. "Exactly what did you say to him? I haven't heard old Clay that agitated since his wife made him take dancing lessons with her."

"I asked him about my dad."

"And he said…?"

"He insisted that there was no other possible conclusion. He was very touchy about the topic."

"No kidding."

"Why? It seems reasonable enough that I would want to hear the facts. I was too young back then to understand what went on."

"He called me after you left his place and asked me to deal with any further questions you have."

"Can I see the reports?"

Nathan shifted in his seat. "Well…"

"It's all public record now, isn't it?"

"Yes…though there's a lot of graphic detail in those files that I don't think you'd want to read."

"Will you show me those files?"

He held her gaze for a long moment, his eyes filled with concern. "If that's what you want."

When their salads arrived, they ate in silence for a few minutes. And suddenly she realized that she was wasting the only opportunity she might ever have to get to know Nathan Roswell better. "Sounds like you have a good relationship with Clay."

"He was my boss for most of the three years I worked out of the Jefferson County Sheriff's Department based in Hawthorne." Nathan smiled. "Tough old coot—when he retired and moved to Ryansville, I think the entire department breathed a sigh of relief."

"Was he good at his job?"

Nathan laughed. "He was like a bulldog and had about as much tact, but yeah, he sure got the job done. The voters loved him because of his tough stand on crime. His employees mostly tried to keep busy and stay out of his way. He didn't tolerate inefficiency."

"So he'd already moved here when you were assigned to cover Ryansville?"

"Right. And now he's become a good friend. We play chess over lunch, he talks about the old days and how much he misses the action. I nag him about his health and keep him in touch with what's going on." A corner of his mouth lifted. "And give him a place to hide from Dora for a while. She'd keep him moving twenty-four hours a day if she could—but he hates shopping and household chores."

Sara thought about Clay's labored breathing when she'd seen him earlier "He doesn't seem to be in the best of shape."

"He's overweight, and forty years of heavy smoking didn't do him much good. He's got congestive heart failure and has battled lung cancer for the past few years."

"I'm really sorry. It must be hard on you."

Nathan speared a piece of lettuce, studied it, then set the fork down. "I don't like to think about it. He's become like a grandfather, almost. My family isn't all that close."

When the main courses arrived, Sara stared in wonder, then took a single bite of her fish and closed her eyes to savor the delicate, sweet flavor.

"How is it?"

She met his laughing gaze and felt herself tumbling headlong into territory she'd sworn to avoid. This man, this time, were all wrong in so many ways. Yet…he couldn't have been more right for her, either.

Beyond his rugged, impossibly handsome face there was his humor, compassion—and solid core of integrity that told her he was a man she could count on. That, and the fact that just being near him made her skin tingle, told her she was in deep trouble.

"What, no comment?"

"Perfect. Altogether too perfect for words." *And the fish isn't bad, either.*

Behind Sara's chair, a set of open bookshelves filled with plants rose from floor to ceiling, providing greater privacy for a table in the corner.

A familiar voice on the other side murmured something, then laughed with giddy delight at what her male companion said in return. *Jane?*

Knowing how lonely her friend had been, Sara took another bite of her fish, trying to tune out the couple's private conversation.

But then the man's voice came through the divider more clearly. *Robert Kelstrom?* So Jane's blush had meant something, after all, Sara thought with an inward smile. *You go, girl.*

Unless…Robert was part of the scheme to deliver drug shipments in the Minneapolis area.

"You suddenly seem awfully quiet," Nathan mused, giving her a thoughtful look. "Anything wrong?"

"No, not at all." She eyed his plate. "Except that I might have stolen the rest of your meal if you hadn't finished it."

He laughed. "We can order a second round if you'd like."

The voices behind Sara rose, then Robert clearly told Jane to lower her voice. Distracted, it took Sara a moment to answer. "Um…I'd better not. But I'll definitely come back if I can figure out how we got here."

"Maybe you'll join me again sometime?"

"Yes. I'd like that."

On the way out, Nathan rested his hand at the small of her back, and once out in the parking lot, he opened the door of his cruiser for her. She hesitated before getting in, transfixed by his pensive expression and the certainty that if she moved toward him, just a little, he would kiss her.

Even though the car was at the far end of the lot and they were out of view, the thought was as frightening as it was exciting, because she had no doubt that there was something far more compelling here than simple lust.

He searched her face as if looking for a signal. With slow, deliberate care he moved his thumb along her jaw and then slid his hand to the back of her neck and drew her closer. "I've wanted to do this for a long time," he murmured.

Her heart lurched as his mouth descended on hers, gently seeking at first, then he gave a low groan and deepened the kiss into one filled with need, and wonder, and a depth of desire that completely stole her breath.

He lifted his head and gazed deeply into her eyes, then rested his forehead against hers. "Guess I shouldn't have...because now I only want more."

From behind them came the voices of people heading toward their cars, and he stepped away with a heavy sigh.

Once in the car, he started the engine, then rested his head against the headrest and closed his eyes. "I don't do casual affairs."

"I don't, either," she murmured.

"In a small town, that sort of thing would undercut my reputation with the teenagers and just about everyone else."

"I understand—you don't need to worry. We'll forget this ever happened."

"Forget?" He looked over at her, and the heat still smoldering in his eyes sent a shiver through her. "I don't think so."

She ached to reach over and run her forefinger over his mouth, to bring him into another kiss.

But a nagging, unwelcome voice reminded her just how wrong that would be. *You're here on assignment. You can't jeopardize your career.*

Forcing herself to look away, she found her breeziest tone. ''I plan to. I'll probably be back in Dallas in a few months, so why make life complicated?''

She could feel his eyes on her. Sensed his effort at control. Then he shifted the car into gear and drove back to Ryansville in absolute silence.

Great job, she told herself after he'd dropped her off at her apartment. *You just had a chance at something that might have been the best thing in your entire life, and you managed to destroy it.*

Knowing she'd done the right thing didn't lessen her deep sense of loss.

CHAPTER ELEVEN

"HEY, KID. THIS IS amazing!" Nathan stood with his hands on his hips, staring at the train set that filled one corner of the Shuellers' basement. "How long did this take, anyway?"

A feeling of pride welled in Josh's chest. "Me and my dad have worked on it since I was six."

"I always wanted something just like this when I was a kid—something my dad and I could work on together. I bet it's been a lot of fun for you two."

"How come you didn't get one?"

Nathan leaned over to admire the old Lionel Southern Pacific diesel engine, tender and box cars. "My dad traveled a lot, mostly. He did get me a train for Christmas, but he had the gardener set it up for me. It's not the same as working on it with your dad."

Josh nodded, understanding completely and even feeling a little sorry for him. He'd heard people talk about how rich the Roswells were, but maybe it was better to have a dad who did stuff with you.

"Tell me about this one here—it looks like it's very special."

"It belonged to my grandpa Tom. He had it when he was a kid. He gave it to me last Christmas, and when he came from Georgia, he helped me build that mountain range at the side.'' Josh pointed to the back wheels of the engine. ''His sister got mad once and threw it. There's dents and it had to be welded, so it's not worth as much as it would be if it was perfect. But I like it because looking at it makes me think of my grandpa when he was little.''

Nathan straightened and smiled down at him. ''You're a cool kid, you know that? So tell me— how's your leg doing?''

''Okay.'' He lifted the hem of his baggy, overlong jeans to show off a heavy layer of elasticized wrap supporting his ankle. ''I got to miss school yesterday, but some kids came over after school with my home-work.'' He grinned. ''They thought it was pretty cool about me having an attack dog and all.''

''You do know that he isn't really yours, right? And that it isn't safe for you to take him out alone?''

Josh gave him a sheepish look. ''Yeah...I never should have done it last time.''

Nathan rested a hand on his shoulder. ''It must have been awfully scary being out in those woods after dark. A lot of grown-ups would be frightened if they'd found Earl like you did.''

Josh didn't want to talk about it. Didn't want to think about the guy's ghost-white face and staring eyes. When he closed his eyes at night, it all came back like in a horror movie.

''Josh?'' Nathan said gently.

''I'm okay.''

''Your mom says you aren't sleeping too well, so I thought maybe it might help if we talked it over awhile.''

Uncomfortable, Josh moved to the control panel and flipped a switch. A thousand pinpoints of light turned on in the buildings and street lamps of the two villages on the table. He moved to another switch, and all three trains started moving smoothly down the tracks.

"Sometimes I have trouble sleeping, too."

His hand hovering over the rheostat controlling the speed, Josh stilled. "Really?"

"As a cop, I see people who've been hurt and people who've died. It's never easy, even when you're a grown-up. You remember those people for a very long time, and you feel sad for them. The first few times, it's even scary—especially if you come up on something you didn't expect to find."

Josh bowed his head. "I knew he was dead. But then I thought about the movies—where some dead guy in a creepy old house suddenly leaps up after someone and kills him, too. All I wanted to do was get away."

"And then you hurt your ankle and couldn't run."

Hot tears burned beneath Josh's lids and started slipping down his cheeks. "That was even scarier. Harold was barking like crazy, and it was really dark, and I wasn't even sure which way to go home anymore."

"But remember how he barked at the kids who teased you?"

Josh nodded.

"He would have fought off anyone who so much as laid a hand on you. You were completely safe with him there, Josh. I know you felt helpless and scared, but he never left your side until Sara came looking, and then he went to get her. When you think about that night, remember that a well-trained police dog was at your side and nothing could have hurt you. Except," Nathan added with a smile, "that rock you tripped over."

Scrubbing furiously at his tears, Josh nodded again, his trembling lips forming into a smile.

"I think you two were real heroes out there. Harold knew someone was in trouble, and you were brave enough to go after him without even a flashlight. If Earl had still been alive and needing medical help, you two might have saved his life."

Josh felt the heat of embarrassment warm his cheeks. "I only went 'cause Harold did—I knew I had to get him back."

"And that was a brave thing to do. You put that dog, and Sara's love for him, above everything else." Nathan extended his hand for a shake.

After a moment's hesitation, Josh awkwardly stuck out his own hand in response.

"My office is just two blocks away, and my door is always open if you need to talk about what happened, okay? Or you can call me. Promise you'll do that?"

"Promise." Josh hadn't heard anyone come down the basement stairs, but when Nathan turned to leave, Sara was standing by the bottom step.

Nathan must not have heard her, either, because he took a sharp breath and nearly tripped.

"I just came down to see how Josh was doing," she murmured.

Nathan didn't answer, which was weird because everyone knew the deputy was always polite even when he was arresting someone. Instead, he just nodded at her, then disappeared up the stairs.

"Looks like you're having quite a few visitors," she said as she walked over and hugged Josh.

"Yeah."

"How's the ankle? Are you going to be up for trick-or-treating on Sunday?"

"You bet! By then I won't even need the bandage." She had the nicest smile, though she didn't seem as happy as usual.

"Have you heard yet about the nativity scene?" The good feelings in his chest melted away, leaving only the weight of disappointment. "A letter came yesterday."

"And?"

"I'm a shepherd boy."

"Aw, sweetie. I know how much you wanted to be Joseph."

Hearing "sweetie" from anyone else would have made him clench his teeth, but Sara looked as if she felt even worse about the news than he did. "It doesn't matter."

"Well, of course it does! You were so excited...." She hugged him again, then stepped back with both hands on his shoulders. "But you still have a part, and lots of people don't get to be in it at all."

"Yeah, I guess."

"And next year—hey, you'll be even taller and look even more like a Joseph. With your experience this year you'll have a better chance, right?"

"Were you ever a cheerleader or something?"

She laughed. "Are you kidding? I was a scrawny kid with freckles and glasses, and I never got picked for *anything*. I just figure it's always good to look for a bright side when things don't go the way you hope."

Long after she left, Josh watched his trains run through the villages and countryside scenes on his train table, and thought about the two grown-ups who'd come to see him. They were both just about the nicest people he'd ever met, except for his mom and dad, and he wished he could do something nice for them in return. But what could an eight-year-old kid do that would matter?

He thought about it all morning, but it wasn't until afternoon he realized that he already knew what each of them wanted.

Now he only had to figure out how to make it happen.

AFTER VISITING JOSH, Sara loaded Harold into the Bronco and headed out to Dry Creek Road. Once again she stood at the locked gates of Stark's Salvage trying to catch sight of Leon, and once again the house was dark.

Nathan had gone out to talk to Leon about Earl's death and had called the county social workers. They'd gone out the next day and the day after that, but apparently Leon had refused to cooperate with their assessment efforts, and now he seemed to have disappeared. Where could he be?

Concerned, Sara had left a message for Nathan yesterday morning. Later he left a message on her machine, saying that he'd gone over to search. There'd been no sign of Leon, but the guy was known to take off now and then, so it wasn't all that unusual.

Nathan had talked to the head social worker, and she'd felt Leon could probably manage independently with a few visits from Social Services. He'd also need some assistance with business matters and housekeeping chores.

Pathetic as a middle school-girl with a crush, Sara had listened to the deep resonance of Nathan's voice on that message three times before catching herself and abruptly erasing it. *Foolish dreams and useless wishes.*

Harold bumped against her leg and whined softly, his tail wagging. "So you think we ought to do this? You're not just wanting a share of my lunch?"

She'd picked up half a dozen ham-and-cheese sandwiches, a bag of chips and strawberry pop at a café downtown, just in case. The thought of encountering Leon was a bit unsettling, but maybe he was out here hiding and confused and hungry.

She'd considered, then quickly dismissed the thought of asking Nathan to come with her. His message had suggested that he'd found the trip out here to be a fool's errand—and there'd been no warmth in his voice, either.

"Come, Harold." Sara edged along the multistrand tangle barbed-wire fencing until she reached a section with several downed wires. After helping the dog through, she crouched and squeezed between the sharp barbs.

"Leon—are you here?" she called as she and Harold scouted the piles of scrap metal, rusted car bodies and farm equipment. She knocked on the metal siding and tested the padlocked doors of one storage building after the next.

Everything was bolted tight, just as Nathan had said. At the house, all the doors and windows were locked. "Guess I was wrong," she murmured, surveying the property one last time. "Let's head for home."

They'd only gone a few feet when Harold abruptly whined and sat down.

Sara halted and spun around just as something flashed around the corner of the house. "Leon? Is that you?"

She waited several minutes, then circled the house from a distance, but found nothing—not a hint of the hulking figure of the man who'd given her the note a week ago.

"I'm putting some food on the fence post," she called. "Then I'm leaving, so you come out and get it."

She backed toward the front gate and left the paper sack on top of the thickest fence post, then sent Harold into the Bronco and took a final look back. Leon was here—she could feel it. If he was this spooked by company, was it safe for him to be here alone?

She drove half a mile down the road and waited for twenty minutes, then cruised slowly past without stopping.

The lunch bag was gone, and there was no litter on

the ground as there might have been had an eager raccoon helped himself to the food.

"So you *are* here," she said softly. "Now we just need to make sure you're okay."

OVER THE NEXT THREE DAYS Sara continued her surveillance of the Sanderson plant by night and she brought food out to Leon by day. He never came forward when she drove up to the gate. But after she left, the food disappeared almost immediately.

On the fourth day she heard the music.

"Leon! This is Sara—are you here?" She stood at the gate, the lunch bag in her hand. She shouted her question more loudly, then waited a few minutes and tried again.

The music stopped. A curtain fluttered. A full minute later, the front door slowly creaked open, and Leon appeared.

"I brought your lunch," she said. "But I heard such beautiful music that I wanted to stay and listen. Do you play?"

From his tousled, graying hair to his battered, run-down boots, he was unkempt and dirty. But when his mouth lifted into a fleeting, gentle smile, the childlike quality touched her heart.

"Are you doing okay?"

He just stared back at her.

"Are you hungry?"

His expression brightened at that, so she knew he understood. Tonight she would check whether Ryansville had a meals-on-wheels program. Then she'd check with Leon's social worker; with Leon's lack of cooperation during his assessment, the woman may not have identified his needs.

Sara watched as Leon slowly descended the stairs and started àcross the yard, but stopped a few feet from the gate.

"Do you remember me?" She waited, hoping he would speak, but he gave only a slight nod. "Can you tell me your name?"

"Le-on," he said after a long moment.

"Well, Leon, here's your lunch. I hope you like it today. It's turkey, is that okay?"

He didn't answer, but when she stepped back away from the gate, he moved closer and took the sack, then nodded his thanks and turned away.

"How did you learn to play the piano so well?" she called out. When he looked over his shoulder at her, the sad and lonely look in his eyes made her heart turn over.

"Momma. She died, too."

"I'm so sorry, Leon. It must be hard, being out here alone. Would you like to be where there are other people to talk to?"

"No!"

He definitely had no problem comprehending her words. With an angry slash of his hand, he threw the sack to the ground and strode to the house, then disappeared inside, slamming the door behind him.

With a heavy heart, Sara called Harold to heel and headed for the Bronco. Leon clearly wanted his independence, but he probably wouldn't be able to enjoy it much longer if he didn't accept some help.

CHAPTER TWELVE

HAROLD HATED GOBLINS, Sara knew. He always had.

Whether two feet tall or four, the sight of them drove him absolutely crazy, and witches, warlocks and creatures from outer space didn't do much for him, either.

"Sorry, bud," she said as she stepped out of her apartment on Sunday evening. "This time you've got to stay home—at least until all the monsters have gone to bed."

She took a deep breath, grinned, then went down the steps two at a time. Back in Dallas, she lived in a gated apartment complex that sometimes seemed more like a rabbit warren than a real home—the parking lot was usually full, spaces were hard to find. People came and went so quickly that her neighbors were perpetual strangers. Halloween never brought trick-or-treaters to her door.

Here they weren't likely to show up at her door, either, because the apartment over the garage wasn't even visible from the street. But droves of kids would be going from door to door, and it would be fun to see the night unfold. Zoe had asked her to escort Josh.

At the Shuellers' front door, she knocked and then

stepped aside as a group of preschooler's scampered up the porch steps.

"Wow! Let's see—a fairy, a bride, Cinderella…" She frowned. "And what are you?"

"A bat." The child lifted arms draped in black to show off her wings. "A vampire bat."

Sara grinned over her head at Zoe, who'd come to the door with a bowl of treats and Timmy on one hip. "These guys are great!" she said. "How many kids do you usually get?"

"Forty, maybe fifty. It depends on the weather." Zoe turned over her shoulder. "Josh, Sara's here. Are you ready?"

Another set of trick-or-treaters had arrived and left before Josh appeared at the door, looking a little sheepish. "What do you think?"

He wore a black cape and vampire teeth, and the white makeup on his face was liberally doused with fake blood. The large rubber gloves on his hands were tipped with curved talons.

"I think you look *really* horrible. Great job with the blood—did you put it on yourself?"

"Yeah." He met her gaze, then looked away. "I could go by myself, you know."

His mother shooed him out the door. "I'm sorry, Josh, but no. Your dad has to work late, and I have to stay here and watch the door."

"Guys my age don't have a grown-up with them. They go with their friends."

"It might be different next year—and I'm worried about that ankle of yours."

"But it's fine!"

''What happens if you stumble in the dark and twist it again?'' Zoe's face brightened as another contingent of costumed kids started up the walk. ''You two go on, now. Have fun.''

Josh trudged down the porch steps past the oncoming group, then waited for Sara on the sidewalk. From his furtive glances up and down the street, Sara knew he was embarrassed.

''You know, I think I'll just stay way behind. How's that sound? No one will even guess that I know you.''

He nodded and cast her a grateful look, then started off down the street, his limp barely noticeable. At the sixth house, he arrived at the door just as two aliens turned to leave. His stride faltered, and Sara saw him pull back as if wary of his reception.

She moved closer and rested a shoulder against a tree at the edge of the street, out of sight but close enough to intercede.

''Hey, dude—pretty cool, you finding that dead guy,'' one of them said with a note of awe. ''What was it like?''

''Yeah—you saw him up close and everything?''

Josh shrugged. ''Yeah.''

''Weren't you scared?''

''It was pitch-black...except for a little moonlight. Harold went crazy barking—''

''That big German shepherd you had?''

''Yeah.'' Warming to his story, Josh's voice grew melodramatic. ''He was going ballistic, so I thought there might be guys out there waiting to kill anyone they saw. Then I hurt my ankle and couldn't run. I figured I was a goner for sure.''

''Wow!''

The two boys stood awhile, peppering Josh with questions, then one of them gestured down the sidewalk. ''Wanna come with us?''

Josh slid a surreptitious glance in Sara's direction and she shot back a double thumbs-up, then he grinned and joined them. She dropped back a little farther after that, sauntering along as if just taking an evening stroll.

She smiled at Josh's increasing animation as he and the boys stopped at each house. He deserved a good time, she thought. Things hadn't always been easy for him.

At the next corner the boys halted, then took a right on Pine at a faster clip, passing two or three promising homes with porch lights lit and carved pumpkins displayed in the front windows.

She saw the reason as soon as she reached the same corner and spied the flashing lights of a patrol car and a group of people standing at the end of the next block.

Even from this distance she recognized Nathan's tall, imposing silhouette. He stood beneath a street lamp, his feet spread and his hands on his hips, and it didn't take much guesswork to know that the group of boys in front of him had been up to no good. Finally they moved off in different directions, their steps slow.

When Josh and his friends drew closer, Nathan turned and looked at them. Then she could have sworn that he lifted his gaze beyond them and saw her, as well. Feeling more than a little foolish, she caught up to them.

"Are you going to arrest those guys?" Josh asked, staring at the shattered pumpkins strewn along the sidewalk.

"In a manner of speaking."

"But they all left!" one of Josh's companions exclaimed.

"I know who they are and where they live. They're all going to show up at my office tomorrow after school with their parents." Nathan lifted a brow. "Or else."

Hovering a few yards away, Sara grinned.

"What do you think, guys?" he continued. "When these homeowners took all the time to buy and carve their pumpkins, is it right to come by and destroy what they did?"

Three heads shook vigorously.

He glanced at his watch, then reached into his patrol car and turned off the light bar. Suddenly the street seemed dark and quiet. "You don't have much more time—so you'd better get moving! The newspaper said trick-or-treating would end by seven-thirty."

The boys waved and moved on to visit the houses nearby, and Sara started after them.

"So how did you end up trailing three boys tonight?"

Nathan's voice, warm and low, stopped her in her tracks. After that kiss and her cool brush-off, she'd expected him to barely acknowledge her. "Zoe wanted someone to go with Josh and I was happy to help. This brings back a lot of memories of when I was growing up here.''

After aiming his remote at the cruiser to lock the doors, he leaned a shoulder against the street lamp, his face unreadable. ''I haven't seen you around since Tuesday.''

He'd been watching for her? Just the thought was seductive, sending an undercurrent of awareness through her. ''I've been here,'' she replied. ''Don't you ever take a night off?''

''On Halloween?'' He sounded serious, but she caught a twinkle of amusement in his eye. ''Not usually. This time of night we have the pumpkin smashers and candy thieves.''

''Tough bunch, I'll bet.''

''You bet. Later on, I need to check for keggers out at the quarry and do traffic stops for drunks. With luck, there won't be any major problems.''

''What do you do when you catch a bunch of drunken teenagers? Handcuff them all to the trees while you're carting loads of them to jail?''

''Nope. They understand the drill. I know who they are and where they live, so they don't dare try sneaking away. Their parents have to come and get them. Then they're all due at my office by nine the next morning with their parents, no excuses. Failure to show means twice the trouble.''

She couldn't help but shake her head and laugh. ''You do a great job from what I've seen. You sure helped Josh. Zoe says he's sleeping better now.''

''Kids see death on television all the time, but the real thing is tough.''

Nathan had handled that discussion with a level of perception and caring that had touched her deeply and evoked images of him as a loving, protective father. All of which made him even more appealing.

''Guess I'd better catch up with the guys,'' she murmured. ''I'm trying to keep an eye on Josh without making it look like I'm baby-sitting. These guys can move pretty fast.''

His gaze swept her from head to toe and a grin played at the corners of his mouth. ''I'll bet you're one hell of a fisherman.''

''Huh?'' The question stopped her short. Fishing?

''Have you been out lately?''

Not since she was a child, when her dad had taken her out in his old boat with its rusty engine and the two leaky spots along the bow. ''Fishing? In the fall?''

''You bet. Super time for walleye and northerns if you know where to go. Want to join me?''

''When?'' she asked cautiously.

''Tomorrow afternoon. The water's warmer then, and the fish are more active.'' His eyes glinted with amusement. ''Don't worry—we'll be fishing and nothing else. If you want to come along, you can pick up a license at the Bait 'n Burger out on the highway. It's open until ten tonight.''

''You don't have to work tomorrow morning?''

He glanced up at the crescent moon. ''I work around fifty hours a week, sometimes more, and put in a lot of late nights. Nobody will question my schedule.''

''You don't have a relief deputy?''

''Sure—for two days a week and vacations. During the hours I'm off, the PSAP dispatchers send county deputies over here for 911 calls.''

She knew, from the preliminary reports and other documents Allen had given her, that he was referring to the central 'public safety answering point' for fire, emergency and law enforcement in the county.

''So,'' he asked. ''Are you on for fishing or not?''

''I...guess so. Where's your boat?''

''Lake Ryan. Take Main through town, then go south on the highway to Fox and follow it to the lake. When you hit the shore, go left half a mile. Can't miss it. How's one o'clock sound?''

There was nothing romantic about slippery fish and fresh bait, and really, it had been so many years since she'd done something like this. But just like Halloween, the experience might be another taste of nostalgia, a trip back to the innocence of her childhood before everything had gone so terribly wrong. What would be the harm?

''Okay, you're on,'' she called over her shoulder as she started after the boys. ''See you tomorrow. One o'clock.''

They'd go fishing and then she'd get back to work. Nothing would change. She smiled to herself, thankful she had such complete control of her emotions.

Some women might take one look at Nathan's

killer smile, or the warmth and humor in his hazel eyes, and fall right under his spell.

But she definitely wasn't one of those women.

THE HALLOWEEN FESTIVITIES ended and the town was dark and quiet by eleven o'clock.

As she headed for her usual lookout on the hill with Harold at her side, Sara wondered if Nathan was busy rounding up teenagers at the quarry and telling them to report to him tomorrow. One look at their tall, imposing local deputy would probably sober most of them up fast.

The moment she took up her position, though, all thoughts of Nathan disappeared. Something was definitely up.

The plant was always shut down on Sundays, with both the front and back gates securely locked and only a weekend security officer present to patrol the facility.

Tonight the guard's car was missing from its usual spot by the side door. In its place was a dark double-axle truck, which was backed up to the door. Three, no, four figures in dark jackets were lugging boxes from the truck, stacking them on dollies and wheeling them into the building.

Her pulse quickening, Sara reached for her backpack and withdrew her Minolta, then crouched behind the rocks and snapped a series of photographs.

Through the viewfinder she saw one of the men suddenly stop. He pivoted, turned toward the hill where she hid. Then he gestured sharply, and his cohorts started moving faster. Could he have seen a reflection from her camera lens?

Their actions confirmed what she already knew—

they weren't here for normal business deliveries and they were concerned about being caught.

Sensing her increased tension, Harold lifted his head and whined, then rose to his feet as she snapped another set of photos. He growled softly.

At that moment a flash of light caught her eye. Farther down the hill, a beam arced through the trees and then disappeared. She heard the sound of a twig snapping.

Had she been spotted?

She shoved her camera equipment and notebook into the backpack, shouldered it, then grabbed Harold's leash and slipped around the rock to head farther up the hill. She'd studied possible escape routes during daylight hours, knowing that this moment could come, but in the darkness every footstep had to be cautious.

Avoiding the main trail, she picked up a narrow deer path that wound through the underbrush before falling down into a clump of aspen. There she would have a better view of the surrounding terrain.

The beam of light swept through the trees behind her. Closer now, it sent strobelike flashes through the dense trees.

The sharp crack of a rifle split the air. Once. Twice. Behind her, she heard the impact of a bullet against a tree.

Her mouth dry and her pulse hammering, she ducked into a heavier stand of trees farther up the hill.

The shooter was down by the plant and even with a night sight couldn't be taking accurate aim, given all the trees and underbrush. If they had a man up here, would they risk shooting in this direction?

Whatever was going on, she wasn't going to wait around to find out.

Her breath grew ragged, painful, as she fought her way through brambles and low-lying bushes with Harold on his leash behind her. Whining, he balked several times, but she called his name sharply and continued on.

The swing of that flashlight and the sound of footsteps behind her kept her moving.

The rifle cracked again.

Behind her, the light disappeared and total silence descended.

From down below came the sound of agitated voices, then the sound of an engine starting. Tires crunched on gravel as a vehicle moved off. Toward the back gate, probably, though she couldn't see anything from where she stood.

She stopped behind the trunk of a massive oak and leaned against the rough bark to drag in huge gulps of air. Harold whined more insistently and nudged her leg as he looked behind them.

Maybe her follower wasn't part of the group down at the plant. Perhaps they'd seen the flashlight beam, panicked and taken aim, and hadn't seen her at all. So who else was up here—and why?

If there were teenagers up here—partying over a six-pack—one of them could be bleeding to death right now. The thought chilled her.

After retrieving a small flashlight from her pack, she withdrew her Beretta from its holster. This time she swung wider to the north and picked up another deer trail. She moved with caution to avoid making any sound.

Harold pulled back suddenly, shaking his head against the taut leash and pulling to the right.

She rested a hand at his shoulder to quiet him and stood absolutely still. "I hope you remember what to do," she whispered. "It hasn't been that long ago."

Releasing the snap of his leash, she stepped back and gave him the signal to go on alone.

He bounded through the brush, his gray coat instantly disappearing in the dim light. She listened to the fading sounds of him in the brush, then heard him whine.

When she whistled sharply he bounded back to her with his entire body tense and quivering and his tail waving. "You're sure?" she muttered as she followed him off the trail.

He apparently was.

A dozen yards away—from behind an outcropping of rock, she heard a low groan. Only Harold's wagging tail was visible above the rocks.

Still wary, she held her gun extended as she circled wide.

A meaty hand clasped over a blooming dark stain on his upper arm, Leon Stark looked up and focused on her gun with absolute terror in his eyes.

"No," he whispered hoarsely. "*Please,* no."

CHAPTER THIRTEEN

DEALING WITH 250 POUNDS of stubborn male was not Sara's idea of a good time.

She'd quickly reholstered her weapon and reassured him that she hadn't been the person firing at him. Did he believe her? It was hard to tell, because when she'd asked to check his wound, he'd become agitated, then silently lurched to his feet and started for home.

Now he was trudging down the trail, still gripping his bleeding upper arm, still casting wary glances at her over his shoulder. Harold bounced along at his side as if he'd found his long-lost master, his tail wagging gaily and tongue lolling.

"Please, Leon, just let me take a look at your arm. I won't try to make you go to the hospital." When Leon didn't slow down, she added, "Okay, then at least tell me why you were up here tonight."

He traveled another twenty yards before finally mumbling, "Not safe."

"Then why are you here?"

He shook his head as he kept moving. "It's not safe for *you*."

Stunned, she stumbled over an exposed tree root

and nearly fell. "You were up here to protect *me?*" When he didn't answer, she added, "Why?"

They were nearly at the bottom of the hill now, and it didn't appear that Leon planned to give her any answers. But she remembered the other times late at night when she'd sensed someone else was up here. "Did your father ever follow me, Leon?" she asked softly.

Leon's head bowed a fraction.

So Earl had watched over her, as well. But why? Given Leon's limited verbal skills, she'd probably never know, but what mattered most right now was Leon himself.

Taking him to the hospital with a gunshot wound could give rise to some difficult questions, but that was secondary to the risk of infection and permanent damage if Leon's wound was deep enough.

When they reached Dry Creek Road, she knew he would take a sharp left and head for home, where he could lock himself inside. "Leon! You stop right now and listen to me. *Not another step.*"

He faltered to a halt, obviously intimidated by her voice of authority.

"Thank you, Leon." She gave him a nod of approval.

He took a wary step back. "No doctor."

"You don't have to go to a doctor." *Unless it's more than a superficial wound.* "Look—there's enough light right here under this street lamp. Just take off your jacket and roll up your sleeve."

His eyes filled with renewed suspicion. "No doctor," he repeated.

Gritting her teeth in frustration, she rested a hand on his good arm. "I understand that you don't want to go to the hospital. But you're alone now. What happens if you get an infection?"

"I'm okay." But finally, after pondering her words, he peeled off his bloodstained denim jacket. The faded Minnesota Vikings T-shirt beneath appeared fairly clean, thank God. When he pulled the bloody sleeve away from the wound, fresh blood oozed from the small, neat hole near the outer curve of his biceps. Relatively minor, all things considered, and the lack of an exit wound meant the bullet could be recovered.

The shooter had probably aimed at the beam of Leon's flashlight, but given the underbrush, the angle and the darkness, even a powerful night-vision scope couldn't have ensured perfect aim. Leon was a very lucky man. Five or six inches over and the bullet would have hit his chest.

"Let's stop at the emergency room and get that bullet taken out."

"*No.*"

He started off down the road and all she could do was pray that the shooter had decided to flee, instead of coming around to check on who'd been up on the hill. The twelve-round clip in her gun wouldn't be much help against four or five armed men.

After a moment she pulled her cell phone from her

jacket pocket, pressed the power button and started to dial.

At the first beep, Leon jerked to a halt. Turning swiftly, he grabbed the phone, threw it onto the ground and crushed it with his foot.

"Leon!"

Perspiration beaded his pale forehead. Shock? "No doctor," he repeated, his mutinous childlike voice at odds with his massive size. "I'm going home."

Trying to stop him would have been like standing in front of a charging buffalo. Scooping up the remains of her phone, she fell back and watched him start down the road again, then tailed him until he'd made it through the gate and on up to his house.

Men. She fingered the shattered pieces of plastic in her pocket as she called Harold to heel and hurried back to her apartment.

TWENTY MINUTES AFTER she called 911 from her apartment, her phone rang. She hoped it would be one of those anonymous county deputies who covered when Nathan was off duty. No such luck.

"What's this about Leon Stark being injured?" Nathan asked. "I'm out here at his place with the rescue squad, and he's glaring at us through his front window, telling us to go away. He looks pink and vertical to me."

"Um...I just thought someone ought to know. He looked sort of shocky when I...uh...saw him a while ago. There was blood on his sleeve, but he wouldn't talk to me."

"How exactly did he look?"

"A little pale, clammy. He was holding a hand over his arm. I was afraid he might pass out at his place and get hurt."

"Did you see what happened?"

"No. I was out for a run when I found him."

"He seems a little upset with you," Nathan said dryly. "He's been shouting something about you telling on him."

"I tried to convince him to go to the ER and have someone look at his wound, but he wouldn't do it. Since he's all alone in that house, I was afraid to let it go."

An hour after Nathan hung up, the phone woke Sara from a fitful sleep. "I know it's late," he said shortly, "but I need to stop by and ask you a few questions."

Obviously they'd identified Leon's wound. Now she could only hope that Leon hadn't said anything about the gun he'd seen in her hands.

She'd barely stumbled out of bed and into her old terry-cloth robe when she heard footsteps come up the stairs and a knock at the door. A glance through the curtain revealed Nathan standing there, his face tired and drawn.

"What's wrong? Is Leon okay?" she asked as she opened the door.

Nathan raked a hand through his hair, then nodded toward the small kitchenette. "Do you mind?"

"Of course not. Can I get you something? A cup of coffee?"

He shook his head as he sank into one of the chairs at the table and regarded her with troubled eyes.

"How is he?"

A corner of Nathan's mouth lifted briefly. "He might have been wounded, but he sure as hell wasn't weak. Convincing him to come with us to the ER was like corralling a bull moose."

Sara settled into the chair across from Nathan and folded her arms on the table. "You had better luck than I did. Is he in the hospital now?"

"Nope. The doc cleaned and bandaged his wound and gave him a tetanus shot. She also gave him some sort of long-acting antibiotic injection, because she figured he might not remember to take capsules."

"So he wasn't badly hurt?"

"The wound was fairly minor. It's the type of wound that concerns me."

Gone was the relaxed guy who'd taken her to lunch and nearly stopped her heart with a kiss. Now she saw only his professional side—the steady, assessing look in his eyes, the calm logic that seemed to weigh every word she spoke. "I couldn't see much in the dark, and he wouldn't let me get close. What happened?"

Retrieving a small notebook and pen from his uniform breast pocket, Nathan ignored her question. "When did you first see him tonight?"

"Um…" She glanced at the clock on the wall. "Probably fifteen, twenty minutes before I called. Maybe midnight?"

"You were alone?"

She tipped her head toward Harold, who lay on a rug in front of the sink, his head resting on his front paws and his eyes watchful.

"Where did you find Leon?"

"Gosh…I think we were down on Oak, close to Bailey." Within five blocks of there, anyway, she thought, but he didn't need to know those details.

"What were you doing down there?"

"Didn't I tell you on the phone?"

"I'd like to take notes this time."

He gave her an easy smile of reassurance, but she knew he was checking her story for inconsistencies. "Late-night run. With all the trick-or-treaters out tonight, I waited until much later than usual because the costumes upset Harold. The night was so pretty that I just kept going."

"Did you see anyone out on the streets?"

She paused, considering. "Nope—not after eleven-thirty."

"Hear anything unusual?"

"Some people partying at a house along Bailey, coyotes out in the hills, a few backfires, but I didn't see any cars go by."

"Could you tell where the sound of those backfires came from?"

"Hmm…" She gave a small, regretful shrug. "Not for sure, I guess. I didn't think much about it."

"Have you ever seen Leon out on the street late at night when you're running?"

"Never, so that seemed a little strange. Have you?"

Nathan didn't look up from his notebook. "What did he say to you?"

She gave a short laugh. "That's easy. He said no to going into the ER and no to a doctor, repeatedly. That's why I called to report the situation. So tell me, what sort of wound does he have?"

"The docs found a small-caliber bullet imbedded in his arm."

"My God!"

"It was likely shot from a very long distance away. Otherwise this type of bullet would have gone right through. In the dark, the shooter might not have even known Leon was out there." Flipping his notebook shut, Nathan pushed back away from the table, rose and headed for the door. "See you tomorrow at one."

He was halfway through the door when he stopped, rested a hand high on the door frame and looked back at her. "We talked about this once before after Earl died. But just out of curiosity—how would you defend yourself if you were out by yourself some night and someone suddenly came after you?"

"I've got Harold and I've taken a few self-defense classes." She stood and made a show of flexing her muscles. "Though I'd definitely run first and ask questions later."

"And if the guy had a gun?"

"I'd cooperate long enough to figure out how to get away."

"You'd better be careful." He studied her, his expression grave. "There's no telling who fired that shot, but if he fired carelessly once, he could do it again. No one will be safe until I find out who pulled the trigger.''

"LEON STARK got shot last night," Nathan said as he rested his forearms on the white picket fence surrounding Clay's front yard.

Clay glanced up from the stack of mail he was thumbing through. "Is he dead?"

"A minor wound. Looks like a .223."

"He's a crazy old coot like his dad was. Maybe he riled some customer."

"Or he stumbled onto something he shouldn't have."

"Any idea what that could be?"

Nathan shook his head. "Not yet. Leon isn't talking, but I spent the morning questioning people in the area and searching for evidence. I do have one witness who saw him soon afterward and might have heard the shots."

"Credible?"

"I think so. She didn't see anything significant, but she helped narrow down the time and place."

"Local person?"

"Sara Hanrahan. She was out walking her dog."

"I'd sure take anything *she* says with a big dose of salt." Clay studied an envelope, then finished riffling through the rest of his mail and slapped the stack against his open palm. "The moment the mailman arrives is the most exciting event of my entire day. Never should have retired."

"You miss the long hours, late nights and the paperwork, right?"

Clay waved an arm toward his neatly fenced yard and two-story brick home. "There's just so much yard work a man can stand. If you ever need any help with a case, give me a call. You might just save a poor old man from insanity."

"Dora would have your hide if you went back to work." Nathan grinned. The retired sheriff had been known as tough in his day, but no one in town held a candle to his spouse.

"I'm serious, son. Not to get back on the payroll, you understand. Just to keep this old ticker going."

Clay's "ticker" was the main reason Nathan didn't plan to involve him anytime soon. Whenever Nathan ran into Dora downtown, she fretted about the increasing frequency of Clay's episodes of chest pain, and it didn't take a medical degree to see the grayish pallor of his face or hear his labored breathing.

"Sure thing. And in the meantime, you'll be at the office at noon Monday?"

"Yeah." The light of anticipation died in Clay's eyes. "I'll be there. But I'd rather be working."

Nathan watched him head back to his house with a heavy tread and tried to imagine himself facing the change from an active career to full retirement. Nothing appealed to Nathan more than the unpredictable adrenaline rush of being a cop and the opportunity to make a real difference out on the street.

On the way to his place on Lake Ryan, Nathan

called dispatch to let them know he'd be off duty for several hours.

As he turned down his long driveway, he found himself whistling along with the radio and looking forward to his first afternoon off in weeks. Getting out on the boat again would be great—perhaps his last chance this year, before the northern Minnesota weather turned too cold.

But it was more than the prospect of skimming over the crystalline blue waters of Lake Ryan that had him tapping on the steering wheel with impatience as a fat raccoon waddled across the gravel lane in front of his bumper. The moment he turned the last bend and caught sight of Sara's SUV, his anticipation increased tenfold.

She was leaning against the door of her car, her sunglasses propped on her head and her strawberry-blond hair fluttering in the soft lake breezes. Her German shepherd, as always, sat patiently at her side.

She was dressed in a trim navy sweater and boot-cut jeans, but she could have been dressed in tatters and her appeal wouldn't have been any less.

She pushed away from her vehicle and crossed to his car as he parked at the end of the cement walk leading up to his house.

"Is this where you live? By yourself? You could house three families in there, and they'd never see each other," she said dryly, waving toward the house. "I thought we were meeting at some boat dock surrounded by cattails and weeds."

"But this is on the lake, see?" Stepping out of his

car, he rested his forearms on the top of the open door and nodded at the shore, where waves lapped at the rocks. "There's the dock, and that's the boat."

"That's one heck of a boat."

Her tone suggested that she thought he was just another spoiled rich kid who'd grown up needing the biggest toys in town.

"The house once belonged to my great-aunt Grace, but it wasn't an inheritance. I bought it, and now I'm remodeling it, step by step. The previous owners let it go to ruin."

"It's beautiful."

"Not on the inside." He flashed her a quick grin. "I need to change, then I'll be right back. Would you like to come in and see the shambles?"

A faint blush crept into her cheeks. "I'll wait out here."

He watched—mesmerized by the relaxed swing of her hips—as she headed toward the dock with Harold.

It seemed so…right, having her here, as if she belonged. As if he ought to be able to see her out on the dock, her face lifted to the scent of the lake, today and tomorrow and the day after that.

When he'd changed into jeans and a sweater and come back outside, she was standing on the swaying dock and peering into the boat with an expression of awe.

"This sure isn't anything like my dad's fishing boat," she murmured. "Carpeting? Upholstered seats? A console and steering wheel? Sheesh. How fast does this thing go, anyway?"

"Less than two miles an hour if I'm trolling—maybe sixty if I'm in a hurry to get somewhere."

She gestured toward the boarding platform and ladder. "So you can waterski with it, too?"

"That's one reason I got it. This spring you'll have to come out and get up on a pair of skis."

A shadow crossed her face. "Yeah…maybe."

But maybe she'd be back in Dallas by then, and the reminder settled in the pit of Nathan's stomach like a lead weight. "Hop in and we'll get going. Grab a life jacket from one of the storage compartments under the back seats."

"Is it okay to bring Harold?" She eyed the light-gray carpeting. "I could leave him on the shore, I guess."

Her desire to bring the dog was almost palpable. If the carpet had been white silk, he couldn't have refused. "No problem. He'll love it."

In minutes they were heading off into the lake at full speed with Sara and Harold at the bow. A minute later she moved back to a seat behind the windshield. "Brrrr. There's one heck of a windchill out there!" she shouted about the roar of the engine, her eyes sparkling and her cheeks rosy. "But this is great!"

Once past Dawson's Point, Nathan eased back the throttle and let the boat coast to a stop. The wake behind them caught up and rocked the boat as he readied the fishing gear and handed her a rod.

"What are we hoping to catch?"

"We'll troll in the shallows—around six to ten feet of water, where there's heavy milfoil. That's where

the bait fish are right now, so the walleyes and northerns will be there, too.''

''You sound pretty sure of yourself,'' she teased,
studying the red-and-white metal crankbait at the end
of her line. ''Aren't they going to want something
live and juicy—like worms?''

He nodded toward the minnow bucket and grocery
sack on the floor. ''If they don't go for the crankbait,
we'll try frozen smelt or sucker minnows.'' He noticed her shiver and hunch into her life jacket. ''Are
you warm enough? I've got some jackets stowed at
the bow.''

''No, thanks, I'm fine. I love being out here.''

Her smile was so radiant he had the sudden urge
to reach over, haul her into his arms and kiss her
senseless. Exactly what he'd started to do once before
in the parking lot at the restaurant.

She'd blithely said they could forget that the kiss
had ever happened. He'd been hard and frustrated for
the next hour. Now he could either risk another
breezy put-down or he could go after a nice walleye.
He'd probably be better off with the fish.

But while his frustration was growing, she seemed
completely oblivious to anything except being out on
the water. ''I only remember casting and watching my
bobber. I don't think I've ever trolled before.''

''If one of us gets a strike, the other will stop to
help.''

At her questioning look, he added, ''Don't worry—
when I catch something, I'll let you know.''

She laughed as she fed out a few more yards of line. "I think you'll be helping *me*."

The engine purred as they trolled parallel to the southern shore of the lake.

"Did you find out anything more about Leon?" she asked casually after several minutes of silence. "Did someone deliberately shoot at him?"

"I'm not sure anyone could aim from that far away in the dark."

"So it was a random shot?" She shuddered. "Scary."

"Funny thing is, no one else in that area heard gunfire…or a car backfiring, for that matter."

Her grip on her fishing rod tightened. "Maybe no one else was awake."

"Harvey Andersen sleeps with his window open every night of the year, and his house is close to where you found Leon. He says he didn't hear a thing."

"I found Leon in that area," she said slowly. "Of course, he could have been wounded elsewhere and have been on his way home when I found him."

"True."

Halloween night—a few random shots by teenagers after a few beers? Maybe, but he had a gut feeling that there was more to this case than that.

There'd been naked fear in Leon's eyes from the moment Nathan had coaxed him out onto the porch until the moment he'd brought the poor guy home again after visiting the ER. "Did he say anything to you about being harassed lately?"

"Nope." She turned away and faced her line. "He wouldn't say much."

They fell into a companionable silence. Fifteen minutes later he felt a strike—then another—but when he tried to set the hook, the fish was gone.

Sara grinned at him each time he came up dry. "Save your strength for mine," she suggested. "You're going to need it."

He'd admired her easy assurance, her sharp wit. Now, during this time on the lake, he discovered she was the rare, peaceful kind of woman who could handle quiet without desperately trying to fill it.

He found himself watching her more than his own line, taking pleasure in her delight at the late-fall foliage still clinging to the trees and at the azure depths of the lake, where schools of minnows slid past like clouds of molten silver.

Deep in thought, he was startled when she suddenly launched to her feet with a whoop of victory.

"I got one! I got one!"

Nathan put the engine into neutral. "He's gonna take a coupla runs into deep water, so don't fight him too hard."

The fish took off with a high, arcing flash of silver and loud splash at the surface, fighting the hook.

"This is fantastic," she breathed as she reeled him in. "He must be huge!"

Chuckling, Nathan grabbed the net. "They always are, until we get out the tape measure."

She held on to her rod with one hand, reached over to grab Nathan by his life jacket and hauled him closer until they were almost nose to nose. "No. This *is* a big one."

At the intensity in her voice and surprising strength, he laughed outright. "I'm sure it is, ma'am. Absolutely. Only you'd better pay attention or you're gonna lose him."

When at last she drew the fish closer to the boat, Nathan scooped it up with the net and hauled it on board. Harold, who'd edged forward watching with rapt attention, leaped back when the fish flipped and sent a spray of water across his nose.

"Holy cow!" Sara stared as Nathan gently disengaged the hook and stretched the fish out along the ruler markings along the bow. "Twenty-three inches? Isn't that good?"

"You bet. This guy is around four and a half pounds." He hesitated. "You want him, or can I let him go?"

"Oh, please—turn him loose."

Carefully supporting the walleye's weight, he lowered him into the water, held him for a moment, then let him go. With a splash, the fish dove deep and disappeared.

"Do we have any bets on?" Sara said after a moment, her eyes still sparkling. "Like, for getting the biggest—hey, the *only* fish?"

Nathan stowed the net and gathered up his own line. "What are the stakes?" He could think of a few he wouldn't mind, all involving soft music, wine and a nice place with candlelight. His place, for instance.

"A cheeseburger out at the Bait 'n Burger?"

Nathan coughed. "There?"

"Or—" her cocky grin faded into something tentative, sweet, enigmatic "—maybe someplace where the customers don't all wear fishhooks in their hats?"

"I'd like that."

"Thank you for a wonderful afternoon," she whispered. Her gaze dropped to his mouth, then lifted to meet his once again. "I've enjoyed every minute. Every…last…minute."

A man could only resist so much.

He set aside his fishing rod, then lifted his hands and cupped the back of her head, then drew her close. The first taste of her mouth beneath his was sweet. The second was heaven.

Her lashes drifted downward as she leaned into him, and sensation burned through him like wildfire, sweeping away every sense of caution.

He groaned and deepened the kiss, searching. Needing more as he felt her hands skimming over his shoulders.

Something cold and wet moved against his ear.

Again.

And then it growled softly. *Harold.*

Nathan felt like growling himself as Sara broke away, her eyes darkened, her cheeks flushed.

"I, uh, guess he wants to make sure I'm okay."

"Are you?"

Her eyes searched his face. Then she reached for his head and pulled him into another kiss that sent his heart tumbling off into space.

"I—I shouldn't have done that," she murmured, finally releasing him and moving back.

A sense of disorientation slid through him as he stared down at her. "Why not?"

She gave a vague wave of her hand. "Because it's…wrong. We're just friends."

Wrong wasn't the word he'd choose—not when kissing her felt so damn right.

They fished for another few hours, until a chilly, early November dusk settled over the lake, and Harold started to whine and pace the narrow confines of the boat. Sara reeled in a few more walleyes. Too distracted to concentrate, Nathan missed several good strikes, then gave up and just settled back to watch her.

She wanted friendship. Casual distance. He wanted more—and when he paid up on their fishing bet with a good dinner, he was going to see about changing her mind.

CHAPTER FOURTEEN

JANE SMOOTHED BACK her hair and licked her lips, then gathered an armload of papers from her desk. *Everything's going so well I can hardly believe it.*

First there had been the meeting with Ian, the owner of the entire company, the Monday after Halloween. He'd been impressed by her hard work, he'd said. Prided himself on recognizing talent in the ranks. And then there'd been that fantastic meeting a few days later, when Robert and Ian had called her into Ian's office to discuss her future.

Her *future?* She'd just been hoping she could hang on to the job she had until she hit sixty-five. But they'd talked about grooming her for the position of assistant business manager and discussed the rest of her schooling. Who would have guessed? Little Janey Kinney—Webster now, and maybe not as little as she'd been a few years back—moving into management?

At a sharp rap at her door, she looked up to see Robert standing there, slender and tall with his silvered hair and those intelligent pale-blue eyes. Exactly like someone who'd stepped out of the pages of a men's magazine.

"Aren't you ready?" He tapped his wrist. "We needed those reports ten minutes ago."

There might have been a brief flash of annoyance in his eyes, but his voice was as smooth as ever, and it sent a delicious shiver down her spine. *Robert Kelstrom. Mrs. Robert Kelstrom. Jane Kelstrom.*

Now and then she doodled every possible combination of her name and his, while daydreaming at her desk—then ran those pages of dreams through the shredder by her desk to make sure no one saw them.

"Jane!"

He gave her an odd look, and she realized she'd been staring. Heat flooded her cheeks. "Yes, sir—I'm really, really sorry. I just wanted to check the figures one more time."

He disappeared silently down the hall—he was always quiet, because he wore the most gorgeous, buttersoft Italian loafers with soft crepe soles, and sometimes he surprised her by suddenly materializing at her desk without a sound.

She followed him into Ian's office and hesitated, unsure of what was expected. Usually she came in, handed over the documents requested and headed back to her own office. This time, Ian moved behind her to firmly shut the door.

Ian flicked a glance at Robert, then folded his hands on his massive walnut executive desk and gave her a benevolent smile. "Have you thought about what we discussed earlier, Mrs. Webster?"

Excitement started dancing in her midsection. "Oh, yes."

Robert settled into a chair next to her. "It's quite

a change, moving up from the ranks of office personnel into management. Are you up to the challenge?''

"I...I think so."

Ian toyed with the gold pen on his desk. "Robert tells me you show a great deal of promise. You would be working under him, you understand?''

"Yes, sir."

"Allegiance changes when one moves up the ranks," Robert said. "You're no longer just one of the workers—a buddy, who can share confidences at the watercooler."

"I understand."

"Sometimes there can be jealousies when someone is promoted." He turned in his chair and hooked one elbow casually over the back, then met her gaze. "Sometimes there's the temptation to share a little gossip, just to try to keep those old friendships going. You'd have to be absolutely ethical about not sharing inside information about company business."

"Of course. Absolutely!"

Ian chuckled. "Robert is painting a grim picture of something that's a great opportunity. I hope—" The phone on his desk rang. "Excuse me—I told Marcy not to disturb us. This must be important."

Lifting the receiver, he swiveled away to face the window behind his desk.

A minute later he turned back. "We'll have to finish this discussion another day. You agree to the promotion we've offered?''

"Yes—yes, I do."

He gave a vague, dismissive wave of his hand. "Good. Glad to have you aboard." He reached for the files Jane had placed on his desk. "Robert, do you have the bids on the lanolin for the Gardener's Hand Cream in yet?"

Jane rose and hovered awkwardly for a moment. "Thanks...thanks so much, sir. And to you, Mr. Kelstrom."

Neither of them seemed even to notice as she left the room. Feeling a vague sense of disappointment, she headed for the door. By the time she reached her office, though, her excitement started to build once more. She'd been promoted! Robert *liked* her. They'd be working together a lot. Who knew where that could lead?

She glanced at the calendar on her desk and smiled. Robert had taken her out to lunch once already, and Thanksgiving was still two and a half weeks away. Maybe he'd invite her to spend the holiday meal with him—or maybe he'd accept her invitation for the best home-cooked Thanksgiving turkey he'd ever had.

By Christmas, perhaps there'd be tasteful yet intimate gifts. By Valentine's Day, she just might be the happiest woman on earth. Who'd have ever guessed that in such a short time, her world could change so much?

A whisper of doubt curled around her heart, but she firmly ignored it. There hadn't been excitement in her life until now—a marriage she shouldn't have had, years of hard work with little recognition.

She deserved this taste of happiness. Why look for trouble where there wasn't any and destroy the best opportunity she'd ever had?

OLLIE HURRIED into Nathan's office, her face pale. "My cousin Sheila just called. There's been a shooting out at the Lund place on Ridge Road."

Nathan shot a glance at his phone—none of the lights were blinking—then took one look at the horror in his secretary's eyes and grabbed his keys. "An accident? Are people hurt?"

"S…she said it's too late. Both Ria and Vince are dead."

He gave a growl of frustration. In this small town, people often wasted time by dialing the local deputy's office, instead of 911, wasting precious seconds that could mean a difference between life or death. "She knows that for a *fact?*"

Tears welled up in Ollie's eyes, then spilled down her cheeks. "Poor, poor Ria. She's been one of my best friends ever. Who would have thought—"

"Tell me quick, Ollie. I need to get out there." Nathan rounded the desk and took Ollie gently by the shoulders. "What did Sheila say?"

"Sh-she went out there to pick up Ria for the auxiliary luncheon at St. Pat's today. When she got there—" a sob caught in Ollie's throat "—there was blood everywhere. Both of them d-dead."

Nathan released her and pivoted toward the door. "Call dispatch for the county crime-scene unit and the EMTs. Once we get there, we'll decide if we need the BCA to assist with evidence collection. I'm on my way."

Lights flashing and siren wailing, he made it to the small hobby farm north of town in four minutes, but one look at the scene and he knew there hadn't been any need to rush.

Sheila sat sobbing on the back steps of the neatly kept two-story house, her head buried in her hands. She mumbled incoherently as she waved him toward the back door.

Vince Lund, a huge bear of a man in his midforties, lay facedown down on the kitchen floor, a semiautomatic rifle at his side. A trickle of blood trailed from a small, neat wound beneath his jaw, but the exit wound had sprayed the kitchen counter, cabinet and wall behind him.

The halo of evidence around the entrance wound— a tattoo of gunpowder and soot—suggested suicide.

A gleaming brass .223 cartridge lay next to the body. With the amount of powder held in that size of cartridge, the bullet itself was probably buried in the wall.

Pulling on a pair of latex gloves, Nathan stepped past the body and surveyed the living room, where smeared handprints on the walls and a dark-red trail on the floor suggested that Ria had struggled to escape.

He found her faceup on the floor of the largest first-floor bedroom. She was still wearing jeans and a sweatshirt, so she'd never had a chance to get ready for that luncheon.

Was this a murder-suicide? Had Vince cornered his terrified wife, then squeezed off the final shot that killed her? A Colt AR-15 set on semiautomatic fired a three-round burst with a single pull of the trigger. God willing, her death had been mercifully quick.

Hunkering down, Nathan pressed two fingers at her throat and then at her wrist to compare. *Cool,* with early stages of rigor mortis already stiffening the muscle of her neck. Four to six hours, maybe, though the coroner unit would do a more accurate assessment.

Shifting his cell phone from his pocket, he speed-dialed the BCA's crime-scene team, then stared down at her, images of the woman's cheery smile flashing through his thoughts. She and Vince had seemed a perfect couple—happy, joking with each other in the aisles of the grocery store, active volunteers in the community. What could have gone wrong?

Minutes later vehicles began pouring in the driveway. Patrol cars. An ambulance. The local volunteer emergency truck. The Jefferson County crime scene investigation van. It would take hours for the BCA to arrive because of the distance they had to travel.

Nathan stepped back as the homicide investigators and photographers took over. Amidst all the activity he glanced out the open back door and saw Sheila's pale face.

A female officer looped a comforting arm around her and led her away, but not before Nathan caught a glimpse of the absolute disbelief and shock in her eyes.

Yeah, I agree, he told himself silently. *First, Leon's gunshot wound a week ago, and now this. It's always hard to believe these things could happen in your small town, with people you know.*

But there was something more about this case. Something that teased at the edges of his thoughts, just beyond reach. Whatever the conclusions drawn by the experts, he wasn't going to let it rest until he was very sure he had all the answers.

WEDNESDAY MORNING Sara jogged around the block with Harold before finally deciding to stop at the deputy's office.

It had been more than a week since they'd gone fishing together. Since the kiss that had rocked her clear to her toes and turned her heart upside down.

She'd found herself watching for Nathan around town. Wondering what he was doing, where he was. Even worrying about his safety as he went about the business of being the local deputy.

Where the heck had *that* come from? The best thing she could do was concentrate on her surveillance. Watch for increasing activity at the plant. File her reports.

She had no business starting to care about the local law-enforcement officer who could—in the worst of all possible worlds—actually be aware of the illegal activity happening out at the plant. Maybe being paid to ignore it.

But she needed information. The headlines in yesterday's local newspaper had been stark—LOCAL MURDER-SUICIDE—but the articles had offered few concrete facts about the deaths.

In a sleepy little town like Ryansville, where out-of-town guests could warrant notice in the gossip column, this tragedy had filled three full pages with interviews of locals who knew the couple well. All were testimonials to a loving marriage of two people who had been active in their church and the community.

In Sara's casual conversations with shopkeepers, there'd been not one word about any trouble in that relationship or volatility in either spouse. And as of last night, Allen hadn't been able to give her any information on the BCA's ballistics reports. Information that Nathan might already have.

Taking a deep breath, she walked into the quaint little brick building. Ollie glanced up from the papers on her desk without smiling. "He's in his office, but you can go in."

"Thanks."

Through the open door of Nathan's office she could see two stacks of files on one corner of his desk, while three folders were open in front of him.

She studied him for a moment, trying to slow down her pulse. There were lots of guys with dark, wavy hair. Good strong jaws. Dimples. Killer smiles.

Then he glanced up. At the familiar gleam in his eyes and the deep crescents carved into his tanned cheeks, all the resolve in the world couldn't stop the little tap dance in her heart.

"She told me I could come in."

Closing the files in front of him, he pushed away from the desk and crossed one ankle over the opposite knee. Now she could see the shadows under his eyes and the tension bracketing his mouth.

"She's been trying to make me take a break."

Sara pulled up a chair in front of his desk, and Harold lay down beside it as she sat down. "Are you working on the Lund case?"

He gave a noncommittal tip of his head.

"Strange, isn't it? Two nice people, no history of abuse…"

He cocked an eyebrow.

"Well, at least not according to all the talk flying around town," she clarified with a sheepish smile. "I could hardly miss hearing it."

"They were good people. Did you know them while you were growing up?"

"Not that I remember. The paper said they were both in their midforties, so they were more than ten years older than me." She reached down to rub Harold's ears. "Since everyone seemed to like them so well, do you really think they were the kind of people to… I mean, do you really think it was what the paper said? That this was a murder-suicide? Could it have been a setup?"

Some emotion flickered across his face, and she wondered if he'd been thinking the same thing. "The rifle was found at Vince's side."

She considered her next words carefully, then gave a rueful shrug. "I guess I watch too many crime shows on TV. But I keep wondering, would anyone even know if that rifle was his? Someone could have broken in and—"

"You do watch a lot of TV."

"But it's possible?" she persisted.

"Anything is. The county crime-scene unit and the BCA are both continuing their investigations, and so am I."

"What about the bullets?"

"Bullets?"

"Can't you tell if bullets have been shot from the same gun?"

His mouth tightened. "I'm sorry, but with the investigation still going on, I can't discuss the details."

"I understand. I just keep thinking about..." She shook her head. "Well...about poor old Earl dead in the woods. And then Leon getting shot at. Maybe this Vince was really crazy, and no one knew. Maybe he did something to Earl that wasn't that obvious, and then he shot Leon. Can you do ballistics tests or something?"

"As I said, there are investigators working on the case."

"But—"

"If there's something you know about this, Sara, you need to tell me." Nathan's gaze narrowed. "Have you seen something suspicious?"

"No—not at all." She gave him a weak smile. "I just keep seeing horrible visions of poor old Earl, and then think about his son being hurt just a week later. I've started to worry more about being out alone. Maybe there's some psycho running around."

"I don't think you need to worry."

The finality in his voice told her that she'd said as much as she could without making him too suspicious. For now, the rest was in Nathan's hands. "Thanks." She stood, and Harold joined her. "I've been a little scared, but you've made me feel a lot better. Guess I'd best let you get back to work."

She was almost to the door of his office when he called her name. "I haven't seen you around much," he said, rubbing a weary hand at the back of his neck. "Have you been out to see Leon lately?"

"In a manner of speaking." Sara gave a rueful laugh. "I think he's still sulking because I called 911 about his wound."

"He won't talk?"

"Nope. But it's not just me. He won't let the county-funded housekeeper come in to help him, and they've been trying to send him meals for the past week, but he won't accept them."

"Could he be ill?"

"His social worker did talk him into letting her visit yesterday. She says his house is fairly clean, and he looks healthy enough—his wound is healing well. He let her bring in a few boxes of groceries." Sara shook her head. "I hear he's got a well-stocked pantry, though. Earl must have bought canned food by the case."

"So she's not on the verge of trying to have him committed somewhere?"

"No, thank goodness. Apparently he's doing okay so far. He must be lonely, though, so I'm still trying to visit."

"I think that's great." Nathan smiled at her. "Did you get my message?"

"Umm…yes. Sorry I didn't get back to you." He'd left a message on her machine, asking about when he could pay up on their bet—she had indeed caught the biggest fish—but she'd erased it.

The more she saw him, the more she dreamed of impossible dreams. She needed to remind herself that once this case was over, she'd be back in Dallas.

There was no future for her here in Ryansville, and even if there was, she only had to remember the Roswells' sprawling estate and the social circle his family moved in.

There was no place for her in a life like his.

CHAPTER FIFTEEN

"YOU JUST DON'T GIVE UP, do you?" Bernice gave her daughter a grudging smile.

"Nope." Sara held out her mother's long gray coat, inviting her to slip it on. "Just look outside!"

Bernice shot a dubious glance toward the front window and the huge snowflakes swirling lazily past the dark pines across the street. "So it's snowing—the start of a long winter and more snow than we'd ever want, most likely."

"But it's the *first* snow. Isn't it gorgeous?"

"Until you've got four-foot drifts at your front door and mounds so high at intersections that no one can see oncoming traffic until they're halfway through."

Staying cheerful sometimes took a lot of effort. "But it's getting a really late start this year—it's almost mid-November." After helping her into the coat, Sara retrieved her mother's fur-lined snow boots and held them out. "And we're supposed to get three or four inches. You're forgetting that in Dallas, I take home videos if we have any snow at all."

Bernice pursed her lips as she pulled on the boots. "Then maybe you shouldn't have moved so far away."

That was about as close to "I miss you" as her mother ever got, and the hint of loneliness beneath her words tugged at Sara's heart. "Maybe not. Remember how I loved blizzards as a kid? I remember snuggling under my heavy blankets, listening to the school closings on KBRS and praying the announcer would list Ryansville. Remember?"

"I do."

"I can still smell the cocoa and warm oatmeal with cinnamon on those cold mornings. Kyle and I would etch pictures in the frost on our windows, and we'd build blanket forts all over the living room."

"Those days passed by too fast, even though times were hard."

"But they were *good* days, Mom. I have wonderful memories."

"Do you?" Usually Bernice only expressed bitterness over the past, but now her voice held a note of sadness. It trailed away as she tugged on a pair of thick wool gloves. "I always wished things could have been better. Maybe Kyle wouldn't have…"

"You did your best." Sara leaned forward to give her mother a swift hug. "He made his own choices, and there wasn't much else you could have done. I just wish he'd keep in touch with you more."

That wasn't going to happen, though, and they both knew it. His rebellion as a teen had led him into all sorts of minor juvenile offenses, and his mother's pleas had been scornfully ignored. Kyle hadn't been impressed with the warnings of the county deputies, either.

Only by the grace of God and the patience of the

local juvenile-court judge had he avoided being sent
to reform school. Throughout those years he'd blamed
his mother and late father for every scrape.

But this was going to be a *pleasant* walk. Not one
for revisiting the past.

"Are you ready?" Whistling to Harold, who had
curled up by the refrigerator, she led the way outside
and then waited as her mother carefully locked the
door behind them—probably one of the few people
in Ryansville who bothered to do so.

As they started down the sidewalk, Sara savored
the cool tickle of snowflakes against her cheeks.
"Looking up at them makes me dizzy," she said,
laughing and giving Bernice's arm a quick squeeze.

They'd traveled almost a block before Bernice
sighed and looked over at her. "I...I want to thank
you."

"It's great to be outside, isn't it?" The snow was
falling faster now, and the trees and shrubbery were
covered. "Come January we'll be looking at fifty-
below windchills."

"That isn't what I meant."

They stopped at the corner of Poplar and Main,
where young mothers hurried along the sidewalk followed by children who kicked up clouds of snow with
their boots and licked icy flakes from their mittens.
Drivers cautiously made their way up and down
Main's slippery pavement.

"Which way? Back home, or should we cross here
and keep going up Poplar?" Sara shook her head.
"We should probably get you home before this gets
any heavier."

"I'd like…" Bernice took a steadying breath. "I'd like to go to Bill's Coffee Shop."

Stunned, Sara turned to face her. "Really?"

Bernice nodded. "I'd like a coffee, wouldn't you? I…I think it's time. If you think your dog will be okay?"

"Sure. Harold thought he was protecting Josh the day he barked at people, but I can tie him outside for a little while. He'll be fine."

In front of the shop, she tied Harold securely to a post, ordered him to stay, then followed her mother inside to a table at the front window where she could keep an eye on him.

There were no other customers seated in the dark wooden booths lining three walls. An old guy at one of the tables in the center looked up and waved, then turned his attention back to the newspaper spread in front of him.

Bernice had stiffened as she sat down, her cheeks pale and her gaze fastened on the table, but now she shot a surreptitious glance around the room.

"Just relax, Mom. There's hardly anyone here. I'm really happy you suggested this."

Over steaming cups of black coffee and pieces of warm raspberry pie, Sara chatted about the weather, her high-school class and how the town had changed—anything she could find to fill the awkward silence.

The tension in Bernice's shoulders gradually relaxed. When she'd finished half her pie, she pushed the plate away and studied her folded hands, then tipped her head up. Tears glittered in her eyes. "This is…hard for me."

Sara reached across the table and enfolded her mother's hands with her own. "I know. But it's good to be out again, isn't it?"

"It is." Bernice's mouth lifted into a self-deprecating smile. "I'm even getting a little better at it. Thank you…for what you've done for me. Coming back like this. Being…patient."

"You're my mother. I love you."

"But it hasn't always been easy, has it." Her lower lip trembling, Bernice bowed her head. "S-so many things are my fault. So much of what happened to all of us. To Kyle."

"None of it was. You couldn't have changed anything."

Bernice didn't respond at first. After a long moment, she sighed. "But I could have, more than you'll ever know. I'll carry that guilt until the day I die. And sometimes," she added, in a voice almost too low to hear, "I've even prayed for that day to come."

NATHAN HAD APPEARED at Sara's apartment door Monday morning with a box from Blenda's Bakery and a rawhide chew toy for Harold.

And heaven help her, she couldn't find the words to brush him off. Especially with the aroma of buttery caramel and cinnamon wafting past her nose, and Harold drooling in eager anticipation.

They'd talked for an hour, and now Nathan was leaning back in the chair across from her with that sexy, lazy grin, recounting some of the more amusing aspects of being a small-town cop.

She no longer doubted that he was an honest cop, but that didn't change the fact that she'd be leaving after her assignment was over. A fact that was proving more difficult to remember with every passing day. Friendship was okay. Anything more wouldn't be wise.

Yet just listening to his low, resonant voice sent little shivers dancing across her skin. Memories of that last kiss...

"Seven o'clock all right?"

Shaking off her thoughts, she lifted her gaze and found him studying her, his eyes filled with amusement. "What?"

The creases in his cheeks deepened. "Dinner, this Saturday." Glancing at his watch, he rose and took his coffee cup to the sink. "I've got to run. There's a town council meeting in ten minutes."

She caught up with him at the door. "Wait...I don't think—"

"I owe you," he interjected, a twinkle dancing in his eye. "The fishing bet, remember?"

"It really isn't necessary."

"Oh, yes," he murmured. "It is."

Everything around her faded as Sara stared up at him. His eyes were warm, compelling, filled with unspoken sensual promise.

He lowered his mouth to hers. Gentle, searching. Asking, rather than demanding, but when she responded, he deepened the kiss into one that left no doubt about what he wanted. And Lord help her, she wanted it, too.

She reached up to curve her hands behind his neck and draw him more fully against her.

Reality returned slowly.

With the pressure of his bulky duty belt against her thin shirt.

The cold steel of his badge.

"I've got to leave," he murmured against her ear.

"Wait a minute—"

"Saturday evening, seven o'clock?" He was out the door and down the steps before she could utter the right words.

Standing in the open door, she watched him drive off, leaving tracks in the fresh snow. As his car disappeared, she dissolved into helpless laughter. He hadn't asked—he'd sidestepped the invitation and then made it impossible for her to refuse. How could anyone say no to a man who could kiss like that?

"For a deputy, you are one sneaky guy," she muttered as she shut the door.

And one she wished she could get to know a lot better.

THE NEXT DAY, Sara knocked loudly on Leon's door, then took a step back so she could watch for any movement at the front windows. At her side, Harold sat with his tail sweeping broad arcs in the snow, his gaze locked on the door.

"Come on, Leon, I know you're here. Harold says so. I've got something for you."

Silence.

The guy sure was stubborn. It had been more than two weeks since he'd been shot, and she'd stopped by nearly every day, but he refused to open the door to her. The social worker and public-health nurse had managed to examine and dress his wound twice, but he'd stood at his front door and hadn't let them come in.

The housekeeper who'd been sent to help him twice a week hadn't gotten any further. Now she simply brought out a box of perishables—dairy items, bread, ground beef—from the county-run food pantry twice a week and left them on his porch. Heaven only knew what kind of squalor existed in Leon's house, but at least he accepted the food.

"A present, Leon!" Sara called out. "Don't you want to see what it is? I've got some treats, too. If you don't answer the door, Harold and I are going to eat them ourselves."

His tail wagging faster, the dog whined and rose to his feet. A minute later the front door opened a few inches and Leon scowled out at her.

"This is for you." Sara held up the shiny, crimson-wrapped package. "But I won't hand it through the door. You have to come out."

He seemed to ponder the situation, then finally the door squealed open and he came out onto the porch. When she handed him the package, he stared down at it for a full minute.

"You can open it," she said softly. "Do you need some help?"

Without taking his gaze from the package, he shook his head once, his expression changing to wonder as he examined the package from all sides. Had he never received a present? Had old Earl just let birthdays and Christmases pass without acknowledgment?

Finally, with deliberate care, he unwrapped the package to reveal a cardboard box inside. "Just be careful, Leon. It might break if you drop it."

The foam inner lining seemed to baffle him, but when he finally got through to the object inside, his eyes lit with wonder.

She'd found a music box in the shape of an old upright piano at a store on the edge of town. Maybe the twenty bucks had been a bit much for something that might easily be lost or damaged in Leon's house, but when she'd seen the name of its tune on the box, she'd had no choice.

Now when she showed him how to gently wind the key and a tinkly version of "Für Elise" filled the air, his face folded into a wide grin. "Remember this? I've heard you play it on a piano. Maybe someday you can play it for me."

He edged a half step away, suddenly wary, and she knew he was on the verge of bolting into the house. Rather than lose the ground she'd just gained, she lifted the grocery sack at her feet. "I'm leaving now, Leon. There are a few things in here you might like."

On her way to the front gate she heard the sounds of paper and cellophane rustling, and the music box playing its tune once again.

When she glanced back, Leon held a package of Twinkies in one hand, the music box in the other.

She'd never seen such an expression of awe and delight.

Step one, Leon. Before she left town, she was going to make sure that he had more to look forward to than endless weeks alone in this shabby place.

THE MOMENT SHE ARRIVED at her apartment after a run with Harold on Friday afternoon, Sara walked into her bedroom and checked her fax machine. *Yes!*

She grabbed the paper and spun around to sit on the edge of her bed, then toed off her shoes and curled her feet beneath her.

Throughout her nine weeks in town, she'd maintained her surveillance as ordered. She'd faxed regular reports to the DEA office in Minneapolis and the local office in Fargo about the activity she observed, but had heard little back in return.

This fax was from Special Agent Allen Larson, and it was typically brief:

> BCA reports ballistics same on both the Lund and Stark cases. The AR-15 was registered to Vince W. Lund June 15, 2001. Prior to owner's death, not reported stolen. No criminal record on either of the Lunds.
>
> Also, a Seattle division office report indicates a major shipment is likely immediately after New Year's Eve. Will notify you, pending further information.

Grabbing the pillows from the head of her bed, she punched and fluffed them into a soft mound and then flopped back and closed her eyes.

So she'd been right. Except this still didn't answer all her questions. The Lund obituaries revealed that Vince had worked in the factory for more than a decade and had been an elder at Grace Lutheran for the past several years. Active on numerous other committees in the church and community, he'd been an upstanding guy.

Though he could have fallen on difficult times financially. Or could have been lured—or coerced—into something he normally wouldn't do.

On the other hand, perhaps he'd rarely used that rifle, and it had been stolen—maybe even by someone he knew well. There had to be a number of insiders at the factory who'd be only too happy to frame someone else.

Grabbing her laptop from its hiding place in the closet, she hooked it to the phone line by her bed, called up her e-mail program and fired off another message to Allen:

I need financial histories on the Lunds, fast. Outstanding loans, liens, their credit rating, lawsuits—anything you can find that could be a significant stressor.

If the couple had died in a murder-suicide situation, that was terrible enough. If not, the case was a double homicide, and that meant a ruthless killer was still on the loose in Ryansville.

And then it would be time to involve the local law.

As AWFUL AND SCARY as it had been, finding a dead guy in the woods sure made things different for Josh at school. Word had spread about the day Harold had tried to eat the Weatherfields alive, too.

Kids who'd ignored Josh at lunch now jostled with each other to sit at his table. Some of the girls even looked at him with awe. Weird.

The Weatherfield boys hadn't changed a bit, though. Except maybe for the worse—and that took a lot of doing.

"Hey, frog-face. Been out playing with any dead people lately?" Thad gave him a sharp elbow to the ribs as the entire student body flooded out the main doors of school and headed for home. "Must be pretty bad if your only friends have rigor mortis."

Ricky, standing at the big double doors, stuck out his foot as Josh passed. Thad shoved the small of his back.

Airborne, unable to control his fall, Josh saw the bright colors of kids' clothing flash by as the concrete stairs rushed up to meet his face.

His glasses flew off as his backpack hit the back of his head. Pain blasted through him coupled with rage from countless moments like this—two boys ganging up on him and making him feel like a big joke.

All around, he heard kids gasp. One of them snickered.

Being the smallest kid in fourth grade hadn't seemed like such a bad thing when he'd been offered the chance to skip third, but now he knew the truth. There wasn't ever going to be a day, for the rest of his endless days in school, that he wasn't being picked on for being the youngest-smallest-weakest kid in class. Not unless he did something about it.

The scrapes on his knees burned. Something warm and metallic filled his mouth. And…oh, no! One of his front teeth felt different. Sharp and jaggedy.

The Weatherfield boys—one his age, one a year older, and both outweighing him by a whole lot—stood behind some other kids, looking smug.

Without thought, without looking left or right for teachers, or the principal, or anyone else who might try to stop him, Josh threw his backpack aside and barreled toward them, his head lowered and fists clenched.

The other kids immediately scattered. A lot of them started yelling. But none of that mattered. All he could see was Thad's stupid grin—then his look of disbelief as Josh kept coming.

When he rammed into Thad's midsection, the older boy folded like a bent straw. The momentum carried them both backward and right over the tubular metal railing along the stairs.

Thad landed on his back in a prickly bush, screaming like a girl, with Josh on top of him. "Don't ever, ever mess with me again, or you're gonna be sorry! I've had it—do you hear me?" With every word, Josh pummeled him furiously in the ribs, all of his anger and humiliation blocking out everything else.

At the firm grasp of a hand at his collar, Josh belatedly remembered Ricky. With a roar of rage, he twisted around and tried to lunge at his other enemy…

…and came face-to-chest with the principal. A former University of Minnesota wrestler, Mr. Swenson was a middle-aged guy who still carried a lot of muscle. Being sent to his office was a punishment spoken of with the greatest dread.

"Come with me." Swenson's grip on his collar didn't lessen. "Now."

His harsh words fell like bombs. And suddenly the tooth that hurt and the blood in Josh's mouth and everything else turned his legs to rubber. He bowed his head and trotted along meekly, dimly aware of the stares and whispers as Swenson marched him up the front steps of the school and down the gleaming hall to the main office.

Dottie, the school secretary, looked up in disbelief as they passed her desk. "Joshua?"

"Call his mother. And get the school nurse. I think she's over at the middle school."

Josh had already felt fear. Now he felt sick. Like he might throw up his lunch.

He could face any punishment here, but the look of heartbroken disappointment on his mom's face would be far, far worse.

Mr. Swenson marched him into his office, released him, then stepped back and took a good look. "Need the bathroom?"

Josh took a hard swallow. "N-no."

"Then sit there." He gestured toward the stiff wooden chair in front of his desk, then moved behind the desk and sank into his own chair. He folded his hands on his desk and stared at Josh. "Mind telling me what's going on?"

It was so unfair. So totally unfair! Josh shot a quick look out the window. The Weatherfields, as always, had gotten away with their cruelty. And now he was facing a lifetime of detention. Or maybe he'd even be expelled.

But ratting on them would only make things worse. He stared down at the scrapes on his hands and numbly shook his head.

"Tell me."

Josh blinked at the tears burning beneath his lids. He would not let anyone see him cry. But at the odd note in the principal's voice, he ventured a quick glance at him.

The man pushed a box of tissues across the desk. "Here, son. Take care of that lip."

Holy cow. Instead of towering anger, there was almost…sympathy in the man's eyes. Sympathy? That couldn't be. Even kids at other schools had heard about the principal at Ryansville Elementary.

One corner of Mr. Swenson's mouth curled. "At least four kids rushed in here a few minutes ago to tell me what was going on. I could barely get past them to go outside."

Josh stared at him, feeling like a rabbit frozen at the approach of a predator. Swenson would have heard a lot, all right. And none of it good.

"Well?"

"I shouldn't have been fighting," Josh mumbled.

"And?"

"I…won't do it again."

"Can you tell me why this one started?"

Josh gave a sharp, single shake of his head, but the

motion made him feel so dizzy his stomach gave a warning lurch.

At a soft rap at the open door, Mr. Swenson shifted his gaze to the secretary standing there. "Did you reach his mother?"

"She's on her way. The nurse said she'd be here in ten minutes."

"And the Weatherfields?"

"I left a message. The housekeeper said Yvonne was at a meeting in Minneapolis, but she'd try to reach Mr. Weatherfield at his office."

At Mr. Swenson's growl of displeasure, Josh's heart sank even further. The one time he'd ever fought back, and the world was going to end.

Minutes later he heard the sound of hurried footsteps, familiar voices at the desk, and then his mother rushed in and knelt at his chair, her face filled with worry.

She rested gentle hands on his shoulders, and if he'd been a few years younger, he might simply have launched himself into her arms. "Oh, honey—what happened?" she murmured. "You've never been in a fight before."

At the approach of other footsteps, Josh looked over her shoulder and found Sara standing just inside the door with Timmy on her hip. "Hi, Josh. Your mom needed a ride over." She glanced at the principal. "Should I wait outside?"

"No, please stay," Mom said quickly. "I want you to."

Mr. Weatherfield strode in a second later, his face twisted into a dark scowl. "What's going on here,

Swenson? I had to leave a meeting with clients from Chicago for this.''

''Have a chair.'' Mr. Swenson waved to the empty chairs arranged in a semicircle in front of his desk. ''Today, there was an attack in front of three teachers and most of the student body. I want you to know that this kind of thing is going to stop. We need to talk about suitable punishment and how to make sure it never happens again.''

Mr. Weatherfield glowered at Josh. ''This kid here? What has he done?''

Josh sunk lower into his chair, wishing he could disappear. Even Mom's hands on his shoulders and Sara's sympathetic smile didn't help.

''It's *your* kids, Weatherfield. I've just learned that they have been almost merciless toward this boy for some time.''

''Boys roughhouse,'' Mr. Weatherfield snapped. ''Anyone knows that.''

''This afternoon they tripped Josh at the school entrance in front of witnesses. He fell down several cement stairs, chipped a front tooth and bloodied his mouth. Your boys could face legal charges if the Shuellers choose to pursue it.'' Mr. Swenson's voiced hardened. ''Dottie? Send in Ricky and Thad.''

CHAPTER SIXTEEN

BY THE TIME Nathan arrived at seven on Saturday evening, nerves had tied Sara's stomach into a knot and she'd bitten two nails to the quick. How long had it been since she'd been out on a real date? A year? Two? Not since before Tony's death.

Nathan stood at her front door looking assured and impossibly handsome in crisp khaki slacks and a forest-green sweater.

Oh, God, I'm overdressed. In her short black dress, a string of pearls and three-inch heels, she hoped she would blend in at whatever restaurant he'd chosen.

"Um…maybe I should change?"

"You look absolutely beautiful," Nathan murmured, lifting a hand and threading it through her hair. "This feels like silk."

He moved closer, until she felt the heat of him, and caught the faint scent of his aftershave. A thrill of anticipation shimmered through her.

"You smell like lilies." He brushed a kiss beneath her ear. "I love that scent." He drew back, his eyes filled with regret. "And if we don't leave now, I won't want to leave at all."

He drove to the Seasons, a beautiful little 1940s-style restaurant on Cormorant Lake, where they ordered fresh walleye and coconut shrimp. Lit only by the candles on each table, the restaurant seemed to be theirs alone, the compelling intimacy broken only by the waiter.

"What are your plans for Thanksgiving?" Nathan asked as the waiter delivered crystal dessert cups filled with a rich chocolate mousse. "Will you be traveling?"

"No, there's just my mom and me. And Kyle, if he shows up, though he rarely does."

Nathan frowned. "No other relatives?"

"Mom hasn't kept in touch with many. Not since…my dad died." She gave a little shrug.

"You and your mother should join my family for Thanksgiving dinner. We usually have a dozen relatives who show up, and at least that many friends."

Her spoon in midair, Sara tried to envision her mother in that setting—or herself, for that matter. "Um, I didn't think you got along with your parents all that well these days," she said.

"They've actually been trying harder, and so have I. No matter what, we never miss holidays together."

"It must have been hard for them when you chose a career they didn't expect."

Nathan laughed. "I think that old saying about absence making the heart grow fonder must be true. They got back from Florida a couple of weeks ago, and I haven't heard a single comment about my coming back into the family companies. Maybe they've finally given up."

Family companies. A good reminder of how different their backgrounds were.

"So," he continued, "what about Thanksgiving?"

She shook her head. "It would be too much for my mom, and I can't leave her alone that day. Thanks, though."

"If you change your mind, the invitation is open." He set aside his napkin, then offered her his hand. "Dance?"

The mousse had been fantastic, but the sensory pleasure of each decadent bite didn't compare to the rush of awareness she felt as she stepped into Nathan's arms. Beneath his soft sweater she felt the heavy muscling of his shoulders. The scent and warmth of him surrounded her.

"Since you've refused Thanksgiving," he said against her ear, "you have to say yes to meeting my parents next Saturday."

"I do?"

There were a dozen couples on the floor, but they'd somehow ended up near a corner where the light was dim, and Nathan's back shielded her from view.

Their steps slowed until they were barely moving at all. He reached up to cup the back of her head with one hand, then brushed a kiss against her cheek. When he lowered his mouth to hers and kissed her, she felt her heart stand still.

He lifted her chin with his forefinger and dropped another swift kiss on her mouth, then brushed his thumb along her jaw. "I look forward to bringing you home."

They danced until closing time to the tunes of the Golden Notes, a local group that specialized in big-band music. Perfect for dancing. And all too perfect for falling just a little bit in love with Ryansville's deputy.

Not that she planned to tell him. She'd already received word on her next assignment in Dallas. If everything fell into place, she'd be on her way a few days after New Year's Eve.

The thought no longer held much appeal.

"DID YOU AND YOUR MOM have a nice Thanksgiving dinner?" he asked the following Saturday as he ushered her into his car.

"She agreed to eating at Josie's rather than trying to cook a big meal at noon. We went a little early to miss the holiday crowd, though. They had a delicious Thanksgiving buffet."

He leaned in and dropped a kiss on her cheek, then shut her door and moved around to his side and climbed in. "You said she's been hesitant in crowds."

Sara resisted the impulse to touch the spot he'd kissed. "Um…yes. But she's trying. This time she even talked to a couple she knew."

Nathan drove up Fox, crossed the main highway, then headed out to Lake Ryan. At the eastern shore, he turned north on Lakeshore Road for the final twenty miles of the trip.

"I get the feeling you aren't looking forward to this." He glanced at her, then turned his attention back to the narrow two-lane road. "We could have driven south, instead, and had TV dinners at my place."

And possibly a few other courses she wasn't quite

ready to consider. "Your parents' place is fine. Really."

"You don't sound very enthusiastic." His low laughter and deepening crinkles at the corners of his eyes told her that he understood how she felt. "My mother asked us for dinner, but we don't have to stay long. I mentioned you at our dinner on Thursday, and I think she just wants to check you out."

Great. Seeing the Roswell home would be interesting, but dealing with his family might be...challenging. What were the chances that they didn't know all the details of her family's past?

The house and the grounds were everything she'd imagined as a child—from the sweeping curve of the circular driveway and massive, two-story brick home, to the formal double front doors. In the marble-floored entry hall, the gracefully curved double staircases rising to an open landing could have been something straight out of a fairy tale.

Everything was beautifully designed, artistically decorated in white on white, with touches of black and taupe. And it all left her feeling inexplicably cold.

Or perhaps that sensation came from Patrick and Elena Roswell and their platinum-haired daughter Meredith, who'd radiated disapproval from the moment Sara stepped into their home.

"And your family, dear?" Elena asked politely as she rearranged a linen napkin on her lap. "They're from here?"

The bite of flaky, feather-light dinner roll in Sara's mouth turned to sawdust. "Yes—yes they are. Or were. My father died many years ago."

Across the table from Sara, Meredith's perfectly sculpted mouth twisted into a smirk. "What did you say he did before he died?"

Meredith's intent to embarrass her was clear, but Sara chose to ignore it. "He worked at Sanderson. Before that, he was self-employed."

Nathan leveled a look of irritation at his sister and deftly changed the subject. "I hear you're going to Spain next month. Holiday or business?"

"Business. What else? With father managing things here, I need to do the traveling." She gave an offhand flip of her wrist. "Not that I mind. I love the thrill of the chase. Last month we nailed two new accounts in Washington." She shifted her gaze back to Sara. "And what is it that you do?"

I help keep the world safe for people like you. The thought brought a smile to Sara's lips that she couldn't quite contain. "I'm job hunting right now and taking some time to be with my mom."

"And what you do is…?"

"Accounting." She actually did have the degree, one she'd struggled to achieve through years of night school, and it had come in handy during some of the undercover operations she'd done.

"And there aren't any little office jobs open in town?" The faint look of disdain Meredith cast her brother clearly said, *You can't do any better than this?* "Surely there must be something."

"She's an accountant, Merry," Nathan said. "The same degree you got a long time ago." To his parents he added, "Sara has been living in Dallas for quite a few years. She's hoping to relocate here permanently.''

Patrick, an elegant man in his early sixties, nodded politely, then turned back to cutting the turkey on his plate. He'd welcomed her warmly, though, and on the whole seemed nicer than his wife and daughter.

Elena cleared her throat and continued rearranging her small portions without actually consuming more than a few small bites.

"This is a wonderful meal, Mr. and Mrs. Roswell," Sara ventured after savoring yet another mouthful of the wild-rice dressing. Seasoned with fresh garlic and onion, herbs, and strewn with sautéed mushrooms, it was just as incredible as Nathan had promised. "I appreciate your invitation."

When the pager on Nathan's belt interrupted yet another awkward silence during dessert, Sara could have wept with relief. "Oh, dear. Does this mean we need to leave?"

He must have caught the hopeful edge in her voice, because when their gazes met and held, she noticed an answering glimmer of amusement in his eyes. He studied his pager screen, then shook his head with regret. "I'm afraid I have to. You could stay, though, and finish—"

"No, no. I'll come along. Harold has been alone in the apartment for quite a long time now. I really should get back."

"Harold?" Meredith's mouth formed a moue of disapproval.

"My dog."

Nathan pulled back her chair and helped her up. "Wonderful meal as always, Mother."

"And as always, you have to race off. Surely you must be getting a bit tired of all those demands on your time by now." Elena caught her lower lip between her teeth. "And those awful types you have to deal with—I just hope you're careful, Nathan."

"Most of them are people just like us, and they need help." He rested his fingertips at the small of Sara's back. "I'm sorry we can't stay longer. Sara?"

After saying their farewells, Nathan guided her back to the front hall, where they gathered their coats and stepped outside. Halfway down the wide steps, he pulled to a halt. "Did you really want to leave?"

Narrowing her eyes, she rested one hand on her hip. "That wasn't really a call?"

"Oh, it was a call all right. But the other county deputies are covering it because I've taken the day off."

"So you didn't have to leave."

"Not unless they need me for backup or for local information of some kind." He hesitated. "If you want to go back in, we can—"

"Oh, no." Laughing, she threaded her arm through his and started for his car. "I don't think your family was particularly thrilled by my presence. Let's let them relax in peace."

Once they were back in his car, Nathan started the engine, then gave her a boyish, hopeful smile. "I don't suppose you'd like to see my place on the way back?"

He'd stopped by her garage apartment many times,

but she'd only been to his place once—and then she hadn't gone inside. The big old Victorian had intrigued her ever since.

"I'd love to." She reached into her purse for her cell phone. "Josh and his dad can let Harold out into the backyard for a while."

While she talked, Nathan eased his car around the circular drive and out onto the road that followed the shore of Lake Ryan.

Banks of snow lined both sides of the road, while out on the frozen lake, little villages of ice-fishing shacks were clustered. Snowmobile tracks crisscrossed the ice like a network of unmarked freeways.

As they drove down Nathan's driveway, Sara felt a nervous flutter in her stomach. When he opened the front door of his house, she hesitated, then stepped in and waited for her eyes to adjust.

"I promise I don't bite," he said. "I just want to show you what I've been working on."

Maybe he really did want to show her his house, but the thought of him nipping at the sensitive flesh of her neck with his teeth sent an unexpected shiver of longing through her. She firmly reined in those errant thoughts.

She already knew that being kissed by Nathan Roswell was beyond any experience she'd had—his mouth and strong hands telegraphed such heat and desire that her toes curled and her heart tripped. Dangerous for a woman who'd always prided herself on her self-control.

She moved through the entryway into a central hall with wide, double French doors opening into a parlor at the left and dining room to the right. An open stair-case led to the second story. When he flipped a switch, a sparkling chandelier bathed the varnished oak floors in light.

"This will be lovely," she murmured, peering into the dining room.

In the middle of the room, a cardboard box held a dozen upright rolls of wallpaper, and plastic sheeting still covered the floor. There were lots of windows, and she could imagine them hung with airy lace curtains.

"I just redid the parlor woodwork," he said as he moved across the hall. "Now I need to start going to estate auctions to find the right furniture."

This room had the same oak flooring, but a good portion was covered with a lush Oriental rug in navy and deep tones of emerald and ruby. A massive fire-place dominated the opposite wall.

She could imagine the mantel decorated with brass candlesticks and draped in greenery. A half-dozen Christmas stockings hung from one end to the other. And just over there—in front of the bay window— was the perfect place for a towering Christmas tree and brightly wrapped packages.

Nathan looked at her. "You haven't said anything."

The hint of uncertainty in his voice touched her heart. "I was just imagining the house decorated for Christmas. Some houses simply look beautiful. This house has—" she searched for the right words "—such warmth and character. Stepping inside makes me think of all the happy families who must have lived here through the years.''

He chuckled. ''I don't know much about the other families who owned it after my great-aunt, but she certainly was a free spirit. Raised her children like that, too, from what I hear. I'm not sure Ryansville was ever quite ready for Grace.''

''When will you be done redecorating?''

His smile turned rueful. ''Never. But that's okay— this place has turned into a hobby as much as a home. Want to see the rest?''

With every room she saw, Sara loved it more. The music room, and the sunny sewing room in the back. The huge country kitchen, with honey oak cabinets and windows facing the deep timber to the south. The screened porch off the back entry to fend off the clouds of mosquitoes that would arrive every summer.

That porch would be a beautiful place to curl up with a good book on balmy summer evenings, she thought. *I could serve supper out here at the wrought-iron table, and light candles...*

But of course she would be in Dallas, not here. And someone far more suited to Nathan, someone of his background, would be the one lighting those candles.

Ignoring her twinge of regret, she followed him back through the main floor and up the staircase.

''You'll need to really use your imagination here,'' he said when they reached the landing. ''Five bedrooms—but only one is finished, and the bathroom is still a bit of an adventure.''

She'd already used her imagination too much. The image of having supper with Nathan on the porch and making love in the glow of the lights strung on that Christmas tree had been entirely too real. Almost as if she'd lived here in another time and had finally come home....

He showed her one bedroom after another with exposed areas of lather and plaster, and patches of waterstained wallpaper where the walls were still intact. "I replaced the roof first thing. Now these rooms will need new flooring and drywall."

"Would it take long for a contractor to do all this?"

"Maybe not. But I'm doing it myself."

"Why?"

With a shrug he moved down the hall to the last bedroom. "I guess because I want to feel I've really accomplished something. Not," he added with a twinkle in his eye as he opened the door, "that I don't entertain the thought of help when every muscle aches and I'm living on ibuprofen. Oak flooring is a bear to install."

The other bedrooms needed a lot of work. When she stepped inside this one, she gasped.

This was Nathan's bedroom, and in here everything was complete. And whatever she might have guessed about his taste, this proved her wrong.

This wasn't the cold, formal study of whites and neutral tones she'd seen in his parents' home, a precise artistic display. This was a masculine room, yet beautifully done.

Here the walls were painted palest yellow. The burnished gleam of oak flooring and massive oak furnishings were a perfect foil for the bright patchwork quilt on the bed. A huge, lush fern hung in front of a bay window facing the lake. The open doors of a towering armoire revealed a television, DVD and an array of state-of-the-art stereo equipment.

She stepped into the room to take a closer look at the framed, stained glass hanging on brass chains in one of the side windows.

A good two feet square, the superbly wrought design depicted a lake and pine trees that echoed the view of Lake Ryan outside the window. In unimaginably small bits of glass, the figure of a winsome young woman sat on a bench with an infant in her arms.

"I saw it in a little shop in Stillwater," he said, coming up behind her. "They said it was over a hundred years old. That might not be true, but I couldn't pass it up. Look here." He touched the lower left-hand corner.

She bent closer to read aloud the intricate script etched in the glass. "'In memory of my dear wife Hattie—whom I'll love forever and beyond.' Isn't that sweet?"

"They're together by now. I imagine they had quite a reunion."

His surprising words touched her heart. "He must have loved her dearly. This is an incredible piece of art." She glanced at the stained-glass lamp on top of a rolltop desk in the corner opposite the bed. Two others were placed on the bedside tables. "Antiques?"

"Projects of mine."

"You made them?" Incredulous, she moved to the one closest to the door. "May I?"

When he nodded, she turned on the lamp, then reached back to turn off the main light switch on the wall. Rich, deep colors of every possible hue bathed the room in rosy, subdued light.

"I'm impressed," she whispered. "All those tiny pieces of glass are mesmerizing. How on earth did you do it?"

"I took some classes in stained-glass while I was an undergrad at the university."

His voice seemed lower, far more intimate. Closer than she'd thought. Had he moved to her—or had she drifted nearer to him?

She'd known that everything would change when she came into his house. With every layer revealed, this complex man became so much more than the man she'd first imagined him to be. And with every layer she discovered, she fell in love with him a little more.

"You amaze me," she murmured.

"I think I'd rather kiss you."

The resonant baritone of his voice wrapped around her, calling to the deepest part of her soul, where logic and common sense didn't exist. But until she could be completely honest with him, she had no business going any further.

She forced a breezy laugh and turned toward him. But there wasn't any answering humor in his eyes. They were dark, intense. Hot. He didn't have to say another word to convey what he wanted to do.

Feeling as if she'd waited a lifetime for this man and this moment, she stepped into his arms. And when his mouth touched hers, then settled into a deep, possessive kiss, she knew.

This wasn't about hunger, or desire, or physical release. It was about Nathan and finding love for the first time, and knowing that this night, this week, or even a lifetime would never be enough.

But soon, she'd only have him in her dreams.

CHAPTER SEVENTEEN

SHE FELT A FAINT TREMOR in his hands as he pulled away and stared into her eyes, and knew what his effort at restraint cost him.

"I can take you home right now." A small muscle jerked along his jaw. "This would be the time, if you want to leave."

Transfixed by the fine lines of tension at his mouth and the determination in his voice, she knew he would do just that if she asked. No arguments, no efforts to convince her otherwise.

And that just made her want him more. "I...I'm not on anything," she whispered.

He nodded at the cabinet in the master bath, then swept her against his chest with one arm and gently cupped her head with his other hand. "I think we're set," he said simply, the words a warm whisper against her ear.

Shivers danced down her spine as he trailed kisses beneath her ear and down the slope of her neck, then took her mouth in a fierce possession that shook her soul. Even through the barrier of their clothes, she felt the hard-muscled heat of him, sensed the effort it took for him to leash his driving need.

She didn't want him to hold back. Not now. Not

while there might be so little time to feel him, love him, savor his skin against hers. She held no illusions about long-term commitment. Knew only that the memory of this evening would be the best and brightest she'd ever have, and knew no one else would ever come close.

"Please," she whispered, dropping her hand to release the top button of his shirt.

Her fingers trembling, she fumbled with the first and then the second one. Suddenly her sweater was gone—he'd managed all of her buttons in a heartbeat, and she'd discovered that his hands were oh, so much faster.

"Hey, not fair," she sputtered as he skimmed off the rest of her clothes, trailing kisses across her skin as he went. "With those hands, you could have been a surgeon!"

His voice deepened to a growl as he spoke against her ear. "Guess all the glasswork was good practice for something else."

A thought niggled at the edge of her consciousness, a warning that she had to tell him something. Something important, and honest, before it was too late. But the thought flitted away when he stepped back and slipped out of his own clothes, and stood before her as sleek and powerful as any man she'd ever imagined.

From the heavy muscling of his shoulders and chest to the lean, sculpted ridges of his abdomen, he was perfect.

She stared in wonder, then raised her eyes to meet his. "I'm so glad you didn't take me home."

With a single stride he returned to her, pulled her into his arms and kissed her long and hard. When he lifted his head, she felt the room spin in a dizzying rush and then felt the softness of a quilt beneath her.

"Um...there aren't any curtains," she murmured, suddenly self-conscious.

He braced his arms on the bed at either side of her, his sexy grin deepening the laugh lines at his eyes and the creases in his cheeks. "But we're practically up in the treetops, and no one else lives within miles."

"What if—"

"I've yet to meet a squirrel or bird that cared." He reached over and snapped off the lamp, then settled over her again and nibbled at her ear until she giggled. "Is that better? Just you, me and the moonlight."

She reached up and wrapped her arms around his neck. "Thank you."

He laughed, then brushed her hair away from her face. "I just wish I could see you. You are so incredibly beautiful."

Beautiful? She knew it wasn't true. But for now she could imagine the stars and moon shone just for her, and that the heat and passion of his touch would be with her all the rest of her days.

ON THE MONDAY after Thanksgiving, Sara headed out to Leon's place with a box of surprises and the hope that he would be in a good mood.

A month had passed since his gunshot wound, and his resistance to visits from his social worker, a public-health nurse and the housekeeper had remained as firm as ever.

He had, however, discovered the benefit of accepting his noon meals-on-wheels deliveries because he really loved the desserts. And he'd begun accepting Sara's visits because she'd discovered the one overwhelming love of his life—Twinkies.

Sharing a quart carton of milk and a twelve-pack of the sweet little cakes with the cream filling on a daily basis hadn't done much for her waistline, but now she knew the key to his heart.

And today she planned to put that key to the test.

He met her at the gate with a big, toothless grin, but his attention was riveted on the box she held.

"I've got something special for you, Leon. Do you know what day this is?"

His brow furrowed.

"It's a special day. The ladies who come out to help you will be here in a few minutes, and we're going to have some fun."

His grin faded. "Twinkies?"

"You bet. But I've got something more here. Let's go inside to your kitchen table and see what we've got in this box, okay?"

Once inside, she glanced around. The interior of the little house was plain, the furnishings clearly items that had been discarded by other families. Though Leon didn't dust or clean the windows, the dishes were always washed and he kept the floor swept.

He moved to a chair at the table and sat down. "Twinkies?"

"In a minute." Through the window, she saw the

three middle-aged women approach the house, their expressions cautious.

Leon saw them and shot to his feet. Sara reached into the box and gave him a small package of Twinkies. "Don't go, Leon. Please."

As soon as everyone had crowded into the small kitchen, Sara lifted a birthday cake from the box. "I heard this was your birthday, so we all came out to celebrate. What do you think—isn't it pretty?"

His eyes widened in wonder as he studied the decorations. "Mine?"

Sara had instructed Blenda's Bakery to decorate the cake with a picture of an upright piano. The baker had gone a little further, adding musical notes that Leon probably didn't even recognize, but the overall effect was bright as a rainbow.

When she lit the candles and started a chorus of "Happy Birthday," his hands trembled and tears trickled down his cheeks.

The women exchanged glances. "I wonder how long it's been since someone did this for him," Dorita, the housekeeper, whispered.

"Who knows? Maybe never. But I think we'd better mark our calendars for next year," Linda, his social worker, whispered back. "Poor guy."

Leon's face was lit with sheer delight as he consumed his second bowl of cake and ice cream, but when Sara brought three brightly wrapped packages out of the cardboard box, his expression changed to awe.

He opened the first with the excited haste of a

child, then lifted the lid to reveal a dozen brightly colored fishing lures. He smiled broadly.

"Careful—they're sharp!" Sara winked at him. "I noticed your fishing rods on the front porch and figured a fisherman never has enough of those lures. Think you can catch some big ones?"

He nodded vigorously.

From the other packages she gave him, he withdrew new coveralls, several soft plaid shirts and new socks. The last box held a dozen Twinkies. Laughing, he gathered up his new clothes and hugged them fiercely.

"One more thing," Sara announced. She pulled a five-dollar bill from her pocket and smoothed it out on the table. "Tomorrow, we're coming back, and you can put on your new clothes. Linda and I are taking you downtown so you can buy Twinkies on your own. But better yet, get fresh things like milk and bread and meat. Won't that be fun?"

"By myself?"

"Soon, by yourself. If you're going to stay out here on your own, you have to cooperate with these ladies. You need to learn a few things, and you also need a little help. What do you think?"

He'd folded his arms across his chest and lifted his chin as she spoke. Now his gaze drifted back to the cake and ice cream and the women who were all giving him encouraging smiles. After a long hesitation he nodded.

Feeling as if she'd just won a gold medal, Sara stood and gave him a quick hug. Now she knew he'd be okay. "I feel like singing another round of 'Happy Birthday,' don't you?"

THE RYANSVILLE CHRISTMAS committee marshaled the cooperation of nearly every able-bodied person in town, and by the end of the Thanksgiving weekend, greenery and banners hung from every lamppost on Main, while decorations blossomed in store windows.

Homeowners competing for prizes were filling their yards with Santas and sleighs and reindeers, and had enough lights on their houses to surely make them visible from Mars.

And Nathan, caught in a weak moment, found himself helping on one of Yvonne's committees nearly every night. It hadn't been her batting eyelashes and flirtatious smiles that caught him. It had been the earnest pleadings of the little Shueller boy. The kid, he thought, had a great career ahead of him in either politics or law.

Now he and Josh stood outside the town's community center in a stiff east wind, snowflakes pelting them like icy buckshot, at four-thirty on Wednesday afternoon. The heavy skies were already darkening and a good four inches of snow was predicted, with blowing and drifting, followed by windchills in the minus-twenties.

An excellent night for snuggling up under a pile of blankets with the sexiest woman he knew. A woman who'd taken over most of his waking thoughts and all of his dreams.

During the six days since Thanksgiving, he and

Sara had cross-country skied, snowmobiled and gone out for dinner twice.

The best of all had been the lazy Sunday they'd spent at his house, making lasagna and salads, then playing gin rummy and Scrabble, and watching old movies.

Unlike most of the women he'd dated, Sara preferred quiet nights alone or being outdoors to dinner and dancing at fine restaurants—probably the first woman in years who preferred his company to his bank account.

No matter how much time they shared, he wanted more.

"Come on!" Josh peered at him over an overflowing box of Christmas-tree lights. "We get to do the trees over by the library."

When the boy staggered under the weight of the box, Nathan lifted it from his arms. "Maybe we should wait until tomorrow, kid."

"But it's easier to tell where the lights are if we do it when its sorta dark out. And my mom says the weather will be really bad tomorrow."

"I don't think—"

"Please? We promised!"

"We did?"

"Yep, and it won't take that long." Joshua grinned, then grabbed at Nathan's arm and started toward the library.

Muttering under his breath, Nathan followed. He'd never cared for all the hoopla of the holiday—the true meaning of Christmas he found in church on Christmas Day, not in empty trappings and commercialism.

Especially not in his parents' home, where decorations had always been of the look-but-don't touch variety, and gift giving was a competitive sport.

God only knew how Sara felt during the holidays with such sad memories of her father's death.

But as he walked on, he found his spirits lifting, and by the time he and Josh reached the library, he'd even started humming "Jingle Bells."

Because suddenly everything fell into place.

It seemed as though he'd known her all his life. Funny, bright and compassionate, she was certainly the best thing that had happened to him in years. The thought of her leaving town after the holidays already left an empty ache in his heart—but what if she had a much better reason to stay?

If these trees at the library didn't take very long, he might even make it to Shaw Jewelry before it closed at six.

During his second chorus of "Jingle Bells," he realized that this Christmas might just be the best one he'd ever had.

"IF THIS KEEPS UP, even Santa isn't going to be able to make his rounds," Bernice muttered glumly into the phone. "Did you hear the forecast? Christmas Eve is two weeks away, and we'll probably be buried in snow by then!"

The holidays had been hard for her mother all the years since Dad had died. This year, though, she'd allowed Sara to help decorate her apartment beyond the little artificial tree she usually put on the table by her front window.

"I hope not. I promised Leon that I'd bring him over for our Christmas Eve supper, and I think he's looking forward to it."

"I...I want you to know how proud I am of you."

Surprised, Sara pulled the receiver away from her ear and stared at it.

"You've done a lot for that poor man. More than most people would have. One of my customers brought in a dress alteration and said her niece works in the grocery store. She was telling me about how you've gone out of your way to help him. She says the deputy has been good to him, too."

Sara smiled to herself. *Small towns—nothing goes unnoticed.* "Leon likes his social worker now, and he's doing pretty well these days. I just figure he needs a friend."

"All the same, I'm glad you've helped him. And even though I was a little...hesitant, I want you to know that I'm glad you invited him for Christmas."

Hesitant wasn't quite the word, but after considerable reassurances, Bernice had agreed. Maybe after Sara went back to Dallas, her mother would even decide to befriend the lonely man, and might find others in town whom she could help in some way. Moving beyond her self-imposed solitary world would help her, as well.

"He's incredibly gifted at the piano, though he doesn't read music and says he won't play in front of anyone. I wish I could convince him to try your old upright while he's there. He says no, but maybe you'll be able to talk him into it."

"Maybe. Or maybe he'd be tempted by an extra piece of my cherry pie."

Sara laughed. "You've just come up with a perfect plan."

After their call ended, Sara cradled the receiver, debated for a moment, then dialed Jane's number. Nathan was coming over in a few hours, but there was still time to take Harold for a long walk.

On the fifth ring, just as her answering machine kicked in, Jane picked up. She sounded tired. Or were those tears Sara heard in her voice?

She'd been distant, preoccupied over the past few weeks, declining several invitations for supper or shopping, and had made it clear that she wasn't available over the lunch hour anymore, either.

Maybe she was busy with Robert Kelstrom, Sara thought. The other possibility was a greater concern. Had Jane guessed that Sara had been after information?

"Hey, it's been a long time," Sara said. "Are you up for lunch this weekend?"

"I...don't think so."

"It would give us a chance to talk for an hour or two over something yummy out at Josie's. I'll buy."

"No, I just...can't."

"Are you okay? Do you need me to bring you something?" Worry slid through Sara as she quickly sorted through her suspicions about the various employees at the plant. Maybe Jane had seen things she shouldn't. Maybe she'd been roped into the situation and was afraid. Either way, she could be in danger.

The other possibility—that Jane was knee-deep in

the drug-shipping deal and glad of it—was one Sara didn't want to consider. "Look, you don't sound very good. I'm on my way over, okay?"

"No. Don't do that—I'm fine. I've just got a head cold, nothing more. In fact, I'm on my way to bed for a long nap. Maybe we can get together after the holidays, okay?"

"Sure. After the holidays." *By then I'll be done here, and I'll be gone.*

HE'D STARTED at seven in the morning doing traffic stops on speeders out by the high school. Given the slippery conditions and the tendency of the more inexperienced drivers to try going forty miles an hour in a twenty-five zone no matter what the roads were like, Nathan had figured this would be the best use of his time.

By the time school started at eight, he'd nabbed four students and the French teacher, and had flashed his lights in warning at a dozen others.

After that, he'd left to follow up on two barking-dog complaints, a cabin break-in on Blue Bell Lake and one domestic call down at the trailer court.

He'd just started to head toward Bill's for a sandwich and coffee when a quick burst of static broke the relative silence in his squad car.

"Six forty-five, this is six hundred."

He lifted the mike and pressed the receiver button. "Ten-four."

"Vehicle reported in the ditch on County 63 near Dry Creek Road. A woman driving by called it in on her cell."

"Injuries?"

"Negative. She said she was giving the driver a lift into town."

Not an emergency, then. "Did you run a twenty-eight?"

"Negative. The caller didn't report the plate number. Her cell-phone signal broke up, then we lost her."

"I'm on my way."

Executing a three-point turn, Nathan headed south of town. At the end of Dry Creek he took a left on County 63. Hilly, with a number of curves, the gravel road meandered through a few hundred acres of timber. Eventually it veered to the west and wound through thirty miles of lake country, before intersecting with a highway leading to Fergus Falls and Interstate 94.

The only turnoff back here was an abandoned road leading up to a set of locked gates behind the Sanderson plant. Though Nathan had jurisdiction throughout the county, this was technically outside his contracted area; he didn't come here more than a couple of times a month at most.

Apart from fishermen, hunters and teenagers looking for a secluded site for a kegger, the road received little traffic. Even now, drifting snow had nearly filled in the tire tracks carved through the thick blanket of white. So what the heck was anyone doing back here?

Probably a lost tourist, Nathan decided when he found the 1999 black Sable at the base of the next hill.

The car had likely been going too fast when it

topped the hill, then the driver had hit the brakes and slewed left and right in an attempt to correct the skid. Overcorrecting had sent the sedan nose-down in the ditch.

Turning on the mike at his shoulder, he called dispatch as he got out and approached the car.

"I'm down in a hollow, so my reception won't be good. I need a twenty-eight on…" He nudged away the snow covering the license plate, then read off the number.

While he waited for the dispatcher to run the number, he checked inside. Empty, except for a pile of fast-food wrappers and cups on the floor, and crumpled cigarette packages on the dash.

After checking the vehicle identification number, he stumbled back to his squad car and called dispatch. The answer was brief. It was the type of news he never wanted to hear.

The Sable had been stolen four days earlier down in Minnetonka. The cell call had been traced to a Nina Olson, a middle-aged woman from Hawthorne.

Her body had been found in a roadside ditch outside Fergus Falls, with one neat .45 caliber bullet wound at the back of her head and most of her face blown away.

And the Ford Explorer registered in her name was missing.

CHAPTER EIGHTEEN

AFTER CONSIDERING the situation carefully and discussing it with Allen on the phone, Sara planned to tell Nathan tonight about her undercover operation.

It had been a hard secret to keep from him as they'd grown closer. Now she needed to let him know before he found out on his own, and so he'd be prepared when the big drug shipment came through and other agents arrived.

There were cases where local law-enforcement officials weren't told about an operation until after a raid went down, but she wouldn't let that happen this time.

She'd expected Nathan at seven. When he called at six and told her he'd be late, she understood that he'd had unexpected developments at work.

There were no guarantees of regular hours in law enforcement. A late call at the end of the shift, complications during a traffic stop, accidents or serving as backup for another officer all meant a ten-hour shift could stretch to eleven or twelve.

When he appeared on her doorstep at ten in a ski jacket, sweater and jeans, his face drawn and haggard and his eyes weary, she instantly knew he'd faced more than simple complications.

He'd changed, but he hadn't shaved, and his five-o'clock shadow made him look like some renegade rock star instead of the law.

As soon as he stepped inside, she wrapped him in a hug. "You must have had a bad call," she murmured against his chest. "Anything you can talk about?"

His arms enfolded her in return, and he rested his chin on the top of her head. "No, and it wouldn't be something you'd want to hear if I could. Sorry I'm late. I'm not sure we can get to any restaurants before closing. The only places we could try would be one of the pizza places in town, or maybe your favorite—the Bait 'n Burger."

Laughing, she pulled back enough to look up at him. "Let's skip that one." She reached over to the kitchen counter, snagged the remote control lying there and handed it to him. "You channel-surf and I'll make you an omelet. Deal?"

In response, he pulled her back into his arms and kissed her, then tucked her head against his shoulder. "Thanks."

"Or if you'd rather, go lie down on my bed and I'll call you when it's ready."

Giving her a grateful smile, he headed for the sofa with Harold at his heels. Stood still for a moment, then headed into the bedroom. She assembled the ingredients and then peeked in on him.

He was asleep on top of the covers, Harold curled up at his side.

"You know you aren't supposed to be up there," she chided the dog softly. Harold wagged his tail once without lifting his head, and she didn't have the heart to disturb him. "But I guess maybe you think he needs a friend. I'll give you an hour, and then you're on the floor."

She quietly shook out the blanket at the end of the bed and covered Nathan with it, then kissed him lightly on the cheek. On her way out she unplugged the telephone/fax/copier—the darn thing was noisy, and heaven knew, anything coming by fax was for her eyes only.

The evening hadn't turned out as she'd thought. The dinner didn't matter, but she'd wanted to discuss her job and her work. He had to know that the DEA usually worked closely with a local task force involving the BCA and local sheriff's department, but they also worked some operations alone, and this just happened to be one of them.

He'd understand why she hadn't been straightforward with him. Wouldn't he?

DIMLY AWARE of something nudging at her arm, Sara opened one eye and found herself staring into Harold's eager expression. Wagging his tail vigorously, Harold bounced across the small living area to the door, then trotted back to her, his tail still wagging.

"I know what you want, but why does it have to be so early?" Groggy, her muscles stiff and neck aching, she looked around and discovered she'd fallen asleep on the couch and stayed there all night.

"So that's why you're so well rested, you stinker! You stayed on my bed." Reaching for him with both hands, she ruffled the fur beneath his collar, then rose from the sofa, peeked into the bedroom, and found Nathan still asleep. She shut the door softly, glad she still wore the sweats she'd had on last night, and quickly pulled on her snowboots and down jacket.

In a few minutes she and Harold were outside in the sharp, cold air—fifteen below, according to the thermometer tacked to the top rail of the stairs to her apartment—and heading out into the early light of dawn for a fast walk. Even with heavy clothes and lined boots, the frigid wind knifed through to her skin, and it hurt to breathe.

At the end of the block, she slipped off a glove and reached into her jacket pocket. "Hey, I'm rich!" she told Harold, waving the five-dollar bill she'd found. "Let's hit the bakery, okay? What the heck—we're cold, anyway. What's a few more blocks?"

The town was still asleep, save for the bakery at the far end, and the street lamps and the twinkling Christmas lights in storefronts made the snow on the sidewalk sparkle like sequins. Peaceful. Hushed.

She broke into a jog with Harold bounding along beside her. At the bakery she brought him into the old-fashioned entryway and tied him to a radiator pipe, stamped the snow from her boots, then went through the second door into the light and warmth of the store.

She closed her eyes briefly and savored the sweet scents of fresh bread and cinnamon rolls. The weather forecasters promised higher temperatures tomorrow, with freezing rain followed by up to six inches of snow. She'd buy a dozen rolls, maybe, in case they were snowed in for days.

The thought of being snowed in with Nathan gave her little shivers of anticipation.

Someone seated at one of the small tables rustled a newspaper, then chuckled. "This bakery is a good place to be on a cold morning, isn't it? Try the blueberry muffins."

Surprised, she opened her eyes and turned to find Ian Flynn with a welcoming smile on his face and a cup of steaming coffee raised in friendly greeting.

"Um…yes. It sure is."

He gestured toward the empty seat at his table. "Join me?"

She'd planned to bring the rolls back to share with Nathan, but this was an opportunity she couldn't pass up. "Sure."

When she'd purchased the rolls and a cup of coffee, she settled down across the table from him. "I'm Sara Hanrahan."

He folded his paper and set it aside, then extended his hand across the table and shook hers in a firm, decisive manner. "I've seen you around quite a bit with that dog of yours. You're a friend of Jane's, right?"

He'd been less than cordial when he'd found her alone in Jane's office back in October, and his friendliness now made her wary. "Yes, that's right."

He gave her a conspiratorial wink. "I've heard about you."

A chill settled in her stomach. "You have?" She'd been so careful. No one should have found out. Her mind raced through the possibilities for ending the operation with a reasonable chance of collaring the villains. None of them looked good.

Maybe they wouldn't be able to bring down the whole pipeline, but drug dogs could certainly detect microscopic residue, so at least some smaller players could be taken off the streets.

Leaning back in his chair, Ian took a sip of his coffee. "And I just want to say that I'm happy, real happy. I hope this all works out. You seem like the right woman for the job."

Mystified, she stared at him. "I do?"

"I've told my godson for years that he needed to find a good woman and settle down. His mother tells me you were out at their place for Thanksgiving, and I've seen you two together a time or two."

His words took her by such surprise that she could barely find an answer. "Y-your *godson?*" If Nathan had that connection to Sanderson...

From out in the vestibule came the sound of a door opening and closing, and Harold's eager whines of welcome.

"Well, speak of the devil," Ian said. "Look who's here."

Still reeling, Sara turned and looked over her shoulder to find Nathan standing just inside the door. And in all her days as a cop and then a special agent, she'd never seen such absolute fury.

His eyes blazing, that muscle ticking along his jaw, he barely acknowledged Ian or the startled clerk at the counter. "You and I are going for a walk," he bit out. "Now."

"But we—"

"Now."

In another man, that level of anger would have been intimidating. Sara knew he'd never harm her physically, but she needed to get him out of here before he said anything in front of Ian that might make things worse.

She gave the older man a weak smile. "Don't worry—he just isn't a morning person." Grabbing her bag of cinnamon rolls, she took a quick sip of her coffee, then, grabbing Harold's leash on the way out, followed Nathan to the sidewalk.

She gave him a tentative smile. "I didn't want to wake you, and Harold needed to go out, so I thought I'd get us some rolls for breakfast. She held up the sack. "Want one now?"

"No." His voice was flat. Dead calm. "Tell me how long you've been in town."

"Since the twenty-fifth of September. Why?"

"How long have we been seeing each other?"

A cold wind whipped across the street, flinging icy snow in her face and nearly stealing her breath. It didn't begin to equal the icy fist gripping her heart. *He knows. Oh, God, he knows.* "It was sort of gradual—maybe mid-October?"

"And in that time, would you say you've come to know me well? That you care about me?" His voice lashed out at her, but now she heard the pain, as well as anger. "Or is sleeping with me just part of the job?"

"What?"

"Dammit, Sara. I know why you're here. Did someone suggest that you buddy up to the local cop, or was that your idea?"

"No. You don't understand—"

"It was a good move, I'll grant you that. You never know what you might find out."

"I *never* meant it that way. If anything, getting close to you put my job at risk."

"Oh, sure. I believe *that*." He gave a derisive laugh. "There's a word for women who'll sell themselves as part of their job, and it sure as hell isn't 'special agent.'"

She'd fallen for him hard and fast. Even though she'd tried to avoid it, knowing the relationship was nearly impossible, her heart had refused to heed all logic. She loved him. Well and truly loved him—but now her foolish heart splintered at her feet.

If he'd cared for her at all, he'd have given her a chance to explain. Instead...

"Then you aren't a very perceptive man, Roswell," she snapped. Pain and rising anger clogged her throat, making it almost impossible to speak. "In fact, it's a wonder you can do your job at all. How did you figure all this out?"

"I needed to call Ollie to tell her that she shouldn't try making it into work this morning, so I had to plug in your phone. Not three minutes later the phone rang. I didn't answer it, but when a guy left a message on the answering machine it came over the speaker."

Oh, God. Allen had always been extremely careful—he must have been in a hurry this morning.

"The guy said he tried to fax earlier, but your machine wasn't turned on."

"That wasn't meant for you to hear," she said quietly.

"How could I help it? He said to check your e-mail, pronto. He referred to additional agents arriving tomorrow and a big shipment coming earlier than expected. *Agents,* Sara? *Shipment?* What the hell have you been doing here?"

Knowing that Nathan had such close ties to Ian Flynn, she was glad she hadn't discussed the case last night. Despite everything her heart told her, there could still be a connection, a chance that he might tip off his godfather. "Is that all he said?"

"He mentioned the Sanderson plant. Dammit, half the people in town work down there. You didn't think I should be involved? That I'd want to help? I've worked with the DEA and BCA on countless cases in the past, both in the Minneapolis area and up here."

"I...couldn't."

The anger in his face changed to sheer incredulity. "You thought I might be involved? You slept with me, yet you thought—" He broke off and swore viciously.

"In small towns," she said, "the web of connection and favors can be complex. We're often... careful."

He threw up his hands in disgust. "I have no connection to that plant. I even sold the shares of stock I owned once I was assigned here, just to avoid any conflict of interest."

"Your godfather *owns* the place, Nathan. We didn't know that. He just mentioned it to me a few minutes ago. See? There can be connections that don't appear on legal documents."

"You can't think he's involved," Nathan said flatly.

"Look, I don't know anything for sure, and I can't say any more. Given the situation, I could detain *you* until this is all over. Just as a precaution," she added with more regret than she wanted to feel. "I also need to warn you—any interference or hint that you've tipped off someone here in town, and you'll be arrested on federal drug charges along with everyone else we take down. Even if something happens to me, you've been named in my reports—though I've indicated my belief that you are clean."

His expression turned to granite. "That says it all, doesn't it? Nothing has meant more to me than protecting this town. These people are like family." His voice turned harsh. "Yet you think I could betray them." He shook his head slowly. "My only crime is that I've been incredibly stupid for believing you were someone truly special."

He turned on his heel and walked into the wind toward his squad car, his stride long and resolute, and she knew there'd never be another chance to see the twinkle in his eyes or to hear his wry laughter. She would never again wake up beside the man she'd come to love.

Sara stared after him, then knelt and buried her face in Harold's warm fur. It was just the biting wind that brought tears to her eyes.

Nothing more than the wind.

NATHAN THREW HIS CAR into drive, stepped on the accelerator, then swore as the wheels spun in the snow and the car slewed sideways. He slammed a fist on the steering wheel, then took a deep breath and tried again, this time controlling his fury.

He'd never felt such anger. Never. She'd *slept* with him, dammit. Then turned around and practically accused him of being involved in drug deals. And then threatened to arrest him! He'd done his job with complete dedication, and had gone above and beyond what was expected.

And he'd fallen in love with a woman who'd considered him a suspect all along.

The concept of a heart actually breaking had always seemed a little ridiculous. Relationships came and went, but for him there certainly had never been any real pain involved. Now he knew what it meant, because his heart felt as if someone had ripped it in two.

Feeling adrift, still angry, he went home to shower and change into his uniform, then headed back to his office. Reports—he could always bury himself in those endless reports that had to be filed after every call.

He had quite a stack from yesterday, because he'd been out so late waiting for the BCA crime-scene team to arrive and collect evidence from the Sable he'd impounded in the lot behind his office.

Everything started to fall into place as he stared at the snow flurries outside his window.

Vince Lund and his wife had worked at the plant— maybe they'd discovered incriminating evidence. Maybe they'd even been involved. The BCA and county-crime-scene-unit reports indicated that the deaths had been a murder-suicide, but had there been something more?

And what about the gunshot wound Leon had received? Had he seen something he shouldn't have?

Then there'd been Earl's death. Natural causes, according to his death certificate. But there'd been no autopsy, and the prompt cremation precluded any chance of exhuming him for further examination.

Three local deaths could be explained away, but Nina Olson clearly had been murdered. Sara and her buddies were right—something was going on here in town, and he'd missed it.

Nathan shoved away from his desk and stalked the confines of his office.

As much as it hurt to admit it, Sara Hanrahan was doing her job. Doing what she'd been ordered to do. If he'd fallen for her and expected too much, he could hardly blame her—though dammit, she'd been shallow enough to sleep with him when all she wanted was information.

Or had she?

CHAPTER NINETEEN

THROUGHOUT THE NIGHT, freezing rain hit the windows of Sara's apartment like an endless volley of buckshot. The wind howled.

By morning the lights were flickering and the snow had moved in, heavier than expected. When she took Harold out to do his business, she nearly fell down the ice-coated stairs—even the handrail was slick as glass—and felt chilled to the bone by the time she got him back inside a few minutes later.

By noon, the streetlights came back on and traffic on the streets dwindled.

The storm had barreled across Nebraska and South Dakota, picking up intensity by the hour and closing down all the freeways. Announcers on the radio said Interstate 94 was still open to Fargo, though, and that was the expected route of the drug shipment. Was it still coming?

She hoped so. Since yesterday's confrontation with Nathan, she'd been edgy, impatient. She needed to get away from this town. Everything she saw reminded her of him.

She'd even started packing, so she could leave right after spending Christmas with her mother and Leon. This holiday would be even worse than usual. There'd

be no intimate embrace by the soft glow of candlelight on Christmas Eve. No joy in hearing the carols.
No hopes for a future.

At the ring of her phone she jumped. It couldn't
be…

And it shouldn't be.

What she and Nathan had said to each other could
never be taken back. Whatever her own feelings, he'd
never really loved her, and it was better to know it
now than to fall any deeper herself.

"Allen here. We can't make it to Ryansville."

"What?" Carrying the phone with her, she peered
out the window, but saw only a curtain of white. "I
figured the roads were still okay to the southeast."

"Nope—we've already got a sheet of ice, and the
snow has started. I can't walk two feet from my door
without falling on my ass, and Interstate 94 is closed
from Minneapolis clear up to Fargo. We can't send
DEA special agents from either location."

"If the agents from Fargo can't make it, then the
drug shipment won't get through, either."

"Unless the driver heard about the weather change
and drove like a bat out of hell to beat the storm.
With the freeway gates closed on the east side of
Fargo, he might have tried following the snowplows
on state highways. Not that it would help. We hear
the roads up there are filling in with drifting snow as
fast as they're cleared."

"True. Maybe you should run a check with the
state highway patrol for accidents in case our suspects
had trouble. I'd think they would've holed up in a

nice warm motel along the way, but you never know.''

Allen snorted. ''I can't imagine resting easy out in the middle of nowhere with no backup and a few kilos of methamphetamine to worry about.''

''I just want them to get here and I want to arrest everyone involved.'' She paced the small room. ''There hasn't been any unusual activity at the plant the past few days. When this weather breaks, I'll go take another look.''

''We know the traffickers have been sending smaller shipments to test Ryansville as a major supply route. We'll get 'em sooner or later.''

''Right.'' But next time, there might not be any advance warning, and given how fast someone could drive up, transfer the bricks to a waiting vehicle and disappear, it could be a long time before there'd be another chance this good.

A gust of wind blasted the side of her apartment, rattling the dishes in the cupboards and sending icy fingers of cold air through the old window frames. The ceiling light flickered again. ''By the way, I just learned that Ian Flynn is Deputy Roswell's godfather.''

''Damn. Does Roswell know why you're in town?''

''He does now—not quite how I'd planned to tell him, though.''

The line fell silent for a moment, and Sara wondered if Allen was conferring with someone else in the office. ''We did a complete background check on him a few months back. Far as we could tell, he was clean and had no connections to the plant's owner or management.''

''Except for the kind of tie that isn't going to be found in legal records.''

''If he says one wrong word, this entire operation is over.''

''I don't believe he will.''

Allan swore again. ''There's almost four hundred miles on Minnesota's western border, so our suspects could relocate and enter the state just about anywhere.''

''It isn't over yet.''

''Don't count on it, Hanrahan. The months you put into this have just gone down the tubes.''

''I don't think so. Do me a favor—contact a judge in Hawthorne and get me a search warrant executable from midafternoon today through Sunday at five in the afternoon. Fax it soon as possible, in case the phone lines go down. I'll request assistance from the County Sheriff's Department if the shipment arrives before the rest of you get here.''

''Don't take any chances.''

''I won't. Just get me that warrant and get up here as soon as you can. One more thing—when this is over, I need you to talk to your sister for me.''

''Deanna?''

''She's a dermatologist, right?''

''She isn't in private practice—she teaches at the medical school.''

''Perfect. I need some information for a friend up here.''

After she hung up, Sara roamed the apartment, restlessly picking up a book or magazine, then setting it down. She packed a few more things. What if the shipment had already arrived?

For almost three months she'd done her job. She'd done extensive late-night surveillance. Carefully questioned the locals. Written and faxed countless reports. Even without employment at the plant, she'd collected enough data to clearly document unusual activities. But it wasn't enough—and she didn't want to fail now.

Given the storm, it was likely that Sanderson would cancel its second shift and send the first shift home early—maybe even close on Saturday, as well. Reaching for the small radio on the counter, she turned it on to KBRS to listen for the local business closings.

This might be a perfect opportunity, and she wasn't going to miss it.

JANE SHIVERED into her heavy wool sweater as she buttoned it clear up to her chin. The old stone office building was always cold in the winter, but now with the other employees gone home early and the wind battering at the windowpanes, just the sound of the storm sent a chill through her veins.

Robert's secretary was still on sick leave, though, so Jane had offered to type up his new bid proposal as a personal favor. He'd told her to leave with the others, but she'd stayed behind, anyway, and had rechecked every figure to make sure the document was flawless.

When she handed him the folder on Monday, he'd

see her total dedication and maybe...well, maybe he'd see her in a different light, as well.

But first she had to survive the walk home. Her car had stalled a block from home this morning and she'd caught a ride with one of the secretaries, but now she was on her own.

Lost in thought, her eyes weary from staring at the pale-blue glow of her monitor, she turned to look out the window. The shadow of something moving through the blowing snow outside barely registered. She did a double take, then rose from her desk and braced her hands on the cold marble sill to peer outside.

There it was again, a dark figure, but again it disappeared in a gust of snow.

Odd, because the parking lot was empty. Everyone else had gone home hours ago and the plant was closed. Only management had keys to the plant—and in this weather surely they'd be driving.

She turned and crossed her office, stepped out into the dimly lit hallway and unlocked the storeroom across the hall several doors down. At the back wall, a small window looked down on the employee entrance to the plant.

Someone heavily dressed in a hooded parka stood there. In the waning afternoon light and falling snow, it was impossible to tell whether he was one of the managers or someone trying to break in? Anyone who broke through that door would be able to come down the hallway in search of money, or maybe even the computers.

And there was no one here but her.

The tall shelving units in the room seemed to close in on her. In the dark, shadowed corners, unseen things seemed to watch her as she pivoted away from the window, rushed back to her office and locked the door.

Her heart pounding, she turned off her monitor so its light wouldn't draw any attention.

Fingers poised over her phone, she debated calling 911. Maybe there wasn't an intruder, after all. Would Robert think she was a fool if she called over nothing? What if the guy out there was just Phil coming back to check something? Would he be furious?

With shaking fingers she flipped through the Rolodex by her phone. Dialed Robert's phone number. Three, four, five rings.

From down the hall she heard a thud. Or was it just the wind outside?

An answering machine kicked on. Taking a steadying breath, she left a brief message. Then she rapidly dialed Ian's home number. No answer.

Motionless, she closed her eyes and listened for any sounds, her pulse leaping in her throat. There was no way she was going down the hall to check. Only people in horror movies did things like that—and they were the ones too dumb to live past the first scene.

Her knees shaking, she started to dial 911.

SARA COULDN'T SEE any lights on through the windows of the factory or offices, though with the blowing snow it was hard to be sure. Still, there were no fresh tire tracks on the way in and no cars left in the lot. No surprise there, because Sanderson had been listed among the countless early closings of businesses and schools.

She'd planned to circle the building to look for activity, perhaps a strange car in the lot. Not expecting anything, she tried a few doors at the various entrances.

When a door at the main entry to the plant opened, she hesitated, then cautiously stepped inside with Harold at her heels. Had the door been left open on purpose? She waited for several minutes, listening for any sounds coming from the darkened hallway leading to the offices or from the other side of the door leading into the plant itself. With the warrant in her pocket, she could legally justify her presence, but this would be only a quick reconnaissance.

If the shipment was here, she'd wait for backup before kicking in the doors. If it hadn't arrived, an ill-timed raid would ruin every chance for success later on. The shipments would be quietly routed elsewhere. It might take months to find the new pipeline. And everything she'd done here would be for nothing.

Reassured by the tomblike silence, she slipped into the factory itself. Harold was right beside her, his nails clicking on the cement floor.

The cavernous building was dark save for several red *EXIT* signs and a subdued glow coming from an area to the right. A security light, maybe. Massive production equipment towered above her like prehistoric creatures, casting ominous shadows in her path as she crept along the wall, maintaining her cover behind the machinery and high-stacked pallets.

She intended to check out the storage area where

she'd seen deliveries arrive late at night. Then she'd go back to the warehouse. Maybe the driver coming from the West Coast had raced the storm and had parked his vehicle inside.

If so, she had it made. No one could head out into this storm and get very far, and strangers in a small town stood out like clowns at a funeral. Once she knew the suspects were here, she'd alert the County Sheriff's Department for backup.

Harold growled. From behind her came a single, muted sound of a metal shoe cleat against the floor. Then the quiet click of a gun safety's release.

Harold erupted into a frenzy of barking. Dragging him behind her, she dove behind a row of pallets stacked high with boxes. A single shot rang out as she rolled under a conveyor belt still laden with bottles. Harold yelped. Glass shattered. The whine of the bullet echoed as it ricocheted.

Sara lunged forward, jerked her Beretta from the holster at the small of her back and ran, keeping the dog at her side. Another shot burst through the darkened building as she arrived at the exit, and the door to the hallway flew open.

A burning sensation torched up her right arm. Something clattered at her feet and spun away. The Beretta. There wasn't time to go after it.

I need cover. She darted through the door. Slammed it shut the moment Harold was through it. Then she pushed one of the tall display cases to block the door.

Her pursuer rammed it from the other side, shouting angrily. Sara hurried down the hallway leading to the offices.

The doors were all locked, but just ahead, the human resources door stood slightly ajar.

She slipped inside. Shut and locked it behind her, then dropped to her knees to examine her dog. Thank God, Harold seemed fine. Sara stared down at her hand. Blood dripped in a steady stream from a wound at the side of her palm, but she was too dazed to feel the full extent of the wound. Reaching into her pocket with her left hand, she pulled out her cell phone and hit speed-dial for 911, then raised the phone to her ear.

The extra weapon at her waist might help, but she was going to need help, and fast. The guy in the warehouse could be here any second.

At a faint whimper, she lifted her gaze and turned slowly.

Jane edged forward from the door to the small supply storeroom in the corner, her face pale as the snow and her eyes filled with fear.

"I'm sorry if I scared you," Sara said quietly. "Everything's okay, I promise."

Jane turned even paler. "P-please—"

She lurched forward, and Robert Kelstrom appeared from behind her, a gun in his hand and his face a twisted mask of anger. "Put that phone down!" he snapped. "Now! On that cabinet by the door. If your dog makes a move, he's dead."

Sara slowly lowered the phone, praying Jefferson County dispatch had picked up her call by now. "Take it easy. No one wants to get hurt."

"I should have known you two were in this to-gether. The first time your friend showed up around here—" he gave Jane another shove and she staggered, then caught herself with both hands at the corner of her desk "—I saw trouble. I tried to make it clear that you had to keep quiet. And now it's too late."

Sara raised her voice enough to be heard over her cell phone. "Don't be frightened, Jane. No one is going to get hurt. Not right here at Sanderson—not right in your own office."

"B-but I didn't… I don't know what you're all talking about." Tears slid down Jane's cheeks. "What could I tell? Who?"

Robert jerked his gun toward Jane. "Why were you here this late?"

"R-reports. I was doing your reports."

He swore. "I told you to go home with everyone else. Did you think you could get in on the action? Or maybe you were planning to turn us all in." He waved the gun sharply toward Sara. "You—get over by the desk, next to her."

Sara hesitated. There was no way her cell phone could pick up her voice from there. "Please, don't shoot," she pleaded. From the look in his eyes, she had no doubt that he would pull the trigger. Two more bodies wouldn't matter.

"Now!" he roared. "Move!"

Heavy footsteps approached, the sound of metal cleats ringing out against the terrazzo flooring like a death knell. In a second, there would be one good chance. After that, maybe none.

"Jane," Sara mouthed. "Get down."

The shock and horror on Jane's face grew. "What?" she cried. "I don't underst—"

Releasing Harold, Sara spun back against the wall and grabbed the extra gun from her waistband as the door burst open and Phil strode in. She darted behind him, caught his right wrist and jerked it up high behind his back as she kicked him hard behind one knee.

From the corner of her eye she saw Harold lunge at Robert, jaws snapping. Robert fell against the wall, a single, deafening explosion of gunfire filling the air.

When Phil buckled and stumbled to the floor, Sara rolled away with her gun two-handed and aimed directly at Robert's chest.

And, oh, God—Harold lay at his feet, his breathing shallow and blood welling up on his chest.

"I can drop you before you even start to squeeze that trigger, Kelstrom. Don't think I wouldn't like to do it. You move so much as a millimeter, and you're a dead man. So's your friend here." She glanced briefly at the other man, who was down on one knee. "I want that gun on the desk, and I want you both belly down on the floor. *Now.*"

Phil stared at her in disbelief. "I...I only came because I heard the noise—"

"We'll sort that out later, sir. *Get on the floor.*"

"Look, I never did anything. It was Rob—"

"Shut up," Robert snarled. His eyes narrowed as he stared at Sara without lowering his gun. "I'm not that stupid, bitch. You've got two against one here, and you don't have a prayer."

"Special Agent Hanrahan to you, sir."

His eyes darting left and right, he licked his lips, then swallowed hard. Sweat glistened on his forehead—but he still held the gun steady, pointed straight at her heart.

"I've got twelve agents already searching the factory, Kelstrom. A copter landed a few minutes ago with five more. Whatever you do, this is over. Make it easier on yourself. Cooperate."

He didn't answer, but she could see his panic building. "I never miss my target, Robert. If you pull that trigger, you're a dead man."

At a soft sound out in the hallway, Sara moved to the right so she could get her back to the wall and still maintain control of the suspects.

Robert's gun wavered, then lowered.

"I see you've been busy," Nathan said mildly as he stepped into the room with his own gun drawn.

"This woman barged in here!" Robert barked. "She's been holding us at—"

"I know what she's doing," Nathan said. "Get down on the floor, or one of us will put you there."

Anger glinting in his eyes, Robert awkwardly complied. "You'll be hearing from my lawyer."

"I imagine I will." Nathan retrieved two sets of handcuffs from his duty belt and cuffed both Robert and Phil.

Sara immediately dropped to Harold's side and ran a hand over his fur. His breathing was steady. The wound had entered and exited through muscle, and the bleeding was slight.

After helping Robert and Phil to their feet, Nathan

glanced at Sara, his eyes filled with concern. "Dispatch got one 911 call from here, but the caller canceled it. Then she got one from you—she couldn't hear much, but she thought she heard the word Sanderson. Guess she was right. How's your dog?"

"I think he'll be okay, but I need to get him to a vet as soon as I can."

His brow furrowed as he looked down at Sara's hand. She'd grabbed a wad of facial tissues to stop the bleeding, but the blood had started to soak through.

"Are *you* okay?" He reached out and gently took her hand, then turned it over. "How bad is this?"

"Just a nick—it's all right." The initial numbness was wearing off, and her hand was throbbing, but she couldn't bother with it just yet.

"Holy cow," whispered Jane as she crawled from behind her desk. "What happened here?"

"You'll need to come with us to the deputy's office. I expect we'll have a lot of questions." Sara raised a brow at Nathan. "You do have your squad car here, right?"

"Outside." His eyes twinkled. "With all of those other DEA cars and the helicopter."

Jane's mouth dropped open. "You're kidding! Here?"

"Nathan, take Jane and Robert on out. I need to discuss a few things with Phil before he leaves."

As he left, Robert's warning glare at Phil told Sara she'd chosen the right man.

She waited until the others were at the end of the hall. "Okay, Phil, you have a couple of options. Listen close—because your decision is going to make one hell of a difference to your future.''

PHIL DIDN'T TAKE LONG to weigh his options. As the full ramifications of his involvement began to sink in, he became a font of information. He gave names. Revealed when the delayed shipment was to arrive. And accused Robert of killing the Lunds after they overheard too much and threatened to call the sheriff.

By the time the two drug runners from the West Coast pulled in early Sunday morning, the Jefferson County Drug Task Force, the regional BCA special agent, the BCA's crime-scene unit and a drug dog were already in place. Harold was recuperating at the local vet's.

"Ten kilos of meth—a total of seven people in custody. That's quite a haul," Nathan said as he watched the last of the cars pull away. "You were a success."

"I did the local legwork," Sara said, "but this investigation will continue. The DEA has an interest in the case because we figure this bust will lead to a major drug pipeline coming into the upper Midwest. We got a good start here—the driver and his buddy were only too ready to cooperate to save their own skins. So were Phil and two other guys who work in the plant."

Nathan shook his head. "I just wish the Lunds and Nina Olson were still alive," he said heavily.

"With multiple homicide charges and this trafficking case against him, Robert will never be free again. Your godfather seems to be in the clear, however."

"Did you question him?"

"Nope. Several other agents did, and they've been going through his records. Maybe he would have caught on to Robert's activities in time, but it's lucky he hadn't yet. He might have been eliminated like the Lunds were."

Nathan gave her a humorless smile. "Ian never cared much for Robert, but he did think the man was a good manager. Big mistake."

Nathan looked so weary that she wanted to put her arms around him. Instead, she flipped through the papers on her clipboard and kept her distance. "One last thing—Allen just told me that they've picked up the guy whose Sable was left out on County 63. A highway patrol saw a vehicle matching the description of Nina Olson's Ford Explorer and ran the plates. The suspect is with the Vice Lords gang out of Chicago, so he probably came up to do business with Robert. When he ran into the ditch, he didn't think twice about killing someone for another set of wheels."

"Another case of someone innocent being in the wrong place at the wrong time."

"The one case that we can't find a connection to is Earl—so maybe he did die of natural causes. I'm still looking into it, though."

A burst of static came from the mike clipped to Nathan's shirt, followed by the details of a shoplifter call-out at Mitchell's Hardware.

He pressed the receiver button. "Ten-four."

"I guess you've got to go." She wanted to say so much more, but the words wouldn't come. He'd been coolly professional during the past few hours, as if she was a complete stranger. As if they'd never touched. What was left to say?

He jingled the squad-car keys in his pocket. "I suppose you're heading to Dallas now?" His voice was emotionless, distant. He could have been talking to a fellow officer or any civilian on the street. If not for the hint of sadness in his eyes, no one would guess that they'd ever met.

"I leave on Christmas Day. I'll have to come back when these cases go to trial, though."

"Take care." He turned, walked to his car and drove away without a backward glance.

So it was all over.

Well and truly over, both the reason she'd come back, and the reason she might have had for staying. And now there were six long days until she could return to Dallas and try to ignore the empty place in her heart.

CHAPTER TWENTY

AFTER PATROLLING the gaily decorated, crowded blocks of Main Street, Nathan headed toward the south end of town. With Christmas Eve just four nights away, holiday songs filled the air. Children were brimming with anticipation while their parents appeared rushed and distracted.

For Nathan, the holidays were now just another period to get through. The arrests down at the Sanderson plant and the arrival of the DEA and BCA teams had made headline news—far more excitement than Ryansville usually saw in a year—but now the suspects were in custody, and the state and federal agents were gone. Sara was down at the DEA office in Minneapolis. And Nathan could only wonder how he'd been so wrong about her.

He'd been sure they had something together. A future. A partnership based on trust. But all along, she'd figured he might be just another suspect. She hadn't cared for him at all.

Turning up Dry Creek, he cruised slowly past Stark's Salvage as he did almost every day to check on how Leon was doing.

Up on the porch of the old house, Leon paused with a shovel full of snow, shaded his eyes, then dropped the shovel and waved vigorously with both arms, obviously trying to flag Nathan down.

Nathan slowed to a stop, then checked his rearview mirror as he backed up to the driveway. By the time he got out of the car, turned on the radio at his belt and notified dispatch about his stop, Leon was wading through the snowdrifts with a package clutched to his chest.

They met at the gate. "I'll call and get someone out here to blow this snow out of your drive, okay?"

Leon nodded solemnly as he held a crudely wrapped bundle of papers folded into brown paper and tied haphazardly with twine. "For Sara. And for you."

"A present? Thanks, Leon." Touched, Nathan smiled at him, glad to see he looked clean and warmly dressed.

"It's safe now. Not before."

Safe? Maybe Leon had feared he and Sara wouldn't wait for Christmas if they received his present too early. Leon probably figured such temptations were too difficult to resist. "I know you'll have some presents under the tree, too, when you go to Bernice's place for Christmas Eve." He smiled at the man. "How are you getting along? Do you need anything?"

"I'm all right."

"Good. I'll save this package until Christmas, okay?"

Confusion filled Leon's face as he seemed to ponder the concept of waiting to open a gift. Then he nodded and turned away to trudge back through the snow.

He could use heavy gloves, Nathan thought as he drove away. Or maybe a good snowmobile suit to keep him warm while he puttered around his place. There were probably a hundred things the guy needed, and the chance to see his delight on Christmas Eve was something Nathan wouldn't miss for the world.

Even if it meant facing Sara one more time.

NATHAN PACED HIS OFFICE the next evening, then dropped into his desk chair and swiveled around to turn on the radio. He'd put off his paperwork for the past two days. He'd get started, then just set it aside.

Before leaving the office, Ollie had given him one of her lectures on eating and sleeping well enough, and fussed over him like a worried grandmother until he'd been relieved to see her go. And now the office was far too quiet.

Leon's brown-paper parcel caught his eye.

He'd brought it in last night and dropped it there before heading home to shower and change. The twine had loosened one side and the contents had slipped partway out. Yellowed pieces of paper. Newspaper clippings.

No wonder Leon had looked at him in confusion when Nathan had promised to open it on Christmas—this wasn't a present, after all.

Transferring the package to his desk, he untied the remaining piece of twine, then opened it and began to read. The last document, badly typed on a typewriter with a missing *b* key and numerous misspell-ings, was the one that made time stand still. *Damn.*

Leon had said, "It's safe now. Not before." But he hadn't been worried about the temptation to peek at Christmas gifts. He'd been referring to a very real danger—one his father had probably feared for the past twenty-five years.

Earl had recorded countless observations of activ-ities at the plant and had painstakingly written down what he'd seen the night of Frank Grover's death. Clearly he'd wanted to see justice done but had been afraid to try.

And until Robert's recent arrest, Leon had been afraid, too.

AFTER A STOP at the local funeral home, Nathan found Clay Benson at home alone. The retired sheriff met him at the door with a friendly smile that faded as he got a closer look at Nathan's expression.

"Come on in." He coughed heavily. "Dora's over at her sister's place this evening baking Christmas cookies, but I think I can rustle up some coffee."

"No. Thanks, anyway."

"You mind?" Clay gestured toward his favorite recliner in the living room, where two oxygen tanks sat nearby and plastic tubing hung over the back of his chair. "Doc says I got a touch of pneumonia now, and that always makes my heart condition worse. Damn cigarettes caught up with me, after all."

He settled his bulk awkwardly into the chair, then pulled on the tubing, positioned the nasal prongs and started the oxygen. "Makes me feel a little better when I have a bad day."

"I think your day is going to get a bit worse." Nathan reached into his pocket for the photocopy he'd made of the typewritten letter and handed it over.

Sweat beaded Clay's forehead as he began to read. His hands trembled until he finally quit reading and dropped the document on the end table by his chair. "Hogwash."

"Is it?"

"Damn straight it is. Where'd you get a fool thing like that?"

"From Earl's son."

Clay laughed harshly, a sound that spasmed into a fit of coughing. "Now there's a real good source of information. An alcoholic with dementia who's now dead and his dimwitted son. Who the hell is going to believe this?" He shook his head. "I'm real disappointed in you, son."

"I tracked down a copy of the medical report," Nathan added quietly. "But there wasn't one. Then I checked at the funeral home. They still have files going way back, and there was a description of Daniel's condition in his file."

"So?'

"Daniel was brought in DOA on the day of his arrest. Cause of death was listed as suicide but there was heavy bruising on Daniel's wrists and midsection. He was beaten, Clay, probably while still cuffed. And *then* he was hung. I think the mortician was given a reason to keep quiet—and I think you might know why."

Clay's hands tightened on the documents. "I...I wasn't there when he died."

The old man's gaze lifted to a sepia-toned photograph of a toddler with dimples and curly hair that hung above the fireplace, then he closed his eyes and leaned his head against the back of his chair, his skin taking on an ashen hue.

"I swear I didn't hurt him," he said after several minutes. "I only had to walk away from the jail cell at my office for an hour or so."

Nathan had hoped it wasn't true, but now bitter disappointment welled up in his throat. "So you let someone else do it."

"Dammit. After our baby was born with a heart defect, we poured every cent we had into trying to save her. I had no choice. We needed the best doctors, the children's hospital in Minneapolis." Clay's voice broke. "That money gave us another two years with our baby girl. Wouldn't you have done the same?"

"Do you want a lawyer?"

"You think I'll live long enough for a trial?" Clay coughed again. "The doc says I'll be lucky to see Easter."

"Tell me what happened."

The old man lay back in his recliner and sucked in oxygen for several long minutes. "You'll make sure no one hurts my Dora?"

"If this is all true, the suspects will be in prison for the rest of their days."

"It's true," Clay said on a long sigh. His breathing grew more labored. "There's a tape recorder. In the back bedroom. I might as well tell you…because I sure as hell could use a little redemption before I die.''

''I CAN'T BELIEVE I was so naive,'' Jane said glumly, staring into her cup of Earl Grey. She glanced at the other patrons in Bill's and then lowered her voice. ''I thought…well, that maybe Robert was falling in love with me.''

Sara gave her a sympathetic smile. ''That wasn't your fault. Robert was a self-serving jerk who led you to believe he cared so you'd cover for him if someone questioned what was going on. Any man who'd do that deserves what he gets.''

''What's even worse is that I'd convinced myself that I loved him—a man capable of murder!'' Jane shuddered. ''There must have been signs—how could I have been so blind? The only good thing is that I've finally learned my lesson.''

''Which is?''

''I married a guy who didn't love me and wasted a lot of years. Then I tried to find love with another guy who couldn't have been worse—but I was lonely, and he was simply *there*.'' She took another sip of her tea and then put the cup down. ''I don't need a guy just to make my life complete. If anything, I'm better off alone.''

''Until you find the right one,'' Sara said gently. ''And that will happen.''

''Maybe. But if not, that's okay. I'm thirty-four, and it's time I did something more than just hope Prince Charming will come along. I've decided to go back to school.''

"That's wonderful!"

"On Tuesday Ian assured me that my new job as assistant manager is still secure. When I told him about going to college, he offered to cover my tuition for either the community college in Fergus Falls or for correspondence courses. I could keep working part-time that way, then take a leave of absence when I transfer to the university for my last two years of a business degree." Jane's face brightened into a shy smile. "He said I was too good to lose."

"Then he's a smart man. I really look forward to hearing about how you like school."

Jane's gaze dropped to her cup. "I…I can hardly believe what you do, why you were here." There was awe in Jane's voice, and also a touch of hurt. "I mean, I feel sort of stupid, not guessing…"

"It was my job not to let you guess. But you know what? I'm really glad I came. Meeting you again and having you as a friend these past months has been really special. Maybe we can keep in touch?"

"I'd like that. A lot." Jane glanced at her watch. "Oh, gosh—my lunch hour is nearly over."

"This one's on me." Sara withdrew three five-dollar bills from her wallet and dropped them on the table, then rose and pulled on her jacket. "You're going to do well, Jane. I'm really happy for you."

Out on the sidewalk, Jane paused at the bumper of her car. "What about you? Are you going to be okay?"

Sara held up her bandaged hand. "Nothing at all, really. No nerve, tendon or bone damage so I was lucky."

"Where will you go?"

"Wherever my work sends me," Sara said lightly as she pulled on her mittens. "I'll spend tomorrow with my mom and Leon for Christmas Eve—maybe even with my brother if he shows up, then I'll start back to Dallas after Christmas dinner."

"What about Nathan?"

"What about him? Nothing to tell."

Absolutely nothing.

After spending Monday and Tuesday at the DEA in Minneapolis, Sara had driven back to Ryansville this morning. She hadn't expected any messages from him on her answering machine, and there hadn't been. All four messages were from her mother.

It was for the best. So why did she find herself watching for his squad car or wishing she'd catch a glimpse of him sauntering up the sidewalk? He was probably taking care to avoid her, and counting the days until she left town.

Chuckling, Jane waved a hand in front of Sara's face. "Yoo-hoo, lost in thought, are we? I saw the two of you on Friday when you arrested Robert, and I'd bet my next paycheck that something's going on there. No two people ignore each other *that* much if they don't care."

"We were in the midst of apprehending suspects," Sara retorted. "It wasn't exactly a date."

Jane dug her car keys from her coat pocket and unlocked her car door. "It's a mistake for you to leave, you know. You're throwing away a chance at something good."

"It never would have worked out."

"So you say." Giving a dubious shake of her head, Jane climbed into her car. "Merry Christmas!"

Bright sunshine sparkled across the heavy snow mounded on bushes and tree branches. Colorful decorations twinkled in every shop window, and strains of "Joy to the World" filtered into the street from the loudspeakers in front of the drugstore. Shoppers laden with packages crowded the sidewalks, greeting one another with best wishes for the holiday season.

Giving Harold a quick hug, Sara untied his leash from the lamppost in front of Bill's and started for her mother's place.

Merry Christmas, indeed.

"I BROUGHT PIZZA, Mom," Sara called out as she stamped the snow off her boots and walked in her mother's front door a few hours later. "Are you here?"

The lights on her Christmas tree twinkled brightly in the darkened living room, and the sweet scents of pine and cinnamon filled the air, but Bernice didn't answer.

Slipping off her coat and boots, Sara walked through the living room and found her mother sitting at the kitchen table with a haphazard stack of yellowed documents in front of her.

"Mom?"

Bernice shook her head slowly, but didn't look up.

"Mom—are you okay?" Sara wrapped an arm around her mother's thin shoulders, then looked down at the papers. "What is this?"

"All this time," Bernice whispered. "All this time."

Sara pulled a chair closer and sat down next to her. "What's wrong? Did you save these clippings from when Dad died?"

"No, poor old Earl did. Leon gave them to Nathan Tuesday night." Her hands trembling, Bernice brushed her fingertips reverently across the documents. "When Nathan brought them to me, he stayed several hours."

Sara's traitorous heart skipped a beat. Apparently he'd come when he was sure that she wouldn't be there. "Why?"

"To go through all this with me so I would know what really happened. And now…I finally do. The newspaper clippings just tell the story we've always heard. It's Earl's letter that makes the difference."

Sara sifted through the documents on the table and found one that had been typed. She scanned both sides, then began to read slowly, word by word. "Good Lord, is this true? *Robert* killed Frank and framed Dad. But why?"

"Nathan said he would question Robert and other people that might have known what was going on back then. We both figure Frank either planned to fire Robert or somehow stood in the way of his career."

"And no one ever suspected him," Sara whispered.

"Earl did, but he was afraid to tell. He wrote that letter shortly before he died. He'd been feeling chest pain and wanted to make sure someone finally knew what happened."

"How did he know about Dad…and Robert?"

"Earl's letter says he and Daniel were out hunting and got separated. Daniel found Frank wounded and tried to help, but it was t-too late." Bernice held a hand to her mouth as she gave a deep, shuddering sigh. "That's why the blood was on his clothes. Robert must have seen the perfect opportunity to frame your dad and get away with murder."

"And then later...at the jail?"

"Earl was on his way to go see Daniel, but he saw Robert go in, then Clay left. He figured Robert bribed Clay to leave, then killed Daniel so no one else would ever hear his side of the story." Bernice's eyes filled with tears. "Back then small-town jails didn't have much supervision. The man got away with murder twice."

And again, just recently. Anger rose in Sara's throat, followed by overwhelming sorrow as she imagined her gentle father's horror at finding Frank murdered. His terror at being trapped in a cell, unable to escape his attacker.

Remembering what Clay had said to her back in October, Sara closed her eyes. "Dad never did drink, did he?"

"Of course not! He hated the taste—he didn't even like communion wine. Why do you ask?"

"Clay tried to tell me Dad was drunk the night of Frank's murder. Another lie. I don't understand—surely the coroner's report would have been suspicious."

The pain in Bernice's voice was palpable. "Nathan said some rural counties didn't have a real coroner back then. If they didn't, the sheriff could investigate anything unusual. If he didn't raise questions, the county attorney usually didn't, either.''

"So Robert set it up to look like suicide, paid off the sheriff and probably the mortician, as well. And that was it.''

A tear slipped down her mother's cheek. "All this time…''

"But why didn't Earl speak up sooner?''

"Nathan figures he was really afraid. He'd seen Robert frame Daniel and kill him just a few hours later. He had a retarded son to raise. Earl probably figured no one would believe the word of a junk man over the rising young manager at the plant—especially since Earl was quite a drinker in those days. And if that happened and Robert was set free, Earl knew he'd be next to die.''

Clenching her fists, Sara launched herself from her chair and stalked to the window, then turned back. "I can't wait to talk to Clay about this.''

Bernice shook her head. "Nathan confronted him yesterday. A few hours later, Clay had a heart attack.''

"Did Clay die?''

"He's at the hospital in Fargo, but I hear he isn't doing very well. I know it's terrible to say, but I don't feel sorry for him.''

"So all this time, the awful things people said about Dad…were all based on lies.''

Bernice swallowed hard. "I blamed your dad for killing that poor man, for committing suicide and leaving us alone. But I was sure I'd driven him to it.''

"No, you couldn't have done that."

"Some wife I was—always complaining that we didn't have enough money. That we couldn't buy enough presents for you kids." She gave a bitter laugh. "I was sure he must have confronted Frank about a raise and gone over the edge when the man refused. I thought it was my fault that dear old Frank Grover died."

"Oh, Mom." Sara wrapped her in a fierce hug.

"Maybe that's why I stayed here, even when most everyone shunned us for years." Her voice faded to a broken whisper. "It was no more than I deserved."

"But now people will hear the truth. You don't need to hide anymore, Mom. I'm going to make sure this is covered in the local paper so everyone knows. I'll call Kyle, too."

"I want Daniel's name cleared. He deserves that, after his own wife spent twenty-five years blaming him for something he didn't do."

JOSH APPEARED at Bernice's front door at noon on Christmas Eve bearing a box of decorated Christmas cookies.

The mood in the apartment had been somber all morning, but one look at his wildly mussed red hair and gap-toothed grin, and Sara couldn't help but smile. "Hi, there, kiddo. Want to come in? My mom makes the best Norwegian flatbread and *lefse* in the world. I think she's got a fresh batch of cookies, too."

Closing his eyes, Josh breathed in the warm scents of cinnamon, ginger and nutmeg. "I gotta go home and watch Timmy, so I can't stay." He handed Sara the box he'd brought. "These are from my mom. She wants you to know how thankful she is, even if you made her cry."

Taken aback, Sara stared at him. "I-I'm so sorry, Josh, I never, ever meant to hurt her feelings. I only wanted to help when I gave her that doctor's name."

"No—it was *good* crying! She called the doctor and talked for a long time, and that's when she started to cry."

"What happened?"

He looked up at Sara. "That doctor promised to see my mom really soon, and said that she wanted my mom's records right away. She says there's new laser treatments that can help take away the stain on Mom's face."

"That's wonderful, Josh." Allen had come through with the referral to his sister, who had been working with port-wine-stain patients for several years. "Give her our thanks for the cookies, okay? Wait a minute— let me send some gingerbread men back with you."

He was shifting from one foot to the other on the entryway rug when Sara returned from the kitchen with a half-dozen gingerbread men she'd put on a paper plate and slipped into a plastic bag.

"So are you all excited about Christmas Eve?"

"You bet! Mom says it'll be warm enough that we can walk to church. I love it when the moon sparkles on the snow, and the stars are twinkling. There must be a gazillion of 'em! And all the Christmas lights are really cool this year."

Back in Dallas, the stars never seemed as bright,

nor as heavily strewn across the heavens as they did this far north.

He was right about the lights, too—almost every house in town was draped in lacy icicle lights or the big, old-fashioned multicolored bulbs. "I'm glad I could be here."

His face fell. "Mom says you're leaving tomorrow."

"I need to. I have a job back in Dallas, and an apartment."

"Couldn't you move?" His wistful gaze strayed toward Harold, who was curled up in front of the sofa, fast asleep. "There must be lots of things you could do here."

She'd thought of that a lot over the past week. The quaint charm of her hometown. The pleasure of walking the familiar streets, seeing people she recognized. The value of spending time with her mother. The breathtaking beauty of Minnesota's lake country and the vivid contrasts of each season.

But as much as this place called to her, staying was not an option. Nathan lived here. She'd see him around town, and there'd always be that corner of her heart that cared too much. It would be far better to make a complete break and slip back into the anonymity of the big city where absolute dedication to her career was all that really mattered.

"You are coming to see me, right?" Josh insisted.

"What?"

"At the nativity scene. Down in the town square. I, um, have something for you, and I can give it to you then."

His face was filled with such hope that she had to smile. "I'll bet you'll be the best shepherd ever. What was the time again?"

"The animals will be there from three to seven o'clock, and we have the actors there just before all the churches have their Christmas Eve services. So you'll have to be downtown, anyway, right?"

She bent to give him a quick hug. "I wouldn't miss it for the world. You're a cool kid, Joshua Shueller. I'm going to miss you."

"Come at six, okay? We all have lines to say. Promise?"

She crossed her heart. "I'll be there."

DARKNESS HAD FALLEN by four-thirty, and now, as Bernice and Sara stood in the gathering throng at the live nativity scene in the town square, fat snowflakes began to fall.

Sara had hoped for clear skies and a heavy blanket of stars on her last night here, but the snow was beautiful—silvery sequins dusted the bright woolen hats and coats of everyone in the audience, and the little ones stood with their heads tipped back and mouths wide open, trying to catch snowflakes on their tongues.

Her brother Kyle had claimed he had to work over the holiday and couldn't get away—but Sara had heard his voice break after she told him about their father and Robert. With time and luck, maybe new bonds could be forged and they would again be a family.

In the crude wooden lean-to, a Jersey cow with big,

liquid brown eyes and long lashes as pretty as a girl's stood patiently in a heavy bed of straw. Three fat sheep lay in front of the manger, and the cast of long-robed shepherds and kings was already in place.

The actors—high-school students—self-consciously picked at their costumes and searched the audience for their friends, then gave surreptitious waves to the people they knew.

"Where's Josh?" whispered Bernice. "Isn't he here?"

Sara scanned the players again, more slowly this time. "I don't see him. Maybe he—"

Sara heard her mother gasp. "There's Kyle," she said.

Even into adulthood, Kyle Hanrahan had retained an air of insolence. With his wavy, copper-colored hair and lean, hard features, he might have been mistaken for some rising new movie star, but the perpetual sneer was no affectation, and drawing him into conversation was like slogging through cement.

But now, there was something different, something almost vulnerable in his eyes as he stopped next to Bernice and gave them both a self-conscious nod. "I couldn't get here any sooner."

"Merry Christmas, Kyle," Sara murmured. He'd never been good at giving or receiving demonstrations of affection, but she stepped forward, anyway, and gave him a hug. "It means a lot to us that you came."

Bernice hugged him next, and the two of them stood for a long moment in that embrace, their eyes closed tight.

"All this time," Kyle said. "Everything that people said…"

Bernice stepped back and held his arms. "We've wasted a lot of years. Maybe now we'll all have new beginnings."

"There was an article in the newspaper this morning," Sara added. "Front page. The Lund murder charges are pending against Robert Kelstrom. That, plus his federal drug charges, will keep him off the streets until the day he dies."

"It's starting," a child cried. "Baby Jesus is a real baby!"

From behind the lean-to, a pretty girl stepped forward as Mary, holding a snow-suited baby. Behind her, holding a long staff, came a boy dressed as Joseph, his expression somber and his cheeks red.

Sara stared at him in wonder, her heart lifting with joy. "Look, it's Josh!" she whispered to Bernice. "He got the part he wanted!"

The crowd fell silent as the actors moved into position.

Shifting his weight, Josh white-knuckled his staff and cleared his throat, then squeezed his eyes shut tight as if saying a fervent prayer for help with his lines.

Someone in the audience tittered. Several others whispered, "Shhh!"

Then he opened his eyes and his young voice rang out through the night. "And it came to pass in those days that a decree went out from Caesar Augustus, that all the world should be registered.…"

Even the little ones in the audience stood in rapt

attention at the sound of his voice and the deep emotion behind his words. As proud as if he was her own son, Sara beamed at him, then glanced through the crowd and spotted so many people she knew.

Being here was like being with family, she realized. Shared histories went back for generations, and friendships went on and on.

Across from her she saw Jane. And over there, Timmy, nestled in his dad's arms. Zoe's and Bob's faces radiated pride and love as they listened to their older son's performance.

And then she saw Nathan.

Taller than those around him, he stood at the edge of the crowd in a black, full-length wool coat dusted with snowflakes. His dark hair ruffled in the fitful breeze. Though his lean face appeared haggard and drawn, a smile curved his mouth as he watched Josh.

As if he sensed her looking at him, Nathan turned and met Sara's gaze. Even at a distance she could see the anger that still simmered in him, coupled with regret and determination.

Not that it mattered. What they'd had was over, and the fact that he thought so little of her was of no consequence. Once she got back to Dallas he'd surely be easy to forget.

"...and she brought forth her firstborn son and laid him in a manger because there was no room at the inn."

Josh's shoulders lifted as he gave a great sigh of relief and a quick pump of his hand in victory.

A ripple of applause spread through the audience, then another as one of the shepherds stepped forward.

"Now there were in the same country shepherds living out in the fields..."

Sara grinned at Josh and gave him a thumbs-up. He grinned back at her, his eyes shining.

Despite the fact that the baby Jesus wore pink and fussed in the manger until his—or her—mother surreptitiously slipped a bottle of formula to Mary, the entire production was so touching that Sara felt joy swell in her chest.

She gave her mother's arm a quick squeeze and looked over to find tears glittering in Bernice's eyes. "Aren't you glad we came? Hey, look over there— it's Leon."

The man stood at the back of the audience with a sweet smile on his face as he watched the cast of the nativity scene disperse. He'd dressed up for the occasion—his jeans were clean, and his social worker must have taken him shopping, because he wore a new coat and his hair had been cut. When Sara waved at him, he waved shyly in return.

"Let's go get him, okay? He can go into church with us so he isn't alone, then he can walk home with us." Sara started toward him with her mother, but a hand touched her sleeve, and she turned to find Josh behind her with two wrapped Christmas presents in his arms.

"Hey, kiddo. You were the absolute best Joseph I ever saw! When did you get the part?"

Suddenly shy, he kicked at the snow beneath his boots. "Last week. It was supposed to be Ricky Weatherfield, but Mr. Weatherfield said it wasn't fair that his wife always chose their boys, and he made sure I got the part, instead.''

"So how are you getting along with those kids now?''

"Better. The principal and their dad talked to them.'' He gave her a conspiratorial grin. "But I think it's 'cause I finally got mad and wouldn't put up with 'em anymore.''

At a shivery sense of awareness, she glanced up and found Nathan approaching, his face grim.

"How are you doing, Mrs. Hanrahan?'' he asked, looking past her to Bernice.

"Good. I want to thank you for all you did. I'm still trying to grasp it all.'' Bernice patted his sleeve. "You've given me the best gift I've ever had.''

"I thought you should hear this from me first— Clay passed away early this morning.'' A sad smile lifted a corner of Nathan's mouth. "I know you wanted him to pay for what happened to your husband. If it's any consolation, he told me that the regret and guilt stayed with him every day since.''

Bernice wrapped her arms around her waist. "I…I guess maybe he served a sentence of his own. Sometimes that's even worse, dwelling on mistakes and wishing you could change the past.''

Kyle's mouth hardened. "What about Kelstrom?''

"We're still investigating, though we turned the information over to the county attorney. I expect additional charges will be filed against him on the two homicides back in the '70s.''

Josh looked back and forth between Nathan and Sara. "My mom's going to be calling me soon, so I need to do this.'' He held up the two packages in his arms. ''You've got to have these tonight.''

''I'd better go fetch Leon,'' Bernice murmured. ''Will you excuse me?'' She turned and nearly bumped into Ollie Neilsen.

In the past, Ollie would have walked away. Now she offered a tentative smile. ''Bernice, I saw the newspaper article. I've judged you wrongly for twenty-five years, and I'm truly sorry. Can you ever forgive me?''

Bernice gave a deep sigh. ''I need forgiveness myself. I was Daniel's wife, and I believed he was guilty, too. All those years, wasted on being hurt and angry…''

''There'll be changes here, I promise you.'' Ollie hooked her arm through the crook of Bernice's elbow. ''I heard you mention Leon. Let's go find him.''

''Kyle, come with us.'' Bernice took his hand. ''I think Josh wants time alone with Nathan and your sister.''

As Sara watched them move through the crowd, relief washed through her. A number of people acknowledged Bernice and Kyle with a smile. Several of them spoke. Things were changing for her mother already, and the family had Leon and Nathan to thank.

Josh waited a few moments, then handed the biggest box to Nathan. ''Merry Christmas.''

''Are you sure this is for me?''

He nodded. ''I've been thinking about this for a long time.''

Nathan carefully untied the lopsided red bow and

slid a fingernail beneath the criss-crossed adhesive tape welding red-and-green Santa paper to the box. "You did a great job of wrapping," he murmured. "But I really had no idea you'd do this, Josh…"

He removed the top of the shoebox and stared at the contents for a long moment. "Josh, you really shouldn't have. I know how special this was to you." Holding out the box so Sara and Josh could see inside, he lifted out Josh's antique Lionel Southern Pacific diesel engine. "You should keep it and give it to your own boys someday."

"No." Josh shook his head vigorously. "I remember you saying that you wished your dad had done things with you. And how Christmas gifts didn't mean a lot just 'cause they were expensive. You've been really nice to me, and I thought maybe if you had my train engine, you'd know that my grandpa loved it when he was a kid, and my dad did, and I do, too. I wanted you to have something that was loved a lot. So maybe…well, maybe you'd feel different about Christmas."

"I…I don't know what to say. This is the nicest gift I've ever received."

"I told my mom and dad, and they said it was okay." Josh grinned. "If you start collecting model trains, I'll even come over and help you get set up."

"You are a very special kid, Josh," Sara murmured. "I can't think of a more wonderful gift."

He grinned as he handed her a slender package. "Now you can open yours."

Mystified, Sara carefully unwrapped her package. Inside the tissue, she found a scraggly piece of greenery. "This is…really pretty, Josh. I bet I can arrange it with some nice candles, or put it on the wall."

"No. Don't you remember my uncle Pete in West Virginia?"

"Your uncle?" She thought for a minute, then chuckled. "The mistletoe hunter?"

Nathan glanced between them. "The what?"

"Mistletoe grows high up in the trees where he lives," Josh explained, "so he blasts it down with a shotgun. I wrote to him way back in October and told him I needed really special mistletoe—the kind that works really, really well."

"Honey, this is so sweet of you." Sara gave him a big hug.

"I figured…maybe with the strongest kind, you and Nathan, well…" He shuffled his feet in the snow. "I don't want you to leave. You were so nice to me and all… Can't you stay?"

"Josh!" Zoe called across the nearly empty town square. "I've been looking all over for you!"

"I gotta go." He looked back and forth between Sara and Nathan. "Merry Christmas!"

Sara watched him run across the snowy square to join his family. "My mom must have already walked to church with Leon. I guess it's time for me to go, too." She looked at Nathan once last time, memorizing the lean planes of his face, his resolute chin. The beautiful hazel eyes that now were sad and dark and fathomless in the dim light.

"Maybe it isn't," he said slowly.

"What?"

"Maybe it isn't time to go. Not just yet." He

reached out and brushed snowflakes from her hair, then moved closer and cupped her cheek.

His hand was hard and cool. Gentle. A hundred images rushed through her thoughts—of Nathan kissing her in the moonlight. Of his hard muscled body. Of his kindness and sense of honor. But standing with him again—maybe even kissing him on Christmas Eve—would only make the leaving harder.

"I think we already said our goodbyes," she said, stepping back. "Things seem to be pretty clear."

"Do they?" He laid Josh's gift on a park bench a few feet away, then moved closer to her. She found herself against the rough bark of a tree with her own gift clutched to her chest. "I've been thinking about what you said," he continued. "And about what I said."

"Oh?"

"And I think there were some very confusing points."

"Such as?"

"I have to admit I was surprised when I discovered you were here on a surveillance assignment." He moved a little closer and braced a hand on the tree, then tipped up her chin with a forefinger.

Warmth flooded through her veins at his touch. "No kidding."

"And I have to admit I was also…surprised when you thought I might be involved in Robert's drug trafficking."

"I didn't think that, but…" He bent to brush a kiss at her temple, and she lost her train of thought.

"The fact that you planned to arrest me when I

tipped off all of my cohorts in crime was the hardest to accept."

"I was only doing my job," she whispered. "I couldn't risk—"

He lowered his mouth to hers and kissed her until she felt dizzy and her knees turned weak, and only the tree behind her kept her from sinking to the ground.

When he lifted his head, he searched her face as if looking for the answers he needed. "I overreacted because it hurt so much—I knew I was falling in love with you, and then to discover that you not only didn't care, you even thought I was as bad as the guys we arrest every day."

"That's not true," she protested. "I—"

"I know." He took her package of mistletoe and put it on the bench with his own gift, then pulled her into an embrace and kissed her until the snowy world around them faded out of existence, and only his mouth, his warmth and the beat of her heart existed.

"I want you to stay," he murmured against her ear. "I want to go fishing with you and lose every bet I make. I want to wake up in the mornings with Harold on the foot of the bed and with you at my side, and four or five little Roswells down the hall. I want you with me until the day I die."

"Four or *five*?" She laughed a little, as all her doubts were swept away and only the reality of this man, this honorable, beautiful man, remained. "Boy—wait'll Josh hears about his magic mistletoe. He'll never believe it!"

Amusement glimmered briefly in Nathan's eyes. "I

know you have a career in Dallas. But the DEA has offices in Fargo, or there's always another branch of the law, if you want to keep working. I love you, Sara.'' His voice was low and rough with emotion as he looked at her. ''Will you marry me?''

Church bells rang through the frosty night air. Above them, the clouds had drifted away to reveal a brilliant array of stars—and one that was far brighter than the rest.

She felt a deep sense of peace. ''Nothing would make me happier,'' she said simply.

And then she kissed him with all the love in her heart.

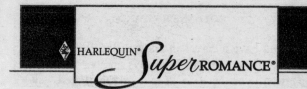

HARLEQUIN *Super* ROMANCE®

presents a compelling family drama—
an exciting new trilogy
by popular author Debra Salonen

THOSE
SULLIVAN
SISTERS

Jenny, Andrea and Kristin Sullivan are much more
than sisters—*they're triplets!* Growing up as one of
a threesome meant life was never lonely...or dull.

Now they're adults—with separate lives, loves,
dreams and secrets. But underneath everything that
keeps them apart is the bond that holds them together.

MY HUSBAND, MY BABIES
(Jenny's story)
available December 2002

WITHOUT A PAST
(Andi's story)
available January 2003

THE COMEBACK GIRL
(Kristin's story)
available February 2003

HARLEQUIN®
Makes any time special ®

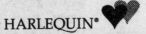